Sir
Coffin
Graves

ENJOY!
LEINAD

Sir Coffin Graves

Book 2

A Novel

Leinad Platz

Mill City Press, Minneapolis

Mill City Press, Inc.
322 First Avenue N, 5th floor
Minneapolis, MN 55401
612.455.2293
www.millcitypublishing.com

ISBN-13: 978-1-63505-035-6
LCCN: 2015916627

Typeset by A. M. Wells

Printed in the United States of America

Prologue

*"History ... is a nightmare from which I am trying to wake."—
James Joyce, Ulysses*

I met Jill when she came into the furniture store where I worked.
She was looking for a curio. I could hardly speak—I'm not even
sure I did—and I was taken with both her looks and personality. In-
fatuation at first sight, for sure, and when I finally got up the nerve
to ask her out, we had a great time. And it wasn't long before I
was in love, and it was obvious she was in love with me.

Through my nineteen years, I have always had very vivid
dreams. But after meeting Jill, they became horrific as well. They
played out showing various scenarios, all of them ending terribly:
Jill killing an old man on a couch, Jill drowning a middle-aged
woman in a bathtub, Jill nearly decapitating a former news anchor
with a baseball bat. But the worst of all was not a dream. The
worst of all was when I found Jill dead.

Her death was a mystery—no sign of . . . anything. No gunshots,
no bruising, no stab wounds, no sign of strangulation. Nothing.
And when her body disappeared, the mystery deepened.

My father owns the Rest Haven funeral home and mortuary,
so it was also a surprise when her body turned up there. I dug her
grave, but only for show. I had discovered my father had been

burying empty caskets for years—who knows what he did with the bodies—so I did the same thing and had Jill's body cremated.

My friend from the furniture store, Patrick, agreed to help me start up a new business venture: Removing the empty caskets through tunnels we discovered under the cemetery and refurbishing them. I could then sell them to other funeral homes. Yes, it was a shady business. But I really saw it as a passive-aggressive way to get back at my father.

My mother died when I was four—he said it was from food poisoning. After I discovered his secret office with Patrick one night, I found evidence that her death was not all that innocent. I also found he'd had dozens of previous wives—and children—all of whom died under mysterious circumstances, simply for the insurance payouts.

But that office turned up other secrets as well. Hundreds, maybe thousands of artifacts that pointed to his involvement, if not participation in some of the most dreadful events in U.S. history. The Chicago Fire. Lincoln's assassination. Jack The Ripper. Even Hitler's death. Yes, I know it all seems too incredible to believe. I had a difficult time accepting it—not even mentioning that for him to be involved in those incidents meant he was hundreds of years old.

Then I discovered, somewhat to my relief, that he was not my natural father at all. But that relief was diluted by realizing he had not only killed my adoptive mother, but my birth parents as well. I also found out his real name was not the very plain-sounding "Henry Davis", but the mouthful "Lord Harod Dunraven."

And he tried to kill me. He would hire and send men over to either attempt arson, or having me shot in the head. I got to them first and became just as violent as the men I killed. "Dear ol' Dad" —even ordered Ginger, the horse I'd had since childhood, to be slaughtered. The rotten bastard.

I experienced other changes as well. I was summoned to a clandestine meeting in the Nicaragua jungle where robed figures told me I was now a Soulmadd—a secret group that . . . well, I don't know what. Except they seemed to be Christian based, and as part of my initiation into the group, I received a brand on my chest like a glowing tattoo. The woman who was my nanny, Sylvana, after my mother died seemed to be a member of the Soulmadds, though I never actually saw her face. She exhibited special healing powers, and after my trip to Nicaragua, I gained them too.

Yes, it's all too much to believe. And I would laugh if they hadn't happened to me.

I became friends with the man who own Burkfelt Jewelers, and his help and insight was invaluable, especially after Patrick was kidnapped and tortured by a group directed by Dunraven— The Regulators. After I rescued Patrick and tried to heal him—his injuries were very severe—Mr. Burkfelt gave us a safe-haven, only to be shot by the Regulators. I did my best to heal him as well, and he seemed to fully recover. Which was when it was my turn to be kidnapped at gunpoint the mysterious group in black.

To say I don't know what's going on is an understatement. But so much has happened that I do know there is no turning back.

The only question at this point is whether I'll survive it.

Chapter 1

"But I say to you, love your enemies and pray for those who persecute you, so that you may be sons of your Father who is in heaven; for He makes His sun rise on the evil and on the good, and sends rain on the just and on the unjust."—Jesus Christ

I stand in the middle of the room, the urge inside me to RUN! is almost overwhelming, even though the five men are no longer a threat. They won't be hurting anyone ever again.

I see my clothes piled off near the far wall, and quickly collect them, slipping out of the room and into the chilly hallway. I don't bother to stop to put them on, I just need to go. Something tells me I'm not out of danger, and standing around naked is not wise.

I'm not sure how I killed them. They made me strip, and the leader pointed to a nail on the wall, saying it's where he would hang my balls. I remember trying to negotiate, offering him the gold buillion, then adding however much money he wanted. He seemed receptive.

But I knew it was useless. When one of the other men said I was offering some kind of religious mumbo-jumbo, I told him to shoot me.

And then I could feel it. A power. An energy surge building up from deep inside me. And BAM . . .

A bright light. A sharp tinge of pain, and then unconsciousness.

I woke laying on the floor, the five men laying there also. But I was the only one to get up.

I hurry towards the end of the hallway, where the elevator is, and press the button. I keep looking back down the corridor as if the dead men will come back to life and finish their job.

The doors of the elevator clunks open, and I step in, dropping my clothes on the floor. I push the button labeled 1, then slip on my underwear. It's not a fast trip, so I'm mostly dressed by the time it shudders to a stop and the doors begin to part. I stare leerily as another hallway is revealed, thankfully empty. I pull on my coat, pick up my shoes and socks and head out to find the exit.

I have to think getting out of a high-security building is as difficult as getting in, but as I walk towards the far end, there is nothing to stop me. I don't see any cameras, but that doesn't mean they're not there.

And then I hear it. A distinct *click*.

I stop, and listen. It's difficult to tell which direction it came from. I consider my options.

There are several, each involving opening one of the plain, blank doors that line the passage, but that's it. I choose the one on my immediate right.

The room is empty except for a long, overturned table.

Click, clunk.

Someone is coming, probably many of them. I step into the room and shut the door behind me. The darkness is complete, and I quickly shuffle over to where I estimate the table is lying. My foot kicks it, and I step around the end, then lie down behind it.

I can hear them. Muffled talking. A door slams. The sound of what might be radio static and disembodied voices.

I hold my breath.

The door opens.

Silence.

My heart is pounding so hard, I'm afraid whoever opened the door can hear it.

"Clear," a man says, and the door slams shut.

I wait a few more seconds before attempting another breath. I listen.

Eventually, the voices become distant, then are gone. Still, I wait.

The quiet is more unnerving. I don't know if they're just waiting me out, or have moved on.

I'm still holding on for dear life to my shoes and socks, so I sit up and put them on, my senses attuned to anything.

I stand hesitantly, then step quietly around the table and across the cement floor, arms out to feel for a wall or door. I reach the wall and touch my way to the only exit. My fingers find the doorknob, and I begin to turn it, slowly. I know if I do it with deliberate gradual movement, it won't make a sound. Eventually, the latch is completely retracted and I pause before pulling gently to open the door. I move it until there is the slightest sliver of a crack, and draw my face close to peer out.

Nothing. No one.

I pull it wider, looking farther down the hallway. Still nothing. Now for the tricky part: Looking the other way, towards the elevator.

Again, as slow as I can, I move my head until my right eye can see the all the way down.

They're gone.

I step out, and quietly close the door behind me, then hurry towards the door at the far end.

I pause, my hand on the knob. What's on the other side? More men?

I turn it carefully, and push it open slightly. I see part of a truck. I ease the door open wider until I can see the cab. It's empty.

I swiftly open the door, step out and close it behind me.

Then I run like hell.

* * *

There really is no easy way out. The only thing I can think of is through the main driveway of the Meadows Polo Club—the same way they brought me.

As I run, I keep watch for anyone, but the place is deserted. At least for now.

I make it to the main entrance and see the tall, imposing metal gate is closed. Then I see, off to the side, a metal door. I race to it, praying it won't be locked.

God is good.

I rush through it, then out onto the public sidewalk, sprinting past the cemetery—the place I had lived for all my years—and finally to the corner. I pause at the signal, huffing and puffing like a locomotive, and see a police cruiser in the left turn lane. Both of the officers inside are watching me.

I wave at them and wait for the light to change.

I am apparently presentable enough to not look like I just mugged someone or robbed a liquor store.

The light changes, and they turn down the street, ignoring me.

* * *

I don't know what happened to my cell phone. I don't know where Patrick or Mr. Burkfelt went—but I suspect they didn't wander far from the motel, if they left at all.

I get my bearings and walk down the sidewalk, purposely not drawing attention to myself. It's cold and looks like it's going to rain. I mentally try to judge how far I need to go to get to the motel. Is it a mile? Five miles? I'm not really sure.

Occasionally, I come across another pedestrian. I keep my eye out for a white van like the one that held the Regulators who kidnapped me. A woman comes around a corner towards me. She is incredibly ugly. I feel kind of guilty thinking that, but she's wearing too much makeup and not enough clothes.

"Excuse me," she says, her bosom appearing as if it might break free of her tight top at any moment. "Do you have the time?" Her face is pockmarked and scabby. She smiles and what teeth are left are yellow and crooked. Her lipstick is some kind of neon pink.

I don't know what time it is. I can only guess it's the afternoon, but I'm not even sure about that.

"No, sorry," I say as I keep walking. And then I see it . . . a white van. It pulled out on the street, then turned left, away from me. *Ace-1 Contracting* the lettering on the back says.

A white van, not *the* white van.

The ugly woman yells something from behind me.

I just keep going.

* * *

It's another fifteen minutes or so before I find the motel. Mr. Burkfelt's ancient car is still there, and much to my relief, I can see Patrick in the driver's seat.

I walk up and tap on the window. He jumps like a little girl in a haunted house, then his face breaks into a gigantic smile. He practically leaps out of the car and hugs me.

"Dude, we thought you were dead."

"I thought so too," I say, grinning. I look around and check the street. It's clear. "We should get going."

Chapter 2

"Sanctuary, on a personal level, is where we perform the job of taking care of our soul."—Christopher Forrest McDowell

Patrick has packed our few things in the car, and Mr. Burkfelt is settled uncomfortably in the backseat. I slide behind the wheel.

"Which way do I go, Mr. B?"

I peek in the rearview mirror to gauge his reaction. There's a small grin.

"Do you mind if we went to my home so I can change? I'm not fond of bloody clothes."

"No problem. Left or right?"

"Left." A pause. "You can call me Malcolm if you like."

I nod. "'Malcolm Burkfelt' sounds like an agent in a spy movie."

He chuckles. "Lately, I've felt like a character in a spy movie."

We pull out into the growing snowstorm, with Mr. B giving directions to his home.

I hate driving in the snow, so I was careful—although part of it was making sure there was no white van following us.

"So how did you get out of there?" Patrick asked.

"Well," I said, carefully coming to a stop at a red light, "I first tried to negotiate with them, and when I realized that wasn't going to work . . . it got weird."

"What's new?" Patrick said, shaking his head.

"What happened?" Mr. Burkfelt asked from the backseat.

I did my best to explain it, even though I wasn't sure what happened.

"An energy beam?" Patrick said.

"Energy burs—at least that's the best way I can explain it."

We travel the rest of the way in silence, but soon we're in a pleasant older neighborhood, neat and clean and quiet. The house itself is an old-style white house that looked it was from the 1940's, but very well kept. We help him inside and he makes his way into the back while Patrick and I wait.

"We need some of our stuff—or at least do laundry," Patrick says. "All I have in that gym bag is another pair of sweatpants, and some underwear."

"Yeah, we should go shopping."

He's quiet for a minute, realizing we're not going home. "It kind of reminds me of my old life, running from the cops, from gangs, living in abandoned houses. Not my favorite memories."

I don't reply, feeling a little bad for being the center of his problems. And now Mr. B's, not to mention my own dilemmas.

We sit in the living room, which is like someone's grandpa would have decorated it—an orange and black couch with some kind of odd design, a huge cuckoo clock, a large ornate coffee table, a hutch with a lot of porcelain knickknacks, the TV is not a wide-screen, but an old 26" tube-type, and in the corner facing the TV is a recliner that, while clean, looks ten years past its prime. But it looks comfy.

"Is he married?" Patrick asks.

"His wife passed away a few years ago."

"Any children?"

I think about this. "I don't know."

"So he's all alone?"

"As are we all."

Mr. B, a.k.a. Malcolm 007, shuffles from the back into the

living room in a fresh suit jacket, white collar shirt under a brown sweater. A fashion plate he is not.

"I need to pack a few more things," he says. "If you would like to watch television or fix yourself something to drink, please help yourself."

"Thanks," I said as he turns and disappears again.

We sit and wait some more.

* * *

As we make our way to the car, in a heavy snow, I feel somewhat relieved noticing Mr. B was moving better and seems to be in less pain.

"Where are we going?"

"Pull out and go left."

Fifteen minutes later, and without a white van in sight, we are in a nicer part of Chicago, an affluent area full of big properties with big homes. One stands out, a massive dark Victorian-style mansion that sits on a slight hill making it seem even more prominent. It would look great in a movie.

"Pull in the driveway and go around to the back."

In the rear is a large garage, where I park. As I turn off the engine, I am startled by a large figure that comes up and fills the glass of the driver's side window, making me jump.

"Holy shit," Patrick says.

I look over to the passenger side and see another big dog was there, looking in.

"Roll down the window," Mr. B says.

"Are you kidding? They look hungry."

"Just a little."

"A little hungry, or a little kidding?"

"Roll the window down a bit."

I do, and Mr. B says "Symbian, Voltar, off."

And both dogs disappear.

"They're friendly," he says. "They know the difference between us and them."

Mr. B opens the rear door and gets out. I watch through the window as Symbian—Voltar?—wags his—her?—tail. The animal has a dark gray coat and matching eyes. It was fit and muscular with an odd elevation running along its spine.

"It's safe," Mr. B says. "You can get out."

I open the door warily, and the dog approaches, smelling my foot as it touches the ground. The tail is still wagging. I get out and look down at the beast. It sits, looking up at me as if in anticipation of a treat. I reach out and scratch its head. Satisfied, he gets up and walks out of the garage. I see the other—a duplicate except for the brown coat—join his partner.

"Specially trained Thai Ridgebacks," Mr. B says, leaving it at that.

Patrick gets out of the other side, looking wary. "I hope 'specially trained' means they won't chew our legs off."

"Not yours," Mr. B says with an odd smile.

We make our way towards the looming house, the dogs leading the way, entering a large laundry room, a couple of dryers spinning clothes around and around.

"This is The Manor House," Mr. B says. "It will be your new home base and sanctuary."

The dogs lead us down a hallway, which opens into the largest kitchen I have ever seen. A lot of counter and open space. A dozen chefs could work with some room to spare.

"Damn!" Patrick says.

I turn, thinking he's commenting on the kitchen, but see instead that he's swinging his arm.

"Stupid ass fly! Where the hell does a stupid ass fly come from in this weather?"

"I wouldn't try to hurt it, if I were you," Mr. Burkfelt says. "Even though I don't think you can." Then he turns to leave.

Patrick and I exchange looks. His expression said *What the fuck?* I just shrug. We follow Mr. B into another hallway.

The first floor is well-appointed, a lot of dark wood furniture on dark hardwood floors in the different rooms we pass.

As we come to the end and turn a corner, a woman stands in an all-white gown, matching her hair. "Hello gentlemen," she says, holding Gizzi in her arms.

"Sylvana!" I approach and hug her. Gizzi snorts and wiggles happily. Symbian and Voltar don't seem as impressed as they calmly lay comfortably on the floor.

"It's good to see you Collin. I'm sure you and Patrick are both tired and hungry." She turns, and a man appears through a doorway. "He will take you to your rooms."

"What is this place?"

"A sanctuary. It has secret powers and is protected from on high. Only Soulmadd Orbs and their guests can get inside. You are safe here."

"What are 'Orbs'?"

"I can answer your questions later, when you've been refreshed. Go. Relax. I'm sure you will find the accommodations appealing. Caesar, if you would escort our residents to their quarters."

Caesar, who is in his late 20's, dressed in a suit, and looking something like a male model, turns and exits the way we had come. The three of us follow—five, if you count our new companions, the dark gray Symbian walking beside me, the brown Voltar next to Patrick.

We go up a grand staircase, which opens into another maze of hallways. The place seems to go on forever.

At the first door, Caesar stops and opens it. "Professor Burkfelt, enjoy your stay."

"Thank you," he says, disappearing inside.
Caesar then leads us to the next door across the hall. "Mr. Williams," he says, opening the door, "we are glad you're here."

"Me too," Patrick says, going inside, Voltar in tow.

"Later, bro," I say.

We then go to the door to the right, and Caesar opens it. "Mr. Graves, I'm sure you'll find everything to your liking."

"Thanks," I say, stepping inside, letting Symbian through before closing the door. I look around at a room that is both elegant and homey. A couch and a chair form an L shape in a corner—probably what they would call the "sitting area"—and a large, appealing bed sits in the middle of the room. A desk is off to the left, with a computer all set up. A fireplace glows warmly, and I am surprised to see Jill's curio positioned next to the window. Inside were many of the mementos I had of her—but the framed portrait is still missing. Still, I get a little choked up seeing it.

Symbian nestles onto the carpet near the fireplace and curls up. I go to the window, the drapes open with sheer curtains behind them. I open them, seeing the north side of the large property, the next residence about a hundred yards away.

A dressing area leading to the bathroom is off to the right. Decorated in a tan marble with both a tub and a shower, I see a TV mounted on the wall. I step back into the dressing area and open the closet, surprised to see it has clothes in it. As I go in, I realize they are my clothes—someone had collected them for me.

I go back to the living room and look around again. Odd, there is a TV in the bathroom but not here. I then see a remote control on a nightstand. Next to it is my cell phone, which I had lost, or thought I lost. I pick it up, stick it in my pocket then grab the remote and press the power button. A panel over the fireplace slides open and a big flat screen monitor appears behind it. The picture comes on, showing a commercial for a woman's skin product.

I kick my shoes off and lay on the bed. I could get used to this.

* * *

Out of the shower, I dress in some fresh clothes and go downstairs. Symbian happily follows. I promptly get lost, wandering down different halls, seeing more of the house than I anticipated.

"Symbian, I'm lost."

The dog wags its tail and looks at me, panting slightly. Then he begins walking down a hallway, and I follow. After back-tracking, we find Patrick already in the kitchen, sitting at the counter, chowing down on a huge plate of spaghetti and meatballs. I pet Symbian, wishing I had a treat to give him.

A chef behind the counter, as if anticipating my concern, holds up a dog biscuit and sets it on the counter, winking at me.

I pass it to Symbian, who takes it and pads over to his friend Voltar, who is resting comfortably near the wall.

"Will you be able to finish that?" I ask Patrick, staring at his gigantic helping of food.

"Sure. It's all about the pacing," he says twirling noodles on his fork.

A middle aged man in slacks, polo shirt and apron smiles at me. "What would you like, Mr. Graves?" he says in a British accent.

"I'll have the same if it's not any trouble."

He smiles and nods, and I take a seat next to Patrick who was biting a meatball the size of a baseball.

A large bowl matching Patrick's appears in front of me. "Would you like anything to drink?"

"Water is fine."

Sylvana floats in—at least that's how it seems in her long white gown.

"I hope you found everything to your liking."

"Yes, it's very nice," I say as a glass of ice water is placed in front of me.

"Yesh farry nigh," Patrick tries to say around a mouthful.

"Good. We will have a day or two before I anticipate events will turn. The Red Sky is forming, and action will need to be taken."

"Red Sky?" I ask after my first bite.

"Yes, I am sure there are coming judgments and discernments that you may not understand at first. If Dymortis is successful, the legend is a forty-day storm after the Red Sky will cover Manor House with a thousand feet of dust and dead 'Black Souls,' sealing the Manor. If this happens, it leaves no choice but for the Soulmadds to abandon the Earth." She pauses. "I hope to spend time with you to help sort through your questions. At the moment, I will leave you to your meal, and then I will arrange a tour, which, unfortunately, may bring more questions than answers, but it should nevertheless be enlightening."

She smiles thinly, then glides out of the room.

"Is there anything else I can do for you gentlemen?" the chef says.

"I'm good, thanks," Patrick says. "This is wonderful."

"What's your name?" I ask.

"Simon, sir."

"Thank you, Simon, this is very good."

"You're welcome. Please let me know if you need anything." Then he kind of bows, and leaves.

"I don't like the sound of all this stuff—Orbs and Red Sky and Black Souls," Patrick says.

"Yeah, it doesn't seem like things will be getting better. It's ominous."

He holds up his beer. "Here's to coming out of this on the other side in one piece."

I pick up my glass and clink his. "You don't have to be here."

"Where else would I be?"

"Hawaii?"

He points towards the window showing the snow coming down. "And miss out on this?"

Chapter 3

"One of the secrets of life is to keep our intellectual curiosity acute"—William Lyon Phelps

As we finish our meal—Patrick had seconds—I hear the whine of a toy motor. I look to my left and see a red plastic remote control car. It pulls up next to my stool and parks.

A boy of 7 or 8 appears in the doorway. He stands there with an odd expression—mostly blank with curious eyes—staring at me, arms at his sides.

"Hi," I say. "Is this your car?"

"Yes. It's a replica of a 1968 Camaro Z28, considered by some to be the best sedan-sized sports car ever made. However, I prefer the Ford Mustang for pure design aesthetics."

"Wow," I say, "I can't disagree." Then I notice something—or rather, don't notice something. "Where's your controller?"

"Right here," he says, pointing to the ground. The car again comes to life, backing up and turning towards Patrick. The boy's arm follows the movement.

Patrick leans in and whispers: "He's controlling it *with his mind.*"

"A modified form of telekinesis," the boy says.

The car makes a loop in the middle of the room.

"How is it modified?" I ask.

"It utilizes spiritual as well as mental-electrical manipulation," he says flatly as the toy does a kind of wheelie, rising up on its rear wheels and spinning like a top.

"Apollo," Sylvana says as she enters the room, "you are showing off."

"Yes ma'am," he says, agreeing. The car stops spinning and does a donut, the boy's hand twirling with it in unison.

"Why don't you give our new occupants a tour of Manor House?"

The boy's hand drops, the car stops and he looks at us with that odd expression again, but with a slight smile. "Are you brothers?"

"Not by blood," I say.

"But by life," Patrick adds.

A pause. "Will you be my brothers?"

"Sure," I say. "We can always use more."

"Okay." He raises his arm and points towards the opposite door. The car speeds off, and he calmly walks after it.

"I think that's our cue," I say.

We get up and follow, leaving Sylvana behind. Both dogs scramble and get to their feet to join in.

"The first floor is communal rooms for all the residents to enjoy," Apollo says, pausing in front of one closed door. "This is the game room. It features a more traditional gaming experience. Billiards, darts, card games, bowling, table games. While amusing, they don't hold my interest for very long."

"There's a bowling alley in there?" Patrick asks.

"Yes. Three lanes with electronic scoring. A slightly challenging game of physics utilizing speed, accuracy in aiming and proper spin to knock over a series of wooden pins to achieve your score." He turns and faces the door immediately across. "This is the electronic gaming room, featuring pinball, video games and computer simulators. Somewhat interesting if one is tired and not fully committed."

Patrick and I exchange glances. If this kid isn't a prodigy, I don't know what would be.

"Further down this hall, there is the library, a movie theater, and a water room."

"Water room?"

"Swimming pool, steam room, dry sauna, and tubs to experience various levels of temperature and relaxation, from extreme cold to excessive heat. It is a Korean-style spa and no clothing or footwear is allowed. I find it useful for those times I need to disengage from my mental challenges and activities since electronic devices do not function well in that environment. It also has an excellent shower and grooming area." He pauses to consider us, as if judging our current state of cleanliness. "Would you like to relax in the spa? We have some time."

"Maybe later," I tell him.

"Yeah, I prefer to groom myself without other men in the room," Patrick says.

"I understand," Apollo says. "Shyness and inhibitedness are, I find, to be positive human traits in certain circumstances. While courting a potential lover, for example."

He turns his radio car around and heads back the way we came.

"What's a kid doing talking about potential lovers?" Patrick whispers.

"I'm beginning to think he's an old man in a child's body," I whisper back.

"Actually, my body is originally from a local orphanage. Upon the management discovering my absence, they sent out a search team and tracked me down. I had taken refuge in a church and during the altercation, my body fell and my head struck a hard object. I went into a coma and the physicians eventually declared my host brain dead. However, Sylvana had visited and proposed that the failing mind be substituted with a leading scientist and Soulmadd whose body was failing. And so, I became Apollo."

My knowledge of mythology is pretty anemic, but I do recall Apollo being a kind of Greek god. God of what, I don't remember.

"You have already seen much of the upstairs," the boy continues as we stop in what would normally be the living room, but was about three times bigger than any I have ever seen. "It is made up of mainly living quarters. Would you like to see the lower levels?"

"Sure," I say, hoping I don't sound as hesitant as I feel. The last time Patrick and I were in the lower levels of something, it wasn't for a good thing.

Apollo raises his arms and part of the wall where the fireplace sat lowers into the floor. We approach and, looking down, I see it is a long ramp that goes down into the underground. Pleasant lights flicker on, and we begin descending, the dogs trailing us.

"This is the main entrance, but I prefer one of the alternative entries as it's closer to where I work."

"Work?"

"Yes, I'm the chief electronic and mechanical design engineer. I'll show you my workshop, but I think you'll most enjoy the Control Center."

The tunnel turns slightly, and as we reach the bottom, it opens up into a center area surrounded by several rooms with wide openings and windows. A lot of electronic equipment, monitors and blinking lights fill them. Sylvana was standing in the middle of the hub, smiling.

"Yes, Collin, this is The Hub, the central communications and tactical decision center."

I'm sure I look as puzzled as I feel. I've had the feeling before, but now it's almost obvious -- especially since everyone knew my name around here. "Are you reading my mind?"

She smiles. "You are a Soulmadd. We can communicate differently, including telepathy. Now, I am not technically inclined, so I am going to allow Apollo to brief you on our systems." Sylvana turns to the boy/man. "Please proceed. And we would appreciate it if you could keep it at a level we can all understand."

"Yes ma'am." Apollo points his car at the largest room in the center—an area that looks like it could be in a *Star Trek* movie—and we all follow. "This is the Control Center. It's like the brain, where all communications come, and where all is overviewed. Decisions are made and executed."

Patrick and I stand wide-eyed, trying to take it all in. There are monitors everywhere, some showing news broadcasts, some national, some international. Others seem to be security camera feeds of various locations. One looks to be from inside the U.S. Capitol building. Another, a liquor store.

"We are able to access almost all CCTV feeds that exist," Apollo says. "We recently were able to gain access to feeds from most of the international banking and financial institutions, particularly bank lobby feeds and ATM captures. These were excluded from even high-level access, partially due to financial confidentiality exclusions, but mainly due to the ISP blocking the gateways."

"ISP?"

"International Service Patrol. Dunraven's high-level police organization."

"How is that different from the Regulators?"

"Those are his operational team, like the Navy SEALS."

"And the people here are the Challengers?" I ask.

"Yes, the Challengers, which is the collective you see here today, plus thousands of others not present."

"So you hacked into the banking system?"

"That's the simple explanation."

I pause, thinking. "So am I now part of The Challengers?"

"Yes," Apollo says. "We all are."

"You are a Soulmadd, so you are automatically included," Sylvana adds.

"I hope you did a background check," I say, trying to make a joke.

"I have known you since you were four. I think I know you and your character better than anyone except the Almighty." She pauses. "Lord Dunraven is also aware of your character."

"Is he scared of Collin?" Patrick asks.

"Fear is not a word his ego will allow."

The car races out of the room. "Let me show you my workshop!" Apollo says, obviously excited.

Sylvana smiles, and we follow the boy.

It looks like a cross between a laboratory and a garage with a microscope, dozens of tools in varying sizes and capabilities, a large contraption that looks something like an X-Ray machine, and many electronic devices that are unknown to me. On the only part of the counter that wasn't cluttered with gadgets or tools, there are several small, black, pebble-like things that I thought, at first, were raisins. Then I realize they are flies, apparently dead.

Patrick sees them as well. "There's those damn flies."

"Actually, they are miniature drones," Apollo says. "Well, those aren't because they never became operational, but I have created a few that are in beta testing, and have performed relatively well."

"These are the things that buzzed my head," Patrick says. "You were spying on me?"

"Technically, yes. I was running tests, but perhaps I had brought the Flones too close, drawing unwanted attention to them."

"Flones," I say. "Fly drones."

"Yes. Not a very attractive name, but functional."

"We are in the process of determining a method of deploying them at the ISP facilities," Sylvana says.

"The building on the grounds of The Meadows?"

"Yes, where Patrick was captured and held captive." She pauses. "We were able to watch the whole thing, and Collin, what you did was truly heroic."

I have no response. I have no idea what to say.

"Patrick," Sylvana continues, "your intentions were well and true, and your bravery should be admired, but your execution, as they say, sucked."

"Yeah," he says, nodding with a slight smirk. "I didn't think things through very well."

"But that excursion brought us some valuable and sobering information. I just regret the pain you had to experience."

"How was the information sobering?" I ask.

"We were able to deploy three of Apollo's 'Flones' when you went to rescue Patrick. After you left, they were able to explore the facilities, and have helped us to understand, to a large degree, the extent of their abilities."

"And it's worse than you thought?"

"More challenging. One of the Flones was able to connect

to one of the computer systems, and transmitted a map of a good portion of their capabilities." She pauses for several moments. "We know we are up against a very, very strong adversary, but it is now clear they have their hooks in much more than we anticipated—if they do not already out-right control it."

"What are you talking about here?" I ask. "I mean, I know they have much of the U.S. government, from the President down. How much more power could they have?"

"They basically have control of all the network, cable, print and Internet news organizations. There are several hundred media outlets they do not control or have influence over, but their audience is small. The ISP also has almost complete control over the international banking and financial systems, including the United States. The only thing we are unsure of is their influence with the U.S. military. We know they have access, but it's not clear how far up the chain it goes."

"So if they control the government, the media and the money, their power is almost limitless."

"Yes, with the military being the only thing holding them back. But that is looking less certain," a familiar voice behind us says.

We turned to see Mr. B standing in the entrance.

"I know you were contemplating bringing down the President, Collin, and we are still evaluating that. The Vice President, while not Dunraven's son, is in his back pocket. But the military detests the VP. That could be to our advantage."

"Mr. Burkfelt is our historical expert," Sylvana says. "He has been researching and knows more about Lord Dunraven than anyone else. He can fill you in on the background, to give you a deeper idea of what we are dealing with."

Apollo, apparently bored, stands by his flock of Flones sitting on the counter and spreads his fingers, then watches as ten of them rise and hover—but curiously, they don't make a sound. A monitor on the wall broadcasts the perspective of one of the Flones.

"They have cameras in them?" Patrick asks.

"And microphones, as well as the smallest flash drive ever developed," Apollo says, moving his hands out, spreading the

Flones around the room. "They are nearly indestructible."

"Nearly?"

The boy smiles. "We haven't tried to see what happens when it falls into molten lava." He pauses. "Yet."

I clear my throat. "Can I ask you a question?"

"Of course."

"Do we have a chance?"

The boy pauses for a long time, then glances at Sylvana.

In a very weird moment, I pick up their telepathic conversation.

Sylvana: Go ahead. We have no secrets with him.

Apollo: At the risk of sounding like Jack Nicholson, can he handle the truth?

Sylvana: We will see. I do know that anything less than the truth will be more destructive.

Apollo nods slowly. "The short answer is yes. We have a chance. But I have been a Soulmadd longer than anyone alive, and have seen what they can do. Dunraven slaughtered my family. I have gone up against him, directly or indirectly, many times, and have failed many times. But since I am still alive, you could also say he has failed just as often. I, alone, will not defeat him. Nor will you. Together, we have a chance."

I let this sink in. "So, is your motivation a kind of revenge?"

"It was, at one time. But I have moved on. Now, part of it is the puzzle—the puzzle of what combination of things might bring them down. What elements will take advantage of their weaknesses? What *are* their weaknesses?"

He pauses, looking at each of us.

"But mainly, I am committed to this because they believe in a hierarchy, that some are better than others, that some *deserve* better than others. But having lived so long in this life, I have seen that, on this Earth, we all have deep meaning and value, the strong and the weak, the lame and the sturdy. We *deserve* nothing, but *earn* it. It is not up to me to determine someone else's place in the world—nor is it the right of the ISP, though they seem to think it is. Only you and God can decide your destiny . . . and it seems to me, God gives a lot of leeway."

A silence comes over us as we think this over.

"God gave me a lot of leeway," Patrick says, "and I fucked it up. A lot."

"Many have, and will," Sylvana says. I'm a little surprised she didn't chastise him for his language, but I guess that was the point. "But there is always an open door, even if it is through the back way."

Another long silence while we watch Apollo play with his Flones, even playfully circling Patrick's head.

My thoughts turned to, of all things, Ginger. I think of Apollo's lack of revenge and wonder how I could—or if I ever would—reach that level. Rising above it. Not hating.

It is a process, Sylvana's voice said in my head. *Grief is a slow redevelopment of your emotions.*

But they killed Ginger. He killed Ginger.

I know, Collin. But that cannot rule your decisions. It is okay for you to be angry and hurt, but do not act on it.

"What do we do next?" I ask.

"For a short time, we wait," Mr. Burkfelt says. "The ISP and the Regulators will prepare an assault, of some kind, somewhere. We will gather and prepare."

"That sounds ominous."

Mr. B looks at me flatly. "It is."

Chapter 4

"I like the dreams of the future better than the history of the past."
—Thomas Jefferson

"How good are you at history?" Mr. B asks.

"I like it," I tell him, "and I know the basics, but I'm not sure how much I remember."

"It gives me a headache," Patrick says.

We're in the cafeteria, which was more like a diner but featuring just about any food you could ask for. I stick with coffee, as did Mr. B. Patrick ordered a hot fudge sundae. It is roughly the size of his head.

"There's a lot you need to know, but I think you'll both find this interesting. At least I'll try." He pauses, collecting his words. "You understand that Apollo is an old soul in a new body."

We both nod, Patrick with a spoonful of whipped cream.

"Collin, your adoptive father, currently known as Henry Davis, is similar. I've been able to place him under his various incarnations back to the 4th century, A.D. The name that has followed him through time began as Flagito Corvus, which roughly translates from Latin to Dunraven. Lord Dunraven the XIV executes the instructions written for him to carry out—the orders of Dymortis."

I pause, then nod. "He was in a dream. A scary guy."

Mr. B sighs. "Dymortis descended to earth and pronounced upon the youngest Dunraven the cruelest black curse of all—greed. It has empowered him, given him the grand reward of Blacksoul, and the prearranged protection necessary to fleece the flock of humanity for centuries. This genetic flaw now lies among many on earth today, a poisonous noose around mankind's throat—with the exception of the Royal families only because they are secretly shielded and protected by their blood from this evil greedy spell."

"Okay, you're going way too fast. Blacksoul? Royal families?"

"Yes, I'll get to that. Dymortis—through Dunraven—is responsible for throwing the first sharp stone, igniting religious wars that still burn in the world today. Dunraven has intentionally fertilized the seedlings that created the wealthiest bloodlines, collecting over half of the total world's wealth—over five-hundred trillion dollars residing within this single family today."

Patrick nearly drops his spoon. "Wait -- a trillion is worth more than a billion, right?"

"It's a thousand billions," I say. "So, let me get this straight: Henry, the guy I thought was my dad, owns half the world?"

Mr. Burkfelt continues: "The Dunraven's have obtained this position through lies, manipulation and murder. They exploit to serve their real evil master. They have spent centuries dismantling your family's legacy by burning down villages and taking control of the monetary system. Over the years, they slaughtered your bloodline, their aim to victimize, confiscate and eradicate all of your family's cherished ancient scriptures. Their goal was to erase the Royal footprints by sweeping them out of the history books."

"There's that word 'Royal' again."

I find myself drifting off to a recent dream with Jill and Sylvana. I remember them both explaining some of this to me.

Both Patrick and Mr. B are staring at me as I drift.

Mr. B pauses for a long time, sips his coffee, pauses some more, then takes a deep breath.

Patrick kicks me under the table, snapping me back.

"Hello, your Royal highness, welcome back" he whispers.

At that moment, I realize the importance of hearing all

this again. It's to re-gain that valuable knowledge and to fully comprehend what I'm now up against.

"I'm sorry—you were saying?"

Mr. Burkfelt re-gathers his thoughts. "You are now the only remaining living being from the Royal families. Your adoptive father has become impatient as he knows he can no longer reproduce any children of his own, and it has broken the Dunraven family line. He was going to raise you to be his own son, but realized he could never change you. Your adoptive mother did not die from food poisoning, but brutally killed after she let you run down-stairs during a game of hide and seek."

I nod slowly. "Yes," I say simply, not realizing that my four-year-old self had indirectly gotten my mother killed. Not that it was my fault, but it still stings.

Sylvana approaches, looking somewhat sad. "It was inevitable, Collin. He would have put her to death one way or the other—he just used you as an excuse."

"I know, but it's still stupid."

She looks serene and thoughtful. "Because you have the oldest and purest blood, and the secret gift no other Soulmadd has, only you can be the Monarch Soulmadd. I am both yours and Jill's Soulmaddic guardian, sent to Earth to aid you in your mighty quest. At the right time, the true light will call upon enlistments and forces orchestrated by the Soulmadds—and by you!"

All I can say is: "What?"

Mr. Burkfelt leans forward. "Collin, you are the highest ranking Soulmadd, which means you are the Monarch ruling over all nations, presidents, prime ministers, kings, queens and all heads of governments—and even Dunraven. Although he has tried to kill you—and will try again—he cannot put you to death. Your greatest foe is Dymortis—he has incredible powers that only you can challenge. We still have a lot of planning and work to do before the rest of the world loses their freedom."

I sit in stunned silence, not sure what to think, much less what to say. Patrick continues working on his sundae while keeping an eye on me.

Finally, I work up a question for Sylvana.

"You said you are the Soulmaddic guardian for me and Jill. That implies she's alive."

The slightest smile appears on her lips.

"She is not dead. She is just not here."

* * *

There is more to the story. A lot more. Much of it is mind-boggling. According to Mr. B and Sylvana . . .

The symbol on my chest is the ancient Royal Seal. It symbolizes transition, balance, honor, faith, unity, order, patience, stability, creation, longevity, protection, hope, free will, endurance, life and navigation. I think I got all that straight. I now have complete immunity, exempted from all society laws. And I am the last remaining living soul representing the wealthiest Royal family.

Still not sure what that means—too difficult to wrap my brain around—I asked about all the birth certificates I had found. Sylvana said some are altered birth certificates of cast-away orphans signed by fraudulent doctors. The orphans were given new names, fake adoption papers and social security numbers created by unlawful attorneys. The children were then sold to high-bidding families through an embezzling adoption agency.

Orphans were considered "subjects" and referred to only by their market number, embedded with microchips. Some were sold to pharmaceutical companies for testing of experimental drugs, some to medical facilities for new surgical techniques, others to technology companies for experimentation of neurological devices, and even to rogue military agencies to test biological warfare. Many were—and are—sold to the underground pornography industry, or to high-society escort services to play out their sexual fantasies. Others become the tools of terrorists to inflict mass casualties . . . and some used at games of Run For Your Life and indiscriminately shot for sport.

Orphans from around the world are smuggled to their final destination in well-disguised food delivery trucks.

Some of the other documents I saw were laundered life insurance policies showing "natural" causes of death, signed off by coroners on the take and establishing large sum payouts to elite beneficiaries. One of those coroners was the competitor that had tried to kill me. Good ol' Jerry. At least Patrick torched his warehouse.

Jill had been one of the bought-and-sold children, and was one of only three who had escaped the Meadows Club. Apollo was another. Patrick was the third.

"Jill was orphaned at 8 months old as well," Sylvana tells us. Both your birth mother and father were murdered while flying on vacation—and Jill's parents were murdered too. They were ordered to be killed by Lord Harod Dunraven XIII. Your identities were secretly changed.

"It was Jill's love, her pure feelings towards you, knowing the security of never being hurt again . . . and the brave love she felt coming from you is why we granted her wish to be embedded into your soul forever. Jill is a very special Soulmadd. It's true she was sent to meet you, but we never expected her to fall in love with you as completely as she did. Your charm and innocence wrapped a blanket around her soul."

Sylvana pauses, then adds:

"Using children for objects of greed or pleasure will no longer be tolerated."

Mr. B had left briefly, returning with a map. He shows where there is a private airport, secretly landing jets at night. The Global Elite Members then get in vehicles that travel in a secret underground tunnel, running 13 miles to the Meadows Club, codenamed Eagle's Nest. Meadows/Eagle's Nest is the international headquarters controlling the other 600 locations strategically placed around the globe.

Sylvana says: "Soulmadds have been sent back to Earth to find and save both you and Jill, then to assist you in destroying the evil that has fallen onto the Earth. We have a dangerous foe, but only at the precise time will we have just the right opportunity—if our plans are not spoiled.

"Jill as a child was raped and held captive in the Meadows Polo Club, but I snuck her out. I placed her in a mission outside the city, and the ISP believe Jill has been permanently eliminated from the Royal Family—and it has brought Dunraven great joy and an enormous sense of accomplishment. He knows if you escape, his plan may never be fully executed to become the enraged madman necessary to destroy the human race."

But there was more, Mr. B explained. In the eyes of Dunraven, the perfect human son was created, masterfully conceived. The child's life was carefully laid out and built around him, with the brainwashing spinning the infant eventually into the perfect marionette—the President of the United States.

Sent around the world for special education, crafting the ideology, skillfully engineered into a poisonous plan, MacNeill Quinn also learned to turn his lustful mind to prey on little girls and boys. After being victimized, the children were exterminated to protect the allure of the office. As an adult, he lived a ruse of being happily married with a child.

Every one of Lord Dunraven's sons are born with azoospermia.

"What the hell is that?" Patrick asks.

"Basically, they didn't produce sperm, meaning they could not reproduce."

"Why would he do that?"

"To protect his dynasty. His heirs, ultimately, could not challenge him."

"But you said the President—his son—had children."

"Yes, that was a diversion of the man's true being, so he could ascend to the highest level of power in the most powerful country."

The President would sit in the situation room and handwrite executive orders, Mr. B said, following the instructions given by his father to de-Americanize the country. During certain prearranged scenes, the President would dance with his pretend wife or hold his daughter's hand for the cameras. He would look and act presidential on the outside. All the while, he is secretly planning not just the dismantling of the United States, but the destruction of the world.

"By Jill entering your soul, the two oldest Royal families have finally united into one," Sylvana says. "Just like you, Jill has Royal ancient blood, and her family worked with yours many centuries ago—families who nurtured and protected mankind, setting the stage for countless acts of random kindness. Both of your ancestors were the founders, entrusted with ancient scriptures. They obeyed its writings, creating the first monetary system dating back to 700 BC."

"If Jill and I belong to the Royal Family, are we related?" I ask.

"Not in the way you think. The two family lineages were once twelve lines of Royalty, but Dunraven and Dymortis have slowly exterminated all but you."

There is a long silence as I try to absorb this.

"An effective currency and commonwealth banking system was created," Mr. B eventually continues, "established and expanded the civility necessary to peacefully unite the human race into a harmonious society."

"This all seems to come down to money."

Sylvana nods. "You are the wealthiest human on earth . . . not only monetarily, but more importantly in faith."

I shake my head. "I still don't understand."

"You will. Eventually, you will."

Chapter 5

"Never be afraid to trust an unknown future to a known God."
—*Corrie Ten Boom*

Patrick and I decide we are ready for some downtime. First, we try some old-style video games—Asteroid, Ms. Pac Man and even Snake. While they are mildly amusing to me, Patrick is not enthused. He talks me into trying out some more modern titles.

He creams me in Death Cars, takes me out in *HitMan: Karma*, and even when we team up in *WWIV: Annihilation* where we were on the same side battling aliens set to destroy the Earth for no apparent reason, he makes me look like a grandma on sedatives.

"C'mon, Mildred. You throw your grenade like a girl!"

I was tempted to take him out with my laser gun, but figure he's the only thing keeping the aliens from turning me into their lunch.

We move on to bowling—a real game with real balls and real lanes—where I hold my own, and even eke out a win. By two whole points. Of course, he trash-talks the whole time and then insinuates I cheated by using my new powers. Since I wasn't entirely clear on what my new powers are, I just simply grin back at him, then flip him the bird. He looks surprised, then chuckles. I'm sure he got my point.

When we leave the bowling alley, there are a lot more people in the house. Since there are only a handful of Soulmadds—a dozen, including me—I would have to assume these folks were either Challengers, or somehow affiliated. As Patrick and I walk around, we say hello to several, which are a cross-section of just about everyone you could find in America: Young and old, thin and fat, dashing and nerdy, male and female, beautiful and dowdy, black, white, Asian, Latino, Eskimo, Aborigine, Indian—both American and South Asian. Apparently, there was some kind of meeting that had been called.

"Well, I think I'm going to take a nap," Patrick says. "Whipping your ass tired me out."

"Okay. Hopefully, in your dreams you'll be a better bowler."

"And maybe you'll learn to use a controller."

This time I only shake my head at him, and he grins before wandering off in the direction of his room.

I walk around for a bit, see there is a movie playing in the theater, find ten or eleven people in the game room gathered around pool tables, laughing and joking, another dozen or so in the electronic game room, all quiet except for the *beeps* and *boops* the machines make. Near the end of the hallway, I come to the frosted teal doors of the spa, or "Water Room" as Apollo called it. Although a nap sounds good, this seems better, so I stick my head in and peek.

The lobby is mostly warm wood with a large, round reception desk and a young Asian lady standing behind it. She smiles at me.

"Welcome," she says. "Just enter through the doors and place your shoes in a cubby, then continue on to the changing room. No clothing, hats or footwear is allowed, and we recommend removing any jewelry as well. I hope you enjoy your stay."

"Okay. Thanks."

I walk into a small hallway lined with dozens of small doors. I open one—number 72—and see it is a small empty space, just large enough for a pair of shoes. I kick mine off, remove my socks and stick them inside. Then I walk around the corner into what is basically a locker room, only the nicest one I've ever seen, with polished wood doors and padded benches. There is soft music playing, but otherwise everything is very quiet.

I go to locker 72 and see there is no lock. I guess stealing isn't really an issue at Manor House. I begin to disrobe and halfway through realize she hadn't given me a towel. I consider going back out and requesting one, but then decide they must have stacks of towels ready. If there are hot tubs and showers, there must be towels.

I walk out and go to the end, which is a large room that I guess is the grooming area as it has sinks, mirrors, stools and counters stocked with razors, combs, cotton swabs, soaps and lotions. To the right, there is a glass door covered in steam. I open it and walk into a huge room with banks of showers on the left, and ahead a series of pools. A large indoor waterfall pours into a swimming pool. Jets in the pools churn up the water. And off to the right are a few doors, one labeled "Steam Room", another "Dry Sauna", a "Fire Room", and an "Ice Room."

I seem to be the only guest, so I decide to start in one of the pools and just spend some time relaxing. I dip my foot in the first one and find it is ice cold. The next is more pleasant, very warm without being hot, so I step down into it and take a seat. I lay my head back on the edge, close my eyes and allow one of the jets to work on my back.

After a few minutes, I hear the sound of a child's laughter and look to see an Asian man walking in with his 5 year old son, both naked, of course. The boy points at the pool I'm in, his father nods, and the child runs to the edge before taking the steps one at a time. I lean my head back again and rest my eyes.

I begin to consider what might be in store for me. Obviously, I'm expected to play a part in what might be some kind of conflict between Henry Davis—a.k.a. Lord Dunraven—and Dymortis against the Soulmadds and their followers. Good vs. evil. Right vs. wrong. And, it seems to me, Heaven vs. Hell. A battle is brewing, and I suspect it will start small and grow as it escalates.

But what is my role? Am I here because of my history with Henry? Or something else?

I hear other voices, a couple of men talking in a language I don't understand as they draw near to the pools. I remain relaxed, eyes closed, trying to focus.

I wonder if I may be asked to somehow infiltrate the . . . what? What should I call them? The Bad Side? The Evil Ones? *Them?*

It crosses my mind that Sylvana and the Soulmadds might ask me to pretend to join *Them* to find out what they're up to. Act as if I was joining their cause to help *Them* take over. Cozy up to "Dad" to get on the inside?

I'm not sure I can do that. I don't think I'm that great of an actor.

I hear new voices, and am a bit confused. I open my eyes to see three naked women heading for the Dry Spa.

I quickly sit up, startled.

This is co-ed?

I look to my right and see a young woman sitting a few feet away from me.

"Hi," she says.

Unconsciously, I move a little farther away.

"You looked surprised," she says with a slight smile.

"Hi . . . Yes, I wasn't . . . wasn't expecting . . ."

"A mixed gender spa?"

"Yeah."

She nods, still smiling. "When you come from the world to this home of equality, it can be a little startling."

I remain quiet, not sure what to say.

"Just relax," she says. "No one cares." Then she closes her eyes.

I look around as a man walks out of the Steam Room, walking past a woman sitting in a lounge chair. They didn't seem to notice each other.

I feel so naïve. On one hand, I realize it is partially my youth and inexperience. I mean, to be honest, until just a minute earlier, I had never seen a real live naked woman before. Sure, movies, pictures, even dreams—but not . . . *in person.* I just wish I was as pure and perfect as some people think I am.

On the other hand, I understand that no one *should* care. It's not like I'm hiding any secrets under my clothes, and I've always been as comfortable naked as I was clothed—I just always did it alone.

"There's nothing wrong with nudity," the young woman says, as if reading my thoughts. "It's what you do with it that changes things."

I pause for several seconds as a couple of children race by, their father yelling at them to stop running.

"Are you a Soulmadd?" I ask.

"No, I'm Leslie. I've been asked to be your assistant."

"Oh. I didn't know I needed one."

"You probably don't. But I'm here in case you do."

"It kind of felt as if you read my mind."

She giggles. "No, I just thought things through, figuring what you might be thinking. I made a logical guess."

I nod. "I like what you said about this being a place of equality—but you've been asked to be my assistant, which sounds like you're . . . not equal."

"Yeah. There's not a perfect word for it. 'Partner' also leaves the wrong impression."

She closes her eyes again.

Leslie is about my age—eighteen or nineteen—with dark, short hair and a tattoo that looks like a butterfly or a humming-bird on the top of her left shoulder.

I have an assistant, or helper, or whatever. I wonder why.

I take a look at my hands and see my fingers have all turned pruney. I should get out. I still feel self-conscious.

Dope.

I still haven't seen any towels. I guess they figure that if you're going to be wet all the time, why bother.

I take a deep breath and move towards the steps, pausing for a second before climbing out. I glance back at Leslie, and her eyes are still closed. She doesn't care.

I head for the Dry Sauna—trying not to act like I'm hurrying —open the door, and step in . . . only to see eight naked women sitting on redwood benches. A couple look up and one smiles at me briefly, but the rest don't notice and keep talking.

It's about a thousand degrees inside, and is quite uncomfortable, but I take a seat as far away from the others as possible, telling myself to get over the nudity thing. If they don't care, I shouldn't.

I hunch over, hanging my head, feeling the sweat pop up on

my skin, running through my scalp, the heat baking me. But, in a strange way, it feels good.

* * *

In the shower, a male attendant—wearing a tank top and baggy shorts—appears, finally offering a towel, and I dry off before heading to the changing area. I have to admit I got used to the co-ed everything. I didn't even notice Leslie getting dressed at the end of the aisle until I was leaving.

"I'll catch up," she says, putting on her bra.

I wave. Maybe blushed.

I wait in the lobby, though I don't know why. Being polite, I guess.

"Dude."

I look up to see Patrick walking in. "Hey. I thought you were napping."

"Tried. Didn't happen." He stops in front of me, looking around. "So how is it?"

"Weird. You'd love it. Guess what—I have an assistant."

"An assistant what?"

"A girl. A young woman."

"What is she assisting you with?"

"I have no idea."

"Do I get one?"

"Sure. I'll be your assistant."

He scrunches up his face. "You get a woman, and I get you? What would you assist *me* with?"

"Probably keeping you away from my assistant."

He laughs as Leslie walks out from the back.

"You didn't have to wait," she says as she pulled a brush through her short, wet hair.

"Patrick was asking what you're assisting me with."

She looks at Patrick and smirks. "I'm your assistant too."

"Cool. I think—"

A voice intrudes into my head:

Collin, to the lower level please . . . Collin, to the lower level as soon as possible.

"I gotta go," I said and hurry out the door, although I wasn't sure where to go.

"Where do you need to be?" Leslie says from behind me.

"The lower level."

"This way," she says, going to opposite direction.

"What's going on?" Patrick asks.

"I'm not sure."

Leslie leads us into a room that looks like a storage area—metal shelving units stocked with cleaning supplies, paper goods, cases of soda stacked up on the floor. She pulls on a corner of a shelf, and the whole unit swivels out, exposing a sliding door in the wall behind it. She slides it open and points. "Down this way."

We slip by her and I start down the stairs, then realize she's not following.

"Aren't you coming?"

"I'm not allowed down there. I'll catch up with you later." She closes the door, and we continue down.

The door at the bottom opens into The Hub, and several people are gathered in the Control Center. They are all staring at monitors.

"What's going on?"

Sylvana turns, a somber look on her face. "They have arrived."

"They who?"

"The Regulators," Mr. Burkfelt says. "They've surrounded the property."

"Wow," Patrick says as I focus in on the big screen.

What I half-expected to see were men with guns. But there are no people showing on the monitors. Only armored vehicles. And tanks. A monitor on the right side, pointed to the sky, shows a helicopter hovering.

"What do they want?" I ask.

No one says anything. They just continue staring at the screens.

A camera follows as a tank lumbers down the street.

Another camera shows a dark sedan coming around the corner

and turning into the driveway. After several seconds, two men in suits get out and walk up the path to the porch, up the steps, then approach the front door.

"What do they want?" I ask again.

The chair that sat in the middle of the room like Captain Kirk's throne slowly turns, revealing the boy/man Apollo. His face is passive.

"You," he says in his child's voice. "They want you, Collin."

Chapter 6

"What does not kill me makes me stronger."—Johanne Wolfgang Von Goethe

Watching the monitor, we see the two men knock on the door.

"We need sound," a man behind me says. Another man goes to a console and begins working a computer. Seconds later, we can hear the outdoor feed, just in time for the door to open.

Leslie stands in the doorway. *"Yes?"*

"I am Detective Mayler from the Chicago Police Department. I have an arrest warrant for Jacob Davis."

"Who?"

"Jacob Davis."

"I'm sorry there's no Jacob here."

"That's okay. We also have a search warrant." He holds out a paper, which Leslie takes. *"We need to enter and search the property."*

Leslie pauses as she reads the warrant. *"Okay,"* she says, backing away as the two men enter.

"Switch to the interior feed," the man at the console says.

"Put one on monitor twelve," Apollo says, "but leave monitor eight where it is. Add a wide shot of the exterior grounds on monitor nine."

The technician clicks on the computer and the monitors change as requested.

"*I don't know why you're looking for this guy here,*" Leslie says.

"*Do you own this property?*" the detective asks.

"*No, it's my family's.*"

"*And your name?*"

"*Leslie Banks.*"

Turning my attention to monitor nine, I see a pair of white vans drive up the driveway and park behind the detective's sedan. A dozen men exit the vehicles, all dressed in black. Some carry cases.

"The Regulators," I say.

"It's okay," Mr. B says. "They cannot find you here." He pauses. "And even if they make it down here, there are other areas we can utilize."

Some of the Regulators make their way around the outside of the property, but most march into the house.

"*What's this?*" Leslie asks as the men file by her.

"*Specialists to help us execute the warrants.*"

"*I don't really like you storming my home, looking for some random guy I've never heard of.*"

The detective doesn't reply.

At the console, the technician switches several monitors to interior feeds, showing the men splitting up into various areas of the house.

"What will happen when they find all the other people in the house?" I ask.

"They have been sequestered," Apollo says.

I turn to look out of the Control Center to see dozens of people from upstairs making their way towards a tunnel off to my left.

"We have many rooms down here for their safety," Sylvana says.

I return my attention to the monitors and we watch for a long time in silence as camera feeds switch and change, showing the men checking out the many rooms. They overturn furniture, open cabinets and throw the items inside onto the floor, pull out drawers and toss the contents out. It's obvious their intent wasn't to look for me, but making a mess. In the entertainment room, two men remove hammers from a case and began destroying the screens of the computer games. The sound isn't on in those rooms, but it's not needed.

One of the feeds shows a man going into the storage room, and I tense. He stands in the middle for several moments, looking around before sweeping items off a shelf with one arm. He follows suit with several other shelves, eventually reaching the end. Then he grabs the top shelf and tugs, intending to topple the entire shelving unit over, knocking it to the floor. Except it doesn't topple. He tries again, and nothing. But he does seem to notice that it gave a little, and he grabs the brace on the edge, swiveling the unit out, just had Leslie had done to reveal the hidden door.

The man pulls a handgun from his belt and goes behind the shelves. The angle of the camera prevents us from watching clearly what he's doing, but it doesn't take much imagination.

"Seal the stairwell," Apollo says.

The technician makes a few clicks. "Sealed."

We wait.

"Close the sliding door behind him."

Some clicks. "Closed."

"Seal it."

Clicks. "Sealed."

"Seal the storage room."

"Sealed."

"Prepare the deactivating gas."

"Ready."

A pause of several seconds. "Proceed."

"Deactivating gas?" Patrick asks.

"It puts them to sleep. We'll collect him later."

"They'll know he's missing," I say.

"Eventually." Apollo turns to one of the other men in the room. "We need to retrieve the body and reset the hidden passage."

"On it," the man says, leaving.

On the other monitor, the detectives lead Leslie into the sitting room.

"*Maybe we can come to an understanding,*" Detective Mayler says as he reaches down and starts to undo his zipper.

Leslie turns and walks to the window.

The other detective approaches Leslie from behind and grabs her by the arms. Leslie arches her back as he spins her around to face Detective Mayler.

"It won't take long," Mayler says.

I turn to Mr. B. "We have to stop them."

"It's a ploy," he says. "They know they're being watched. They're trying to draw you out."

"But we still need to stop them."

"I will," Patrick says.

I turn to Sylvana, but she has slipped away.

"*Gentlemen.*"

I look back up at the monitor and see Sylvana has entered the room.

Both men, startled, shoved their dicks back in their pants.

"*Ma'am,*" Mayler says. "*We're here to arrest Jacob Davis.*"

"*Leslie, you can go.*"

The young woman crosses the room and walks out.

"*I think you should leave now.*"

"*Not until we have Mr. Davis in custody.*"

"*Then you'll be here a very long time.*"

Sylvana turns and passes through the open doorway, closing the door behind her.

"Seal the Sitting Room," Apollo says.

A pause. "Sealed."

The men in the room look at each other, then go to the door, finding it locked.

The second detective takes a step back, then kicks the door. Nothing happens. He tries again and again.

"*Step back.*" Mayler pulls out his service revolver and fires off a round at the doorknob.

The second detective ducks as the bullet ricochets off into a wall. Mayler then kicks at the door, to no avail.

The second detective pulls out his cell phone. He punches

some buttons. *"No service."*

Mayler checks his phone. *"Shit."* Then he begins pounding on the door and shouting.

I check the other monitors and see the destruction is continuing.

"Prepare Deactivation Gas for the Sitting Room."

"Ready."

"Proceed."

We watch as Mayler continues to shout and pound, while the second detective goes to the window and tries to kick it out. Then he pulls his gun and fires.

"What's that?" Mayler says after the reverberations of the gunshot dies away.

"What's what?"

"That hissing."

They both stand with their heads cocked, listening.

"Fucking gas!"

They begin pounding and shouting and kicking feverishly. In less than a minute, they both stop, staggering a little. Then the second detective topples over, his head crashing into an end table.

"Prepare to seal all rooms."

Detective Mayler holds a hand to his head as if he has a headache, then slumps to the ground.

"Ready."

"Proceed."

We watch the other monitors, where doors suddenly close, the men inside turn, startled, all moving towards the exits at the same time.

"Prepare Deactivation Gas."

Some of the men kick. Those with hammers—one with a mallet—try to use them on the doorknobs.

"Ready."

"Proceed."

A couple of the Regulators are in the kitchen, one in the living room where there are no doors.

"Prepare Deactivation Gas for the kitchen and living room."

"We may not have enough, sir."

"Please do your best."

"Yes sir."

We watch as the other Regulators start dropping. Seven, eight, nine.

I turn in time to see Sylvana enter the control room. Behind her, Leslie passes by, on her way to the sequester area.

"We will need thirty men to move our guests," Sylvana says.

"You've got two here," I say.

"Collin, you will have to stay here for a short time," Mr. Burkfelt says. "It is you they are after."

"But they're unconscious."

He looks past me, to Sylvana. I turn towards her.

She smiles slightly. "A true leader would never ask someone to do something he himself wouldn't do." Then she turns and walks out of the room.

We quickly follow.

* * *

We go into the sequester area—a series of barrack-style rooms with six to eight bunks each—and I pick out thirty men to help move the bodies.

"Where are we moving them?" Patrick asks.

"There is a holding cell at the far end," Sylvana says, pointing. "Do not harm them. Go to the top of the tunnel and wait at the entrance. The doors will open when the gas dissipates." She pauses, as if listening.

The last three men have gone down.

She nods, and I lead the men up the ramp, where we wait. I put the men in small groups and give them instructions on which room to take. Just as I pair the last two with me and Patrick, the doors rumble open.

We file in, the men splitting off to their designated areas. I lead Patrick and the other two men into the Sitting Room where we find the detectives. I go to the second one, who had banged his head on the table, but he isn't bleeding. He would, though, wake up to a large lump.

We lift the man, my hands going under his arms, my helper taking his legs. We follow Patrick and his helper out of the room, down the hall, into the living room, and into the tunnel entrance. We follow three or four others carrying Regulators underground.

Eventually, we get them into the Holding Cell, lay them on the floor next to the others ahead of us, lined up neatly. Out of breath, I ask the guys to disarm our guests.

It is a large, almost cavernous room, capable of holding not only the fourteen men who raided the house, but probably every other person in the house. But not exactly comfortably. Other than a single sink and one toilet, there is nothing but concrete and lights—no beds, no chairs, no tables.

"This one's still sort of conscious," one of the helpers says, pointing at a Regulator.

"Was he from the kitchen?"

"Yes."

"He didn't get the full amount of gas. Can you keep an eye on him?"

He nods.

More file in. We collect all the handguns and a couple of large-blade knives as well.

"Is this all of them?" I ask as two helpers shuffle in with a Regulator.

"Yes sir."

"Okay, file out," I say, and watch as the guys step out to the hallway. Patrick and I are the last, Patrick still carrying the gun from the last Regulator to be brought in.

Near the corner, one of the men in black sits up. The one from the kitchen. Despite looking woozy, he tries to stand—unsuccessfully. He gets halfway up before toppling over onto the two men lying next to him.

"Let's go," I say, and we step out, closing the two large metal doors. Just before they clink shut, we hear the woozy Regulator shout:

"You're doomed!"

We secure the doors, collect the weapons, and head out. None of us say a word.

Chapter 7

"All warfare is based on deception."—Sun Tzu, The Art of War

We sit around a large round table in a conference room. In place of windows, the room is ringed with monitors showing feeds from the Control Center.

"They're only going to escalate," I say, stating the obvious.

Mr. B nods. "We need to act before they react."

"But they don't know what happened," Patrick says.

"Yet," Mr. B says. "I'm sure the folks out in the tanks and armored vehicles are wondering why they've lost radio contact."

Apollo, using one of the monitors to play a video game, says: "We have two options -- wait them out, or escalate first."

We all look at the back of his head while he destroys alien spaceships.

"How do you escalate against tanks?" I ask.

Apollo pauses his game long enough to type into a console and change the channels on a few of the monitors. We stare at the screens for several seconds.

"It's already on CNN," he says. "I'm sure the other cable news channels will follow—until Dunraven orders them off the story."

"I think you need to be more transparent," Sylvana says.

The little boy with an old man's soul smiles, mischievously.

"I posted a little message on social media." He taps a button, and the monitor that had shown his video game changes.

Y R there tanks in a quite Chicago neightborhood?

"I included a screen capture of the street. It went on all the major platforms."

I don't point out that he misspelled *quiet* and *neighborhood*. I'm sure it was on purpose.

Apollo smirks at me. "Of course I misspelled them. If it was perfect, it might not be as believable."

I nod, still a little freaked out that he is in my head. I have to learn how to do that to him.

You can't . . . unless I let you.

He is still smirking, as if he enjoyed my discomfort.

Patrick points. "The other channel picked it up."

Fox News is broadcasting the feed from a local station.

Mr. B points to another monitor. "There's movement on the street."

One of the tanks is rotating its turret as an armored vehicle across the street begins going in reverse towards the intersection.

"They're being called off," Mr. B says.

I feel a buzzing in my pocket and pulled out my cell phone.

Dad, the screen says. I've been meaning to change that.

"Put it on speaker," Sylvana says.

I push the button to answer, then speaker.

"Thanks for calling them off," I say.

"Release my men."

"Why? So they can annoy me again?"

A pause. *"They will leave you be."*

"Who will you send instead?"

"You may think you're immune while you're there . . . but you have to leave sometime."

"Thanks for the warning."

"Release my men."

"Or what?"

A long pause.

"Do not anger me, young man. The wrath will not just be felt

by you."

"As you've already demonstrated."

"*Release my men.*"

I pause for a few seconds. "I'll think about it," I say, ending the call.

"Those guys must be something special," Patrick says.

"Supposedly his elite team," Mr. B says. "They weren't expecting the gas."

Apollo turns up the sound on one of the news feeds.

"*. . . a statement from the Chicago Protection Agency saying that the tanks and armored vehicles were in destination to a location when their GPS malfunctioned, putting them in the residential neighborhood. Basically, they're calling it a technology mishap, and as you can see from the images we're receiving from our affiliate, the vehicles are leaving the area.*

"*Now, there have been reports from the residents there that a sedan and a couple of vans pulled into the driveway of one home—you can see them here in this still shot taken earlier—and that several men got out of the vehicles and entered the home. Now that we're back with the live feed, I'm hoping we can see—yes, there you can see a sedan and two vans still parked in that driveway. Other than a small crowd that has gathered there across the street, there is no other activity we can see. We hope to have a reporter on the ground soon, but right now, we're going to take a quick break . . .*"

He mutes the sound.

"So, as usual, the story is being spun as something different than what it is," I say.

"It is to be expected," Sylvana says. "We have some leverage holding these men. We need to decide what to do with them."

We all turn to look at Mr. Burkfelt, who is frowning.

"It is a sticky situation," he says. "We could just let them go, but that would mean they would be able to see some of our operations here, and that wouldn't be acceptable. Plus, there's the chance one or more might have the opportunity to break free and do some damage, either to our facilities or to our people."

"We could tie their hands and blindfold them," Patrick says.

"That would be one solution—if we had a dozen or so blindfolds and restraints lying around, which we don't."

"Then gas them again," Patrick suggests.

"We're out of the DG," Apollo says.

"Plus, if we did have enough gas," Mr. B adds, "we'd have to drag their bodies out to their vehicles, and there's a lot of press outside now."

We sit in silence for a few minutes, watching the monitors.

"Then we leave them, for now," I say. "Maybe we can arrange to make some makeshift blindfolds and restraints, wait until night, and move them then."

"Or just keep them," Mr. B says. "The longer we hold them, the more leverage we have."

"What if the tanks come back?"

"They won't." He pauses. "They may try something else, though."

"Like what?"

"Sending men on foot to storm the property."

Another long pause as this sinks in. I imagine black-clad men sneaking up in the darkness with rifles.

"Are there any weapons here?" I ask.

Sylvana and Apollo exchange glances.

"We do have a defense mechanism," Apollo says. "But it hasn't been fully tested, and it might draw more attention than the tanks."

"When was the last you worked on it?" Sylvana asks.

"Weeks ago," Apollo says. "It was stable for almost an hour, until a fluctuation forced me to shut it down."

"What are you talking about?" I ask.

"Basically, in layman's terms, a force field. A protective shield. Made up of dense radioactive elements."

"Radiation?"

"Yes, but it's been modified—a focused low-powered non-iodizing form which I've been able to shape in a way that directs the rays into a thin dome that envelopes the property."

"But you said it could draw more attention than the tanks?"

"It glows. It's not very luminous—it's not bright enough to read a book—but it would be noticeable to the naked eye."

Again, we fall silent, all of us thinking.

"They will come," Mr. B says.

"I guess it leaves us no alternative," Sylvana says, looking at me solemnly.

"Uh oh," I say, smiling. But then it fades.

"It is time for you to learn your new powers, Collin."

"You make it sound like a bad thing."

"No, not bad. I just wish we had more time to allow you to work through them."

I look from Sylvana to Apollo, and back. "I don't mean to sound flippant, but how hard can they be?"

Sylvana offers a slight smile, while Apollo giggles.

Chapter 8

"Superman don't need no seat belt."—Muhammad Ali

We enter another cavernous room—one as large or larger than the holding pen where the Regulators cooled their heels. Sylvana had asked for a few of the Challengers to be brought in to help along with Patrick. It wasn't yet clear to me why I needed any help, but then there seems to be a lot I don't know.

I stand in the middle of the room, Sylvana just behind me to my left, Apollo behind me to my right, and Mr. B in a chair way off to the side. In front of me stands Patrick and four others —Leslie, a young Asian woman named Kee, a large middle-aged Hispanic man the size of a Sumo wrestler named Xavier, and a tall, thin black man in his late 20's named Terence.

"I would like to thank you for participating in this experiment," Sylvana tells the group, her voice reverberating in the giant concrete room. "Collin is going to attempt various tests on you. They will not hurt. You may not even know they are happening. Some are mental, some are physical. Please do not be alarmed at whatever may occur, either to you or one of the others. Ready?"

"Yes, ma'am," they all say.

First, let's start with telepathy, Sylvana's voice tells me. *Try to read Kee's thought.*

I stare at the young woman, not sure what I was supposed to be doing.

Find her signature, Sylvana says. *Tune into each individual's actions, reactions, tics and movements. That will give you the channel to their signature.*

Kee starts to appear uncomfortable.

You do not need to stare, only observe.

I look away and notice just as I did that Kee licked her lips.

As I gaze at the cement floor, trying to pick up on anything other signals, I saw her right shoe lift slightly for a moment, then lower. Then, suddenly, quietly:

He's cute. I need to pee. Should have gone before. He has a nice ring.

Good, Sylvana says, mentally. *Now try to insert a thought into her stream.*

No clue how to do that.

Follow her stream.

I try to pick it up again.

I hope we can sit soon. He looks nervous. Is he doing anything?

I think I find it.

YOU CAN USE THE RESTROOM IF YOU NEED.

Her head jerks back, and her hands go to her ears.

Too loud, Sylvana says. *Whisper.*

"Sorry," I say out loud.

"Excuse me," Kee said, then half-runs out of the room.

The others exchange glances, wondering what had happened. Now try Terence.

He's more fidgety than Kee, moving his weight from one leg to the other every few seconds, looking around from me to Sylvana to Apollo to me.

I hope we eat soon. I'm starved. Nice turkey sandwich. Pasta salad. Can we have beer here?

I focus.

If you are of legal age, yes.

Terence blinks madly for a couple of seconds, like he has seen a ghost. Then he smiles.

"Pretty good. Pretty good," he says, nodding his head.

Now try Xavier.

This man is more difficult. He doesn't move. He doesn't blink. He just stares at me, as if with a dare.

We have a stare-down.

I try to tune in, try to pick up anything, only coming up with Patrick wishing he had put some cortisone on his scars to keep them from itching.

I hold my breath for a few moments, but that doesn't work.

I blink.

Xavier blinks.

Then, faintly:

Why is this dude our new leader? Looks like a kid in high school.

I pounce.

Graduated last year.

Xavier doesn't react. Just stares at me with the same blank expression. Then he looks away, his only acknowledgement.

I glance at Leslie. She's smirking. I notice her thumb and finger are absently rubbing against each other.

Must be mind-reading. I wonder if I will feel it.

I don't know, I tell her. *Do you?*

She smile, then giggles.

Good, Sylvana's voice says. *Now try something else . . . something playful.*

At first, I didn't know what she meant. Then I get an idea.

The three men had short hair, or in the case of Patrick, none.

So I try it on Leslie.

Her shoulder-length hair begins to rise.

Behind me, Apollo snickers.

Patrick turns to look at Leslie and says: "Cool."

"What?" she asks, looking around half-alarmed.

"Check your hair."

She put her hands up to the side of her head, then higher. "Oh! Oh!" she says as her fingers tried to bring down her hair, which is standing straight up.

I release the stream, and her hair falls.

She smiles as she tries to make it look right again.

"Patrick," Apollo says, "hold your hand out."

He does, and I find it easy to latch onto his stream. I move his arm out away from his body. Patrick then tugs it back. I move it again. He yanks it back. I try again, but he is straining against me. I grit my teeth and try to focus better. His arm jerks out for a second before he wrenches it back. We do this three or four times, and he looks like he is directing traffic. As he gets used to me struggling with his left arm, I make his right arm rise. For a few seconds, both his arms stick out, like a scarecrow.

"Aw, man," he says, and I let him go.

You know what to try next, Sylvana says.

This will be difficult, if not impossible. But I try.

At first, nothing happens. Then Xavier's arms—which are crossed over his chest—come away from his body as if he is surfing. Terence and Patrick both jump, surprised, as the large man floats a few inches off the floor.

Go ahead, Sylvana prompts.

So, again, I try something that I'm not sure will work—but it does. Xavier floats over the floor, surfing it smoothly as I guide him towards a wall 50 feet away. As he comes within a few feet, I turn him left and slightly pick up speed.

"Hey! Hey!" he shouts, though it's hard to tell if it's in surprise, anger or delight.

As he comes to the corner, I slow him down and bring him to a stop, then lower him softly. When his feet touch the cement, he turns to me and claps his hands, applauding.

"That was freakin' awesome," Patrick says. "You just moved a three hundred pound man around the room at your will."

"Two-eighty, kid," Xavier says, smiling as he re-joins the small group.

"Do me next, do me next," Patrick says.

"Okay," I tell him. "Be careful what you asked for."

And I raise him to the ceiling. A little too quickly. I have to pull back as his head nearly collides with it.

"Careful, dude," Patrick says, nevertheless overjoyed.

I turn him horizontal, then slowly glide him around the room.

"Hey, look at me! I'm Superman!" He strikes a pose with one arm out, like the Man of Steel might have.

"Don't get cocky," Xavier taunts. "There are strings attached."

I bring him down carefully, and he runs back looking like he just stepped off his favorite roller coaster.

"Mr. Burkfelt, if you could assist us," Sylvana says.

Mr. B gets up and walks towards the group. "I'm going to ask you some questions," he says. "Leslie, what is your greatest fear?"

She thinks a moment. "Being in a horrific car accident."

"Xavier, what was your last medical ailment?"

The big man pauses, looking from Mr. B to me, and back. "I had a cyst."

"What kind of cyst?"

Another pause. "You know, a cyst."

"What kind of cyst?" Mr. B asks again.

A pause. "A pilonidal cyst."

"And where was that located?"

"In my butt."

"Your butt?"

"Tailbone."

I turn to Sylvana. *What is the point of this?*
You'll see.

"Terence, have you ever seen a ghost?"

"No."

"Have you ever seen a UFO?"

"No."

Suddenly, I have a kind of twinge, something that makes me feel slightly uneasy.

Mr. B nods at Terence, then goes to the next. "Patrick, how old were you when you had your first sexual experience with another person?"

A slight pause, with a smirk. "Fifteen."

That twinge again. It was an interesting feeling.

Mr. B turns to me. "Collin, do you have any questions for these folks?"

I think for a few moments. "Terence, where did you see the UFO?"

"I said I *didn't* see a UFO."

"I know that's what you said, but that's not the truth. Where did you see the UFO?"

Terence tries to look angry, like I'm calling him a liar. Which I am. Then he seems to deflate a little. "A few years ago. My friend and I were driving from Wisconsin and saw . . . something."

I nod, then turn to Patrick. "And when was your first sexual experience with another person?"

He looks like he is thinking for several seconds, then starts to say something, then stops. He appears uncomfortable.

I wait.

"Um . . ." he starts to say. "I guess I can let you know when it happens."

I nod and turn towards Sylvana. "Anything else?"

"There are some other things we can work on later," she says. "I'd like to thank our little group for helping us with our experiments. We ask that you keep this to yourself. You may return to your quarters."

The three turn to leave, Patrick staying behind. Terence was feeling slightly disappointed that he didn't get to levitate, so I help him along, lifting him up and sliding him to the door.

"Thanks, man!" he says, giving me the thumbs-up before exiting.

"You may notice there are some objects behind you. This will be your next challenge," Sylvana says as I turn to see several items sitting on the floor -- a basketball, a bowling ball, what looks like a cannonball, a two-by-four, a slab of cement about six feet high, and a large steel plate, roughly the same size.

"You want me to move those?"

"No," Apollo says. "Destroy them."

I frown.

"There's a control inside of you that will allow you to disturb the molecular structure," Apollo says. "You are able to manipulate the atoms."

I'm still frowning.

"Think of your focus as water," Sylvana says, "as it dissolves the basic arrangement of the object."

I step in front of the basketball, and stare at it, thinking water. Nothing happens.

"Relax your mind . . . find the channel," Sylvana says.

"But it's an inanimate object."

"Everything has a channel, Collin. Even inanimate objects."

I take a deep breath and concentrate. How do I manipulate atoms?

And then I begin to feel something. A sound like . . . a humming. Very light, very faint. I try to tune in. It seems to come in louder.

"You have found the flow," Sylvana says. "Absorb it."

I focus, feeling a little like I am meditating. And then the humming fills my head. I begin to see the ball as a living, breathing entity, the atoms moving, albeit slowly.

I feel a push from inside me, and the atoms began to move faster, and faster. The top layer begins to melt away. Then, suddenly, the ball pops—nearly explodes. Bits of rubber dot my pants.

I turn my attention to the bowling ball. It is easier to find the flow, but it takes longer to have any affect. After what seems like an eternity—but maybe two minutes—the marbled blue ball begins to shake, then cracks. It's not a clean crack, but it renders the ball useless.

"Not quite destroyed," I mumble.

"You'll get better, with practice," Apollo says.

I stand in front of the iron ball. The flow comes easily, and in less than a minute, the ball literally begins to melt into a molten blob.

"Touch it," Apollo says.

I kneel down and find it cool to the touch.

"Now, split the wood."

"In half?"

"Down the middle."

The long ways.

I concentrate. It doesn't take long for it to begin to shake, but instead of splitting, it bursts into about a million splinters. They explode in every direction, and everyone jumps back.

"Sorry about that. Is everyone okay?" I ask, brushing bits of wood off my clothes.

Patrick and Mr. B brush their shirts, Apollo shakes himself, while Sylvana just stands there, small remnants of the board stuck to her clothes and in her hair.

"You will need to practice some control," she says, straight-faced.

"That was funny," Apollo says.

"For the last two objects," Sylvana says, "you need to pass through them."

"*Through* them?"

"Yes."

I check to see if she is joking, but considering I've never known her to kid around, I know she is serious.

I sigh and step in front of the concrete slab.

"You need to disrupt the molecular structure without dis-solving them," Apollo says.

No kidding.

I concentrate, consider, then take a deep breath.

"You must pass without hesitation so as not to absorb the material," Sylvana says.

Oh good. I could end up with a gut full of cement.

I find the channel and focus. After a while—I lose track of just how long—I feel ready, and step forward. In my eyes, or mind, the slab begins to shimmer. My foot and lower leg disappear into it, and I just step through. I feel nothing but a light buzzing, a tingling along my exposed skin. And then I'm on the other side.

Patrick claps, and Mr. B is beaming. Neither Apollo nor Sylvana seem surprised.

I move to the steel plate and ponder it. I walked through concrete, I can do this.

I find the channel quickly, see the shimmer, wait a few moments and boldly step through. Again the tingling—though this time it stings like needles—but I pass quickly.

Again, the clapping, the beaming, and the indifference.

"Now, there is something I need to tell you," Sylvana says.

"There are a couple of other abilities you have. One is known as The Orb. It is one I can teach you, and will do so when we can leave the building. You are basically able to transport yourself at nearly the speed of light by turning your being into an Orb. I have used it many, many times, and Jill had the power as well. It helped us to travel in a moment to Central America for our clandestine meetings."

I blink, taking this in. "You made me slog through the hot, horrible jungle, with bugs and animals and plants that cut up my legs when I could have just zipped there like Star Trek?"

"You were not ready," she says simply. "There is another power you have, one that I have only been told about."

"Told? By who?"

She smiles thinly, but doesn't answer the question. "It is a power that, as far as I know, only you have. But it is not one you can test nor experiment with. It is supremely destructive, and can only be used under the most necessary and dire circumstances. It is the ultimate damaging power ever imagined."

A somberness falls over me. I recall a term I learned in high school. *With great power comes great responsibility.*

"The power is called The Surge. Think of a nuclear weapon, wiping out everything in its range. Except The Surge only destroys living beings. While inanimate objects may be adversely affected, becoming possibly structurally unstable, it is the sentient beings that will be obliterated. And it is not discerning. It will take friend and foe alike." She pauses. "I do not know how you access it, or direct it—if you can direct it—except that the power comes from the ring."

I look down at my hand. "You mean, it's like some comic book superhero? I point it like this—"

I stick my hand out, fist clenched, ring pointing at Patrick, who gives a little shriek and jumps away.

"Don't worry, I won't obliterate you."

"Uh huh," he says, standing way off to the side.

"Just know," Sylvana says, "that it is a last resort. We do not know exactly what will happen when you use it—if you use it—but it is totally destructive to the living being it is used on."

"My best guess," Apollo says, "is that the tissue either melts or is evaporated."

"So it's a form of heat."

"Possibly, but not one we have a complete understanding of. It may be radioactive, like nuclear fission, or it may be something we haven't conceived of yet."

"Someone has," I say.

"Yes, and He is entrusting it to you," Sylvana says. "He believes you can handle it, and use it properly—if it needs to be used at all—but that does not mean an accident or misuse cannot happen. You are fallible."

She pauses to let that sink in.

"But you, with the other Soulmadds, are our one great hope."

Chapter 9

"Everything you can imagine is real."—Pablo Picasso

I slip out the backdoor, onto the porch, allowing my eyes to adjust to the darkness, my ears to the sounds. I've changed into all-black clothes, even black sneakers. I move to the railing, looking out over the immense backyard, the expanse of grass that seems large enough to play a professional football game. It had warmed up enough that the snow was mostly gone, with only patches here and there. At the far end of the field are trees, that, I suspect, is where the Regulators are hiding and waiting.

There's too much space for them to cross without being seen.

Behind me, Apollo and Sylvana step quietly onto the porch. We simply stand and stare.

After a couple of minutes: *There*, Apollo says, mentally. His arm points generally into the dark.

Yes, Sylvana says.

It takes me several seconds, but I see it—what seems like lumps of grass are moving, very slowly. Four, five of them.

They seem to be under some type of tarp or cloth.

Yes, Apollo says, with others behind the trees, providing cover.

At that moment, I see a flash of what seems a muted flashlight beam—but I only see it for just a split second.

We are probably being watched with night-vision goggles, I think.

Of course, Apollo says. *And a rifle is probably trained on you right now as well.*

I watch a lump rise slowly, then move forward a few inches. I picture a man underneath a dark tarp, wiggling like a caterpillar, pushing a handgun or rifle along the ground with him.

And an IFB, Apollo says.

A what?

Radio earpiece with someone in the trees communicating information.

I consider the possibilities.

Are you ready? Sylvana asks.

I guess.

Okay. You want to focus on where you want to go, feel the energy pull up into your chest, then let it go—like we practiced, only now there are no walls.

Avoid the trees, Apollo says.

Many of the things I learned in that big room will now take place, only more quickly, and without a second chance.

I take a deep breath and then step down onto the narrow brick walkway. I hesitate for a moment, then following Sylvana's instructions, I focus, feel, and let go.

It's only a second, maybe less. I overshoot, lose balance and tumble sideways along the grass, rolling into a tree face-first. I scramble up, scraping dead leaves and dirt off my cheeks, looking around to get oriented.

I'm fifty yards past where I wanted to go—dang, that was fast. I mean—blink—and I was 150 yards from the back of the Manor House. I missed my target, but it might actually be a better position. I can come up behind them, which is much better than zipping into the middle of their little gathering.

Now it's a matter of approaching quietly. At least I won't have to do it under a tarp.

I cover the first 25 yards quickly, slinking behind a tree and looking for my targets. A figure in black, peeking out around a trunk, a contraption on his head—the goggles, I'm sure—and a rifle pointing up. He's off to the left. I scan to the right, and see another, prone on the ground, barrel pointed towards the house.

Suddenly, something appears next to me, making me jump.

Just me, Apollo says. *You can do whatever you need to do, and he won't know what's happening or where you are. You may wish to get closer, to be more effective. I'd also suggest you try neutralizing the man lying down first as he may be more difficult.*

I nod and take a step.

If you wish to go silently, Apollo says, *float yourself like you did with the others, but slowly.*

It was one thing to do that to someone else, but seems more tricky to perform it on myself. I close my eyes and concentrate. It takes several seconds, but I can feel my feet rise from the grass. I look around to see where I want to go, then slide myself in that direction. Moments later, I'm hovering over the man lying on the ground, who has his rifle pointing at the house, covering the other men crawling across the lawn.

Just put him to sleep, Apollo says.

I hold out my hand, fingers spread, then slowly bring them together. I feel a buzzing in my skull, then down my shoulder and arm. The man's head tilts as if he's listening for something, then lays his head down and is out.

"Hey!" It's the man who had been hiding behind the tree off to the left. He's now halfway to Apollo and I, gun leveled at us.

My hand swings around and I make the same gesture. The man's eyes roll back in his head, his knees start to go out from under him—and the gun goes off.

Instead of a loud report, however, it sounds more like a *wwwhhhuuuppp*. A silencer.

The bullet goes wildly astray as the guy collapses into a heap.

I turn my attention to the men in the middle of the lawn who had been inching along under their coverings. Each has stopped. One man has poked his head out and is looking back towards us, but the darkness and shadows kept us hidden.

Another one of the Regulators pops his head into the night

air, looking at the man on the ground nearest to him, whispering something.

We just wait.

The two men exchange words, and keep looking back towards us. The third finally pops his head out to see what's going on.

Behind us, a vehicle's engine rumbles to life. Sounds like a truck. Just as Apollo and I look back to see where it's coming from, the headlights come on. The beams are pointed straight at us, but a couple of trees block them from hitting us directly. I look at Apollo, who appears confused. His eyes wildly scan the scene.

Then I see them: Four men with night vision goggles and rifles pointed at us, coming out from behind tree trunks.

Then everything happens extremely fast.

First, one of the men shouts "Get down on the ground, now!"

At the same moment, Apollo mentally screams at me *Now!*

A white ball of light flashes to my left where Apollo was, and is just as quickly gone.

A shot goes off—no silencer. A clean, clear cracking sound.

I hear, or think I hear, a scream.

I am slow on the up-take, hesitating a second before doing what Apollo had done, and tap into The Orb, instantly transporting myself straight up.

Then I realize why I heard the scream.

There needs to be clear space for The Orb to zip from one space to another. It's not a Star Trek transporter. No way to pass through walls. Or, in this case, tree limbs and leaves.

I am being sliced like a loaf of bread, excruciating pain carving through my flesh.

Coming out of the trees, I lose control, my trajectory spinning wildly, shooting off somewhere towards the east. I feel myself arcing through the air, then beginning to fall, no way to know where I am, or where my body is heading. I can't see. I can only feel the falling, and the pain.

And then I hit the ground.

Apparently, the angle is low enough that I don't smack into it, but roll. It's not grass, and it's not dirt. Asphalt. I am rolling in a Target Store parking lot, coming to a hard-and-fast stop against one of those metal corrals for collecting shopping carts, the back of my head banging against a post.

I just lay there on my side, right cheek resting on the black-top, trying to take back the air that had been knocked out of me. In the glow of the parking lot lights, there's a guy about my age in a jacket under a bright orange vest, holding onto a couple of shopping carts, staring at me.

He doesn't say anything for several seconds, and when he does, it's simply: "Holy crap."

My breathing is beginning to return to normal, and I do my best to sit up. I look at my right arm, but see no damage—the pain that felt like I had been sliced-and-diced didn't show externally, but was still stinging loudly on the inside.

All I can think of, though, was getting back to Manor House. I shakily get to my feet, my head a bit dizzy.

"Should I call 9-1-1?" the guy asks.

"Which Target is this?"

He frowns, not understanding my question at first. "Rockford."

Rockford? That's 80 miles from where I started.

"Which way is Chicago?"

Again he frowns, but then points off to his left.

"Thanks," I say, and immediately slip into The Orb.

I can only imagine the shopping cart wrangler standing there, wondering where I went, and wondering if he had imagined the whole thing.

I am back in Chicago moments later, but apparently need to work on my landings as I again careen off the ground, skimming it like a stone on water. Fortunately, this seems to be a park instead of a parking lot, nothing but grass. And snow. And it was snow that I ended up rolling into.

I lay on my back, staring up at the stars, hearing a dog barking far off to my left.

I turn my head in that direction, and see Manor House basically across the street. I can see men with guns now running towards it, a truck following.

I sit up and try to focus my scrambled brain, considering what I might do. By the time I could get up and run, they'd be at the house. But it was the only thing I can—

Then, there's a loud electrical sound, a snapping, like when a circuit is thrown and the power pops on. And Manor House was suddenly bathed in an odd, pulsing purple glow.

* * *

All I can think is that I had failed. I may not have had enough time to work on my new powers, but I still feel like I had wildly missed the mark. Apollo, apparently, had made it back inside and had turned on the protective field, and I was stuck out here, only to watch.

Some of the Regulators that were running towards the house fell, others stopped in their tracks.

A white van pulls up, and a few more Regulators get out, one of them barking orders.

The men still standing raise their weapons.

"Fire!"

And they do, the rounds going off nearly simultaneously, like an execution squad. But it seems to have no effect.

"Again—fire!"

Same thing, without a change.

As the sounds of gunfire dissipate, I can hear sirens in the distance. The leader of the Regulators hears it too.

"Disengage!"

Several of the men collect their comrades who had fallen, then hurry to the van, piling in, the leader getting behind the wheel. The vehicle starts up, and speeds off.

I watch them drive off, then run to the house—but not too close.

Ffffmmmmmpppphhhh.

And the shield is turned off.

I run to the door, and find it locked. Of course. I pound on it, and a few moments later, it's opened by Leslie.

"Are you okay?" she asks.

"Yeah, are you? How's everything here?"

"Fine. They're waiting for you."

I hurry in and go down to the Control Center and see the group waiting for me. Apollo is sitting in the captain's chair, not looking well.

Symbian and Voltar both approach, the brown dog licking my hand.

"It was a valiant effort, Collin," Sylvana says.

"But I failed."

"There is no success without failure. You are fine. We are all fine."

"Is Apollo okay? He doesn't look so good."

"He is fatigued, but will recover."

Patrick comes up to me, and gives me a handshake. "That was awesome," he says, smiling.

"Thanks, but it didn't feel awesome."

"That's what the awesome people say."

I turn towards the others. "What do we do now?"

Sylvana and Mr. B exchange a look.

"I think it's time to reveal the next level," he says.

Chapter 10

*"Hail to the Chief we have chosen for the nation, Hail to the Chief!
We salute him, one and all. Hail to the Chief, as we pledge cooperation.
In proud fulfillment of a great, noble call."—Albert Gamse*

We sit in a conference room—Sylvana, Mr. B, Apollo, Patrick and me—surrounded by video monitors on the walls showing various aspects of life outside Manor House. It's the middle of the night, and other than an occasional car passing by, nothing is happening. I suspect, though, that the Regulators are not far away.

We're brought coffee, water and light snacks, and I realize how hungry I am as I take a handful of crackers and cheese.

"So when do I need to confront Dymortis?" I ask, hoping I don't sound as reluctant as I feel.

"First things first," Mr. B says. "You need to climb the ladder before you get on the roof. Patrick, could you open the door and see if Dr. Jarminsky is here?"

Patrick jumps up, opening the door and allowing a distinguished middle-aged man in a button-down shirt and khakis to enter.

"Thank you for joining us so late," Mr. B says. "Dr. Jarminsky is—was—a high-ranking official with the Center for Disease Control and Prevention, also known as the CDC. He recently resigned due to moral conflicts with what he was witnessing. We're hoping,

Doctor, that you can bring us up to date on the virus."

The doctor blinks behind rather thick, round glasses, looking at his odd audience of an older lady, and eight-year-old boy, a professor, and me and Patrick—who probably look like high school students to him. "That would depend, I suppose, on your basic knowledge of infectious diseases."

Mr. B chuckles. "Yes, I would think that other than suffering through them, our knowledge is fairly limited. But we'll do our best to keep up."

He blinks some more and stands nervously at the end of the table. "Well, the particular virus you're referring to is a type influenza A that is a mutated strain of a combined aviary and swine derivation created in a laboratory outside of Boston."

"You mean like the Swine Flu?" Patrick asks.

"Yes, but redesigned to be more effective in all human hosts. Swine Flu, or 2009 H1N1, is bad enough on its own, but this new creation is practically immune to antibiotics and other human defenses."

"So this is like H2N2?" I ask.

"You're on the right track, but a little off. The 'H' stands for hemagglutinin, which has, until recently, had eighteen subtypes. And the 'N', or neuraminidase, normally has eleven subtypes. This new strain goes beyond that, and has been classified, internally anyway, as H22N14."

"Wow!" Patrick says, as if he understands any of this.

"The higher numbers are not usually indicative of a stronger strain, just a new mutation. H19N11, for example, was found to have no effect on humans whatsoever."

"But this H22 blah, blah is harmful to humans?" I ask.

"Yes, H22N14 is highly dangerous. One report I read stated that out of sixteen 'patients'"—he uses air quotes on that word —"only one survived, but only barely."

"You're saying this is a lab-created virus?" Mr. B asks.

"Yes, specifically the Palmer Medical Laboratory developed it. Although it is technically referred to as H22N14, it's been given the nickname 'New England Respiratory Virus' and they have attempted to 'naturally' introduce it into the environment." Again, the air quotes. "They're trying to make it look like it is organically occurring when it was purposely injected into controlled situations."

Half a dozen things float through my brain. I start with what seems the most obvious. "Who is 'they'?"

"The government. On orders from President Quinn."

I glance at Mr. B, who doesn't seem surprised. He may have already known.

"This is not just speculation," I say, returning my attention to the doctor. "Not second or third hand rumors passed down from his political enemies?"

Dr. Jarminsky slips a hand into his pocket and removes a flash drive, sliding it on the table towards me. Before I could even twitch, Apollo snatches it away and runs out of the room. Sylvana grimaces, but says nothing.

"On that stick are the electronic documents, including the executive orders from the president directing the CDC to begin its cautious release system. The original intent, it appears, was to have the virus be infected into a small subset of the population, but it proved to move too slowly for the president's liking, so he requested it be released in a more widespread fashion."

Apollo returns with a laptop, the swiped flash drive inserted in the side. "There are a lot of documents on here," the man/boy says, "but I see some files which look like videos."

The doctor frowns and shakes his head. "Yes, disturbing recordings of the virus being injected into 'patients' at C.H.O.C. Upon seeing that was when I decided I needed to resign."

"What's C.H.O.C.?" Patrick asks, though it might as well have been me asking.

"Children's Hospital of Orange County—a facility in Southern California. All the 'patients' which were injected died within three days. The only advantage to NERV, if there is one, is that while it overwhelms the auto-immune system very effectively, it isn't as infectious or contagious as the designers hoped."

"NERV," I say. "That sounds a little too appropriate."

"Designers?" Mr. B says. "You mean scientists, right?"

"Technically, yes, but since their creation is intentionally meant to harm humans, I find it difficult to use the term 'scientists' to describe them. Criminals, murderers, but not 'scientists.'"

"How do we stop them?" I ask.

The doctor offers a prim little smile that tells me my question is naïve, but at least he has the kindness not to say it out loud. "There's too many of them and not enough of us."

I shake my head, disgusted. "I just find it hard to believe there are so many people evil enough to do whatever the president says, apparently without question. I mean, injecting children, and watching them die? *Sick* children? This is like the Nazis all over again."

Again, the prim smile, but this time Mr. B answers: "Money can create very thick scars over a wounded conscience. I would be willing to bet Dr. Jarminsky has a few documents showing substantial payments."

There's a long pause as we all wait for the doctor to confirm this.

"Ashamedly," the doctor says, "I have first-hand knowledge as well."

None of us comment.

"But it wasn't just sick children. It was also tested in a children's home, day care centers and a school in South Dakota. No survivors."

"Why just children?" Patrick asks. "Don't they have the balls to take on adults?"

Dr. Jarminsky grimaces slightly. "The original concept was to infect the children, and the children would infect the parents. That, to them, seemed to be the most reliable method of distribution. But, as I mentioned, the strain proved to not be as infectious as they wished, so they shifted how it will be introduced to the general public."

"And how is that?" Mr. B asks.

"First, flu shots."

A long silence as this sinks in.

"So people go to the doctor to get immunized against the flu and they are instead injected with this . . . this . . . viral poison? That's outrageous!" I say, feeling the heat of anger inside me.

"Not really," the doctor says. "Often, flu shots are little more than a weakened strain of the influenza that is being combatted. Your body can fight the weakened strain, so when it comes in contact with, one might say, the full-strength version, your body is better equipped to fight it. In fact, there are many substantiated cases of people who get the flu from flu shots." He pauses. "They've just . . . well, kicked it up a level."

We remain silent for several moments until Dr. Jarminsky checks his watch. "I should be going. I have a 5 A.M. flight."

"Thank you, again," Mr. B said. "We'll be in touch soon."

The doctor pulls his cell phone out of his pocket and sets it on the table. "I don't think so. Not where I'm going."

"You're going underground?"

"Hopefully deeper than that."

Mr. B slowly nods. "We wish you well. You're welcome to contact us if you need anything."

The doctor gives a sad little smile, then turns and walks out, leaving his phone behind.

More silence. Patrick yawns.

"We should all get some rest," Sylvana says. "We have much to do, and not much time to do it."

* * *

I awake from a dreamless sleep—my first in a while—by being shaken lightly. I open my eyes to see Leslie.

"Hey," I say.

"Sylvana asked me to come get you."

"Okay," I reply, trying to get through the cobwebs of waking up. "I'll get in the shower and be right down."

"I don't think there's time for that. It's fairly urgent."

I rub my eyes. "Alright. Where?"

"The conference room," she says, turning and pulling my pants off the chair.

I pull back the covers and get up, barely aware that I'm naked. I take the pants and pull them on, then sliding on the shirt she hands me. We walk out—me barefoot—and head down to the Control Center, Symbian faithfully following. In the conference room, Sylvana, Mr. B and Apollo are waiting.

"No Patrick?" I ask.

"He is not . . . He needs his rest," Sylvana says, though I know what she was going to say: *He is not needed for this.*

The video monitors are all on, all but one showing the grounds outside, all calm and clear. One monitor, though, has the image of a man, dark hair, clean shaven, glasses, white shirt, blue tie. Behind him is a bookcase.

"Thomas Osborne is the President's National Security Advisor," Mr. B explains. "Mr. Osborne, this is Collin Graves, the adopted half-brother of President Quinn."

The man adjusts his glasses slightly. "Does he have clearance?"

"Of the highest order."

He stares at the camera, at me. I'm sure I don't look the part with my hair probably all askew and looking like a transient they just pulled off a park bench.

"Good morning," I say, taking a seat. I'm pleased to see a cup of coffee in front of me.

"Yes, well, there have been some developments over the last couple of hours," Mr. Osborne says. "The rollout of NERV has expanded and is being introduced to five hundred schools as of this morning."

I pick up the coffee cup. "I don't understand why they are targeting children. In the grand scheme of things, they don't have any power." Symbian walks up next to me and lays his head on my lap. I scratch his head.

Osborne nods. "True, but the thought is to target the parents by effectively neutering them as they mourn the loss of their children. Basically, the intent is to neutralize the grass roots."

"Do we know which schools are targeted?" Mr. B asks.

"Mainly in the rural west where the President has his lowest support, and particularly Texas where there have been rather large pockets of opposition."

"Is there anything we can do to stop it?" I ask as Symbian

walks into the corner and lies down.

"It's already happening. I'm not sure it can be stopped."

"I know I've mentioned this previously, but what about getting this into the media?" I ask. "There are a lot of bloggers who detest the President."

"True, and that certainly is something worth exploring—it just won't stop the plan from being executed. The public doesn't have a high opinion of the media, and even less of bloggers, feeling they are too partisan."

"But if there's evidence, something that can be leaked and difficult to explain away, that would help."

"Absolutely. It just won't stop them."

"How vulnerable is the Internet?" Apollo asks.

"It's not just vulnerable, but fragile," Osborne replies. "There is an internal group working on slowing it considerably, if not redirecting traffic to useless sites. The end game is to turn it off completely, except for high-level government and military use."

I sip my coffee, thinking. "Isn't there something you can do?"

"Mr. Osborne is the highest-level government official that is on our side," Mr. B says. "He has the President's ear, but it doesn't mean the President listens. It is important Mr. Osborne's cover not be compromised. There is only so much he can do without putting himself in danger."

I understand. The most Osborne can offer is passing along information, but not actually being able to do anything. Which also implies his hands are as dirty as anyone else in the administration. But perhaps the scar over his wounded conscience isn't as thick as others under the President's thumb.

"Anything else you can share, Mr. Osborne?"

A long pause. "I've been asked to contact the military and begin the mobilization of martial law."

"Seriously?" I say, more than a little surprised. "Is that even possible?"

"Absolutely. They've been quietly shifting American troops stationed in other nations—Germany, Korea, the Middle East—back to U.S. bases. All aircraft carriers and battleships have returned to their home ports. The National Guard is being mobilized. The FBI, CIA, Secret Service and Immigration agents are being reassigned. Even the Black Ops are being brought in and briefed on their new assignments."

"And what is that? What are their new assignments?"

"There are many different aspects on many different levels. For example, last week they began to close gun stores and shut down gun shows, citing infractions with federal and local codes. They then confiscate the weapons, preventing citizens from new purchases. They've also begun targeting para-military groups in raids nationwide—you may have seen reports of a couple on cable news. They're effectively neutralizing as many potential citizen threats as possible."

"What next then? Are they going to go into homes and take away hunting rifles?"

A short pause. "Yes. That is the goal."

We all sit in silence as we absorb this information.

After another sip of coffee, I half-mumble: "I can't imagine what they'll try to do next."

"It's not imagination," Osborne says. "There are plans to suspend all shipping and trade between all foreign countries, with the ports shut down, citing national security concerns. Of course, they'll say it's just temporary, but it won't be. There are also policies being put in place to have the Federal Reserve stop all trading in the stock markets under the guise of 'protection of compromised computer systems' that terrorists have allegedly hacked into. They haven't, but that will be the story. After that, they'll freeze all accounts —checking, savings, 401k's, IRA's, stocks, bonds, insurance, annuities, anything with money in it. Behind the scenes, the banks will quietly be taken over by the federal government."

"That will create a lot of chaos."

"That's the idea."

I go silent, trying to think. "This all sounds like too much. I mean, how do we stop something like this? It's just so overwhelming."

Thomas Osborne, National Security Advisor to the President

of the United States, takes off his glasses and leans in towards the camera slightly.

"Cut off the head of the dragon."

I stare at the monitor. "Assassination? Is that what you're suggesting?"

He doesn't reply, just puts his glasses on and sits back in his chair.

Chapter 11

"No thief, however skilled, can rob one of knowledge, and that is why knowledge is the best and safest treasure to acquire."—L. Frank Baum

I get to take a shower, shave, make my hair look normal, brush my teeth, get dressed and go back downstairs, my companion following. Despite not being very hungry after hearing all the happy news, I decide to get something to eat. The kitchen is bustling with at least a dozen people either cooking food or in line those waiting for it. Plates with breakfast are being handed over as quickly as people can take them.

I look for the end, which extends out into a hallway, and turn that way to take my place.

"Here," an older black gentleman says. "You can go ahead of me."

"No, that's okay, thanks anyway."

Then another person offers, and another.

I'm being watched and stared at like a celebrity or something.

One teenage girl smiles at me. "Are you the Savior?"

I flinch. "No. No, I'm just here to help."

"They told us you're our new leader."

I have no idea how to respond to this, so I only shrug and

move quickly to the end of the line, Symbian trailing me.

The motherly woman in front of me turns and smiles sweetly. "I'm glad you're with us," she says. "We need some hope."

Again, I'm at a loss as to what to say, and can only manage "I'm glad I'm here."

It only takes a minute to get to the front, and I'm handed a plate filled with eggs, bacon, sausage, toast and hash browns. I couldn't have asked for better.

Symbian and I follow the crowd and find a large dining hall, humming with activity. As I step in, many heads turn and all goes quiet. I stand there awkwardly for a moment before applause breaks out. Some stand and cheer.

Something took place while I was asleep, and I'm guessing it was a briefing about me. I haven't even done anything, and they're looking up to me. The last time I tried to help, I ended up in a Target parking lot in Rockford. I feel my face flush red. I put my head down and look for a place to sit.

"Over here," Patrick yells, waving his hand as the clapping dies off. He's sitting with Leslie and a small group of people our age.

As I sit, they all beam at me.

"Would you do us the honor of saying Grace?" a young man says.

"Oh . . . I . . ." I lick my lips. "Okay. Sure."

They all bow their heads.

Oh man.

* * *

Patrick, Voltar, Symbian and I walk into the Control Center, and out of the corner of my eye, I think I see something scurry away. As soon as I look, of course, whatever it was is gone. Patrick didn't seem to have noticed. Neither did the dogs.

We walk into the doorway of Apollo's workshop and see the little boy sitting on a stool, his back to us, hunkered over something he's working on. There are several other people—mostly men—at different workstations, all tinkering on something.

"Hey," Patrick says.

"Hi," Apollo says without looking up or around.

"Whatcha doing?"

"Fixing my Drat."

"Your what?"

His head comes up, and he swivels around towards us. "My Drat. One of my Drats. I kicked it and it popped a wire."

We walk up to the workbench and take a look. On the countertop is what looks like a robotic rat. It's on its back, feet up, belly exposed, showing wiring and circuitry.

"I need to make it stronger so it won't be so susceptible to feet," he says.

"A drone rat?"

"Yes. A Drat."

"What's it for?"

The boy's eyes twinkle. "I've been told the President has a few phobias, namely bees, spiders and rats. He's okay with snakes, though."

"Henry is terrified of rats," I say. "I remember a problem with rats in one of the storerooms, and when one jumped out at him, he screamed and ran away like a little girl."

The other two look at me as I smile widely.

"Well, it was funny."

"You built this to spy on the President?" Patrick asks.

"Bees and spiders are too slow, and the Drat is big enough to hold more storage and be more flexible."

"So it's more than just a toy to scare the guy," Patrick says.

"Definitely more than a toy. We have produced fifty-seven, and I was hoping they'd be indestructible, but the joints are too fragile." He sighs. "There's always a weak spot."

"Does it bite?" Patrick asks.

"It wouldn't be a Drat if it couldn't bite."

"Collin, Patrick," a voice from behind us says. We turn to see Mr. B. "I think it's time for you to get briefed."

"Sure," I say. "Oh, Apollo, I think one of your Drats escaped. I saw one out in the hallway before we came in."

He frowns. "I wondered where he went."

Patrick and I follow Mr. B to the conference room. I wonder what the topic will be this time.

As we take our seats, Mr. B opens a folder. "Thomas Osborne has sent along some documents, namely executive orders from the President that moves all military, FBI, Secret Service, *et cetera*, under the umbrella of the ISP."

"Tell me about the ISP."

"International Service Patrol. Sounds rather innocuous, I know, but he's built it into the most powerful police agency in the world, and now it's even more dominant. It effectively removes the power and influence of the U.S. military command."

"I've never heard of it," I say.

"It has not been made public. The Regulators are an arm of the ISP, just as an example. Osborne says there is another executive order being drafted that will place all local and state police, sheriff departments and all other law enforcement agencies under the direction of the ISP."

"Is that even possible?" I ask. "I mean, aren't the states some-what autonomous?"

"That has been the concept, until the emergency powers of the President are implemented, suspending the rights of the states, under what will be classified as a State of Emergency."

"And what will be the reason for this 'State of Emergency'?" I ask. "Hackers? Terrorists?"

Mr. B points to one of the video monitors, which is showing the picture of a bird.

"A crow?" Patrick says. "A State of Emergency over a crow?"

"Technically, a raven," Mr. B says. "And not even a regular raven. Those are two-and-a-half to three pounds, with wingspans of four to five feet. This," he says pointing again, "is fifteen to twenty pounds, with wingspans up to twenty-five feet. There have been reports of some being even larger."

"Geez," Patrick says.

"I'm guessing these aren't naturally occurring," I say.

"Correct. They are a Dymortis creation." He pauses. "You've

had dreams, nightmares, of children."

"Yes," I say, and Patrick nods.

"Have you been shown what happens to the bodies?"

I think. "In one, they were just put in the back of a pickup."

"Nothing beyond that?"

I shake my head, as does Patrick.

Mr. B's face sours slightly. "What happens is the bodies are taken to a processing plant." He pauses. It looks like he is trying not to lose his composure. "They are basically . . . um . . . emulsified into . . ." A sniff as he looks away for a few moments. "Uh . . . emulsified into a slurry. They add some other ingredients, and call it CPM—calcium, plasma and marrow." A pause, a sniff. "Excuse me," he says, leaving the room.

Patrick and I are silent for a moment. "Remember when you wondered what your father did with the bodies at the mortuary?"

I feel sick to my stomach.

Eventually, Mr. B returns, trying to smile, holding cans of soda for us. "I believe I got the brands you like."

"Thanks," we say in unison.

"Okay," he says just before we pop the tops, "so, the CPM. It has helped strengthen the mutant birds to the point that they have been released in limited areas on test runs, and the effects have been . . . well, terrorizing." He points a remote control at a monitor and a video begins playing.

It appears to be footage from a security camera on a farm or ranch. Cattle can be seen milling around behind a fence. Suddenly, a gigantic bird swoops down and attacks a cow's head. The animal goes down, and the raven goes after the eyes as the cow struggles unsuccessfully to get up off the ground. A moment later, three other ravens attack, one going after the animal's hindquarters, the other two taking down two other cows. Soon, blood, hide and entrails begin squirting and flying into the air.

The video cuts to another security feed of nice and neat housing tract somewhere in middle-class suburbia with trimmed lawns and clean driveways. A man is walking an Irish Setter when a creature drops from the sky, snatching the dog with its talons and lifting it into the air. The man is jerked up briefly, then tugs on the leash, pulling the dog free. They both collapse on the ground as the bird circles around and comes in a second time.

Another cut, to a city park, kids playing on the slide and jungle gym. A mother is pushing a stroller and I turn my head, trying to stem the urge to throw up. Fortunately, there is no sound. When I look back, the mother has her hands in the air, giving off a silent scream. In the background, two other ravens swoop in and snatch children from the playground, flying out of camera range with their prey.

Mr. B stops the tape.

"We have another hundred videos like that."

"Why hasn't this been on the news?" I ask, still trying to keep my breakfast.

"Good question. Initially, it was, if you remember the spate of cattle mutilations from a few years ago. Conspiracy theorists put it down to UFOs killing livestock, draining the blood. Of course, they couldn't explain why space aliens would need or want cow and horse blood, but extraterrestrials are a much easier explanation than enormous ravens the size of a Pteranodon."

"A what?" Patrick asks.

"A flying dinosaur," Mr. B says.

"So, is there a way to combat these Super Ravens?" I ask.

"Rifles, shotguns, like any other bird."

"How many of these things are there?" Patrick asks.

Mr. B shrugs. "Hard to say. Just a wild guess on my part, but I'd say a few thousand, but it could be in the tens of thousands."

"Who's responsible for . . . creating them?"

"That's a good word. The President ordered their creation, and I believe he controls their release." He pauses and looks up at the blank video screen. "I think he is preparing for a massive attack. The creatures are insatiable, and I expect the slaughter to be extensive at first as the populace is completely unprepared. Once word gets around, I'm sure people will do their best to arm themselves for protection."

"But if Mr. Osborne is correct, buying guns will be nearly impossible."

Mr. B nods. "All a part of the plan."

"I don't understand why the President would want to kill his own people," Patrick says. "I voted for the guy."

We both look at him.

"Well, I would have voted for him if I voted."

"MacNeill Quinn is the biological child of Henry Davis— also known as Lord Harod Dunraven, who is the right-hand man of Dymortis, who is also known as Satan, the sworn enemy of all humans."

We sit in silence for a minute.

"So, what next?" I ask. "How do we cut off the head of the dragon?"

"Well," Mr. B said, "first you have to—"

Apollo walks into the room, followed by a Drat. "Excuse me," he says. "They're back."

Chapter 12

"Knowledge is an unending adventure at the edge of uncertainty."
—Jacob Bronowski

We look up to the video monitors and see men standing in the large backyard. They're not bothering to hide, but standing in a V-formation, the man at the forefront apparently talking. His lips are moving, but we can't hear what he's saying.

Symbian and Voltar walk into the picture, still a good twenty yards from the man. He eyes the sleek dogs warily, his hand moving slowly to the service revolver holstered to his hip. But then he keeps talking.

Apollo takes the remote from the table and presses a button.

" *. . . not be harmed,*" the man is saying. "*We offer a truce, a chance to talk, that is all. We are seeking The Selected One. Lord Dunraven would just like five minutes of his time. He will not be harmed.*"

I look over at Mr. B, who seems amused.

"Is it a trap?"

"Probably. A truce is an odd way to put it since they can't access this building. And what would Dunraven want?"

"To kill me."

"He can't do that. It is out of his grasp now. All he can hope for is to delay or confuse you." He pauses. "No, this is a test by Dymortis, and a rather meager one. He's looking to see how susceptible you are."

I think for a few moments. "Well, susceptible or not, I don't see a reason for meeting with him. There's no point. He wants his men, but he has nothing to offer in return."

Mr. B nods. "That's absolutely right." He gazes at the monitor. "I just wonder how to make them go away."

"I could go out on the porch and yell 'Hey you hooligans—get off my lawn!'"

We all look at Patrick, and he offers his charming grin. Apollo giggles.

"Okay, well," I say, "I think we'll just ignore them for now. Let's get back to what I should do next."

"Have a seat. We'll talk about the End Game."

"You mean there already is one?" I say as I sit.

"Maybe 'End Goal' is a better term." He pauses, thinking. "Have you heard of the Ark of the Covenant?"

"Sure," I say. "It's like a big ornate crate from the Bible."

He chuckles. "That's an interesting way to put it. Yes, a crate designed by God, built by men, one of the most prized artifacts from the early times. It is so holy, that someone looking at it can die. It must be covered so as not to kill those who come into contact with it."

"So it actually exists?"

"That's been debated for centuries, especially since no one has actually seen the Ark and lived to tell about it."

"Like in *Raiders of the Lost Ark*," Patrick says. "The Nazis get torched when they open it."

"Yes," Mr. B says wryly, "just like the movie." He winks at me.

"But you're saying it exists."

"I have no idea if it exists. There are all kinds of people who have said they have it, or know where it is. There's a church in Ethiopia that says they have it in a chapel. Some say it's in a cave in a mountain in the Middle East. Some claim it's in England or Ireland. And, like the movie, others claim the Nazis stole it and it is now secreted away."

"But Indiana Jones got it away from them and it was hidden it in a warehouse," Patrick says. Then he looks at each of our frowning faces. "I mean, if that was, like, real."

"Mr. B, why bring it up if you don't know if it exists?"

"Yes, that may need clarification. It existed, but I can't say it wasn't destroyed."

"Destroyed by who?" Patrick asks.

Mr. B and I exchange glances.

"Dunraven," I say, and Mr. B nods.

"But why destroy it? He likes collecting old shit—I mean stuff like that."

"According to the Bible, the Ark contains the Tablets of Stone, also known as the Tablets of Law. You may know it better as the Ten Commandments."

"He couldn't keep something so holy."

Mr. B nods his head slowly. "Destroying it would help destroy mankind. But there's more you should know, Collin. The Ark had been transported, moved from place to place, temple to temple, for hundreds of years. Some two thousand priests helped carry and guard it until it ended up in Solomon's Temple." He pauses. "You were told about your royal blood."

"Yes. I can't say I understand it."

"Just be assured that your lineage has been traced back ... well, let's just say to the time of Moses. King David and his son, King Solomon are in that lineage. I'll be glad to give you those records when we're done here. But the important point is that the Ark was placed in Solomon's Temple until the Babylonians attacked, destroyed the temple, and took the Ark back with them to Babylon."

"I'm guessing Dunraven was a Babylonian."

Mr. B touched a finger to his nose. "Bingo. He played a major part in stealing the Ark. As it says in 1 Esdras, 1:54, *And they took all the holy vessels of the Lord, both great and small, with the vessels of the ark of God, and the king's treasures, and carried them away into Babylon.*"

"Where's Babylon?" Patrick asks.

"Basically, the middle of what is now Iraq."

"Ah, that explains a lot."

I'm connecting the dots. "So if Dunraven played a major part in taking the Ark, maybe he still has it."

"Maybe. It could still be in Iraq. Maybe the Nazis did steal it, or maybe the U.S. government has it hidden away in Area 51."

"Doubtful," Apollo says from the end of the table where he has been tinkering with his Drat. "Area 51 has been essentially decommissioned, even though it technically never was commissioned in the first place."

"Apollo has spent a good deal of time researching possible locations for the Ark," Mr. B explains. "He's pretty much ruled out the most obvious or unlikely places."

"What if Dunraven did destroy it?" I ask.

"Doubtful," Apollo says. "He'd be dead."

We are all quiet for several moments.

"So, what's next?" I ask. "We can't just sit here and wait for something to happen."

Mr. B opens his mouth to answer, but Apollo beats him to it.

"I need access to the President's phone. His cellphone. I have hacked into the Oval Office's recording system, but obviously, we can only monitor one side of the conversation."

"There's a recording system in the Oval Office?" I ask.

"Since the Kennedy administration," Mr. B says. "Johnson used it, and most famously, Nixon. It's assumed all presidents have used it since then, though there have been denials or 'no comments'."

"I can access the system, live, anytime, using the Plebius back-door hack," Apollo explains. "I optimized the version to make it undetectable to the Secret Service. I even can stream the video feed. But the cellphone would give us access to wherever the President is—not just in the Oval Office."

"How do you get access to the President's phone?"

"For the lack of a better term, a bug. It needs to be inserted, physically, into the phone to intercept the information."

"You can't just hack it like the Oval Office?"

"Plebius is not compatible with cellphone operating systems. I need to have a micronano-transmitter attached physically to the phone."

"So, again, how do you get physical access to the President's phone?"

"I cannot do it, as I would be too conspicuous." Apollo's eyes twinkle. "And since the President does not just leave his phone lying around and is always with him, this does provide a challenge." He pauses, as if to see if any of us have an idea. "I need to be there, or at least within one-thousand fifty yards of the phone, which is the transmission range. We have an office near the White House which receives the audio and video feeds. I would need to be there to connect and optimize the link."

A pause. He still hasn't answered my question.

"It sounds like you have an idea," Mr. B says.

"Yes," Apollo says. "But I do not think Sylvana will approve."

* * *

"It is your choice, Collin," she says, looking rather stern and not at all pleased. "It sounds as if this . . . plan has many more risks than rewards. If you are caught, the ramifications are great. Dunraven would be tipped off, and, of course, Dymortis. It would not end well for you." She pauses. "It just does not sound wise to me."

"We could ask someone else," Mr. B says. "We have several young men here who would be qualified."

"But they would have the same risks," I say. "And they don't have the same . . . they can't do what I can do."

"If you are caught," Sylvana says, "the best case scenario is you are jailed, removed from the picture at least until after Quinn, Dunraven and Dymortis begin to carry out their bigger plan."

"And the worst case scenario?"

"Your death. I would suspect that would be their choice."

"But in the worst case, it would be the same if we send in someone else."

"Yes, but we would still be able to defend the world against their plans."

I take some time to think about this. I'm not sure whether I feel compelled to participate because I feel it is part of my destiny, or I just want to get out of the house.

"I remember a wise woman telling me, not so long ago: 'A *true leader would never ask someone to do something he himself wouldn't do.*'"

She smiles thinly. "True. But I still do not see the over-arching benefit of planting this transmitter. It may give us more information, but not much more than we are already getting."

"It may not be the amount of information," Apollo says, "but that we receive it faster. The faster we receive it, the quicker we can respond."

Sylvana sighs, understanding, but not liking it any better.

"Again, Collin, it is your choice. While I do not give my blessing, I will not forbid it either."

* * *

We go back to the conference room to work out the plans, and one of the monitors is blinking. *Incoming Message* it says in green letters.

Apollo takes to the keyboard and types, and a few moments later the image of Thomas Osborne, the National Security Advisor comes on the screen.

"Hello, Thomas," Mr. B says. "What—"

"I only have a minute, I'm late for a meeting with the President. But there are reports in the media of a flock of some kind of giant bird attacking people in Eastern Europe. I need to attend a briefing to bring the President up-to-date, but I really don't know what's going on. Do you?"

"Actually," Mr. B says, "the President will know more than we do." He pauses for a beat. "They're his birds."

Osborne blinks in confusion. "I don't know what you mean."

"He commissioned them, and is conducting systematic tests."

A pause as Osborne absorbs this. "So how do we combat them?"

"A twelve-gauge shotgun. But a military assault would probably be more effective for more than a few," Apollo says.

Osborne nods. "The report says it's several dozen."

"I would guess the President will approve of such a mission and will say he'll call the general of the Eastern European theater to arrange a few F-15's, but either nothing will happen, or they'll say they didn't find anything by the time they got there."

Osborne thinks this over. "Okay, thanks. I've got to go."

And the screen goes dark.

Apollo is clicking away on the keyboard, watching another monitor. "More reports of attacks in Vietnam, Comoros and . . . Uruguay. Although in the latter, the creatures are being described as 'dinosaurios'."

I frown. "Where's Comoros?"

"An island off the coast of Africa, between Mozambique and Madagascar."

Apollo clicks a little more, and up pops a map of Comoros.

Mr. B is frowning. "I would suspect the ravens have some sort of tracking chip in them," he says. "They would need to keep tabs on them."

"There's a company in New Zealand that manufactures extremely small GPS chips," Apollo says. "They can be tracked by satellite—it would just be a matter of determining the frequency they're using."

He clicks some more, then turns to me. "This might take a while."

"Okay. Maybe I should get ready for my trip to Washington."

* * *

Standing in the middle of my room wearing only our boxers, Patrick and I wait for the "tailor" to return as Leslie sits in a chair off to the side reading a magazine. Our friends Voltar and Symbian are lounging near the fireplace, one watching, bored, the other snoozing on his side.

"You know that . . . thing earlier?" Patrick whispers as he eyes Leslie to see if she's listening.

I shake my head. "What thing?" I whisper back.

"You know, when you asked me about . . . my first time?"

"Oh. Yeah."

"I just . . . you know, I mean . . . we're cool, right?"

"Of course. It doesn't matter to me."

"I just don't want you to think I'm . . . that I brag or anything. Or make shit up."

I smirk. "We're cool."

He nods, and seems relieved. "I hope we get some pants soon." He glances at Leslie.

The door opens and the tailor enters with a pair of black suit jackets on hangers and slacks slung over his arm that looks just like the four other pairs he had brought earlier. He isn't so much a tailor as a guy named Ronald who used to work at a department store, bringing clothes for us to try on.

"This should do it," he says, fastidiously, holding each out for us to try.

I pull it on and Ronald helps straighten it, tugging on the sleeves, then nodding with approval. He then checks out Patrick's fit.

"I think these will work just fine. Okay, off with them, and try on the trousers. I'll be back with the rest." And Ronald disappears the way he came.

We take off the jackets and pull on the pants. "The rest?" Patrick asks.

"I hope shirts, belts, ties, socks and shoes."

Mr. B walks in just as we zip up.

"How's it coming along?"

I do a slow turn. "What do you think?"

"Looks good, as far as it goes." He looks Patrick up and down, then seems to freeze. "May I . . . May I examine your tattoos?" he asks.

Patrick offers a shy smile. "I did get them to get noticed—although I was thinking more along the lines of being noticed by the ladies."

He glances at Leslie, who doesn't look up from her magazine.

Mr. B approaches, staring at the art on Patrick's upper arm. It's an upside-down triangle with an eye floating in the middle, staring. I thought it was interesting, maybe a little odd or creepy, but nothing else.

"Where did you get this?" Mr. B asks.

"At Big Pete's. He was having a two-for-one special. I got the flaming skull too." He swings around to show off the evil-looking head which was in profile with blue flames erupting from the back.

"Yes, quite . . . nice," Mr. B says. "Where did you get the idea for them? Was it some sort of art you had seen?"

"The flaming skull was in a book Big Pete had. I just had him change the flames from orange to blue. Also, it had eyeballs, but I told him to take them out."

"I see. And the eye in the triangle?"

"That . . . well, I know this sounds weird but I kept seeing it in a dream when I was a teenager. I don't know what it means, but I wanted something that was kind of cool and unique. I didn't want something everyone else had."

This had caught Leslie's interest, and she had joined Mr. B to examine Patrick's arm. "The Eye of Providence," she says.

"Yes, only upside-down."

"Eye of Providence? What is that?" Patrick asks.

"The most famous use is probably on the back of a dollar bill," Leslie says. "The triangle is a reference to the Christian Trinity—the Father, the Son and the Holy Spirit. The eye is the Eye of God. I just don't understand it being upside-down."

"That's how I saw it in my dream," Patrick says, sounding a little defensive.

"I'm sure it was," Mr. B says. "The Eye of Providence is possibly based on the Eye of Horus, an ancient Egyptian symbol of prosperity, royal power and good health. The Eye of Providence on the Great Seal of the United States, sits atop a pyramid, which is also Egyptian." He pauses a moment. "Tell me about the dreams, Patrick."

Patrick frowns. "I really don't remember much. It was several years ago."

"But you remembered enough to have a tattoo created from it."

Patrick nods, and closes his eyes, bowing his head.

"Take your time," Mr. B says.

It's thirty, forty seconds before Patrick speaks.

"I'm being chased. Some kind of park or forest. I don't know who is after me, but I know I need to get away. I run, ducking behind trees to look, but I don't see anyone, even though I know they are there. Somewhere. I keep running, and finally come up against a rock wall. A long rock wall. No way over. I'm trying to decide whether to go left or right when a little old man jumps down from out of the trees. He's wearing a tux and top hat and is carrying a cane. He cackles at me. His teeth are rotting and I can smell his bad breath even from ten feet away."

He pauses, licking his lips.

"He points his cane at me. 'You don't think that's going to help you, do you?' he says, and I turn to see the triangle with the eye on the rock wall. But it's not really on the wall, it's kind of floating in front of it. The old man steps forward still pointing his cane. I step to the side as he jabs it at me—but then he swings it at the triangle. It hits it, and the triangle spins like a roulette wheel. The man cackles again as the eye twirls around. But then the spinning slows and finally stops. 'It can't help you, young man! No, no, no!'"

Patrick's voice sounds just like the old man I had experienced —Dymortis.

"Then a beam of light shoots from the eye at the old man, and he screams, evaporating into a mist."

There is a long silence until Patrick raises his head and opens his eyes.

"So, you perceived the eye as something to protect you."

"Yes. I guess."

"You mentioned that the Egyptian eye represented royal power," I say.

"The Eye of Horus, yes." Leslie looks from me to Patrick, to me again. "But it looks quite different. And there's no triangle. I only brought it up because the Eye of Providence may have been influenced by the Eye of Horus, not that they're the same."

"But the eye in the Eye of Providence represents God."

"Yes, the all-seeing God."

"So, this is kind of a jumble."

"Not really," Mr. B says. "While dreams cannot be taken

as reflecting any type of reality, that Patrick saw Dymortis in his dream, and that the Eye of Providence played a part, implies Patrick has been chosen."

"That was Dymortis?" Patrick asks. "He was practically a midget. I could have kicked his ass."

"Yes, perhaps," Mr. B says with a smile. "Until he reached into your chest and ate your heart."

Ronald returns literally pushing a shopping cart. Inside are boxes of shoes.

"Have a seat, gentlemen," he says. "Time for a foot-fitting."

Chapter 13

"Growth demands a temporary surrender of security."—Gail Sheehy

We are standing in the conference room, waiting for Mr. B and Apollo to come and brief us on what we're supposed to do and how we're supposed to do it. We're fully outfitted in our new suits and ties, with shiny black shoes. I suppose we look like government employees, but I can't say I feel like one.

Up on the monitors is the video feed showing the backyard, which still has members of the Regulators waiting for us. They've stopped trying to tell us they just want to talk and we won't be harmed, but they're still milling about, some with rifles slung over their shoulders.

"I wonder how we get out of here," I say.

"Probably an underground tunnel," Patrick says. "Do you really think I'm 'chosen'?"

"It appears so, if Dymortis was in your dreams."

"Chosen by Dymortis?"

"I don't think so. Dymortis—Satan—is an outcast angel who has sworn to destroy humanity."

A pause. "Why doesn't he go after God then? Why us?"

"He can't destroy God, so he seeks to hurt God's creation."

"Then God should destroy him."

I nod. "That's all part of the philosophical debate. Why does God let bad things happen to good people?"

"I wondered that growing up. I would ask God to stop bad things from happening, and they didn't. Sometimes they got worse." A long pause. "After a while, I gave up asking."

"I don't blame you. But in some ways, what happened made you better. I would guess God saw what you would become, and let the bad things happen to help shape you."

Another long pause. "This just isn't the life I was hoping for."

I wait a few seconds. "What were you hoping for?"

He thinks about this. "A good wife, a couple of kids. Writing songs, playing music, making other people happy."

"It can still happen."

He shakes his head, not in denial, but almost disbelief. "Not unless we get through this. Whatever this is."

We stand there for several minutes in silence, watching the men in the backyard walk around.

"Okay gentlemen, it's all arranged," Mr. B says from behind us. "A car is waiting to take you to the airport."

We turn, and his expression changes when he sees our faces. He looks like he's going to say something, but instead just hands us our airplane tickets.

"Do we need to pack?" I ask.

"No, it's a quick trip." A pause as he again considers our mood. "Follow me."

* * *

Apollo and Leslie meet us at the entrance to a tunnel where a pair of electric golf carts are waiting. We climb in and head off to . . . somewhere. In our cart, Patrick sits up front with the driver, while I sit with Mr. B in the back. He hands me a thick envelope.

"Here are your credentials," he says. "Driver's license, Government Issue ID, White House Pass, and encrypted smartphones. Yours is the black unit, Patrick's is white. The pass codes to unlock the phones are your birthdays—your real birthdays, not the ones on the licenses. You can change the pass codes if you like. All the data you need will be on the devices. One of the programs is disguised as a game, but it's actually a direct link to the headquarters here. Use it as a speed dial, text message, and there's even an SOS function if you're unable to talk or type."

"How often should I check in with you?"

"You'll stay in touch with Apollo, he'll keep in contact with us. That will limit our exposure and your connection to us. If you absolutely need to phone us, but it's not an emergency, it will be under 'Grandma' in the contact list. Use the game program in an emergency. Read your cover background in the note section on the phone. The note is password protected. Yours is your favorite pet, Patrick's is the license plate number of his vehicle. For the background cover story, memorize it. Do not deviate, even between yourselves or with other friendly agents you may encounter. Normally, we'd be able to have a few hours to go over this stuff, but today, we don't have that luxury."

"I think we'll do okay."

He nods. "Well, you'll have to. Up top, there will be a car to take you to O'Hare. In Washington, you'll be met by another driver who will take you to your destination."

"How will we know what to do when we get there?"

"That is also on the phone, in a separate note. It should have all the information you need, but it may not be completely up-to-date. In other words, some things might have changed slightly, so you may need to improvise. But we're confident it's extremely accurate."

The carts come to a stop, next to a plain-looking door with a green EXIT sign over it. We get out as Leslie and Apollo join us by the door.

"We're below Hillington Park," Mr. B says. "Take the stairs up to the surface, and you'll find your car waiting in the parking lot." He gazes at me solemnly for several moments. "You know what to do."

"Pay attention, and stay true."

"*Laus Deo*," Mr. B says.

"*Laus Deo*," the four of us repeat, and he shakes each of our hands.

Patrick opens the door and starts up the stairs, followed by Leslie and Apollo, and I bring up the rear. I glance back at Mr. B before the door closes, but the carts have already left.

At the top, Patrick opens the door and steps through, the rest of us following into . . . a men's room. A couple of teenage boys eye us warily, stamping out their smokes as quickly as they can. Since Patrick and I look something like the *Men in Black*, they probably think we're cops. They don't say anything, but one of the kids watches Leslie walk by, grinning as if he has a smart-ass comment ready. I glare at him, and any thought of saying it seems to disappear.

Outside, the park is mostly empty, as is the parking lot. Only a familiar black car idles nearby. The white man with the beard who drove us before gets out of the Lincoln Town Car and opens the rear door. "Good day," he says with a nod.

"Hello," I say as Apollo scrambles in, followed by Leslie. I get in on the other side while Patrick takes the front passenger seat.

As the car backs out, I hand Patrick his stuff. Leslie opens her envelope and hands items to Apollo, and then we all begin reading our information and turning on our phones.

"There are portfolios for the gentlemen in the pockets on the back of the seats," the driver says. I pull one out and hand it up to Patrick. Leslie hands me the other.

"Enrique Cano," Patrick says, reading his new driver's license. "I'm Latino."

"Madison Smoak," Leslie says, sighing, apparently not too happy with the name.

"Tommy Weaver," Apollo says. "Sounds like a kid on a Fifties TV show."

"Justin Congill," I say, deciding not to comment.

For the rest of the ride, we try to absorb our new persona.

* * *

On the flight, we're all in first class, and Patrick takes his seat, looking a little green.

"You okay?"

"Yeah," he says, not sounding convincing. *Never been on a plane before.*

Want me to hold your hand?

He looks at me, unamused. I'm sure a choice profanity was at the ready.

I survived a plane crash when I was just a baby.

You're not helping.

I can ask the flight attendant if they have any adult diapers.

And that's when the profanity came, followed by a smile.

*   *   *

The takeoff was uneventful for everyone but Patrick. He looked as if he might request that diaper on his own, but once we reached cruising altitude, he settled down.

We studied our phones, reading our instructions.

We're breaking into the White House?

Do you know another way to get to the President's phone?

I don't know. Maybe send in one of Apollo's Drats?

Apollo pops up in the seat in front of Patrick, lays his arms on the top, then lays his head on his arms. *Drats don't have opposable thumbs.*

What does that mean? Of course they have thumbs. At least the ones running around my room did.

Not opposable thumbs. They can't take a cellphone apart and manipulate a transmitter into place.

Then why didn't you make them with the right kind of thumbs?

Apollo rolls his eyes as if that's the dumbest thing he ever heard, then drops back into his seat.

*   *   *

After we de-plane and head out to the baggage claim area, there's a man holding a neatly printed sign: *Congill.*

That would be me.

"Hi. Do you know where we're going?"

"Yes sir. Right this way." He leads us out to the curb where a limousine awaits. A driver gets out and opens the rear passenger door as the man with the sign opens the other. We climb in and are soon heading into the nation's capital.

After a brief traffic jam, the car soon pulls up in front of an older building a block away from the White House. Apollo leads the way inside, into an elevator, pressing the L3 button. It opens into a deserted basement with a concrete floor and hospital-green walls. He takes us down a hallway to a door labeled *Electrical*. A fingerprint-scanner is mounted over the doorknob, and he places his little-boy thumb on it. The lock clicks, and a few moments later we're inside, the door closing behind us.

While technically electrical, it's really a roomful of data servers on racks. Apollo leads us through a little maze of them to another door.

"This tunnel will take you under the street, and beneath the White House. Per the instructions, find a purple door marked X7. Inside is an old-style dumbwaiter that will take you into a hidden cabinet in the kitchen." He checks his smartphone for the time. "In about twenty minutes, the kitchen staff will take their break. That would be the best time to enter."

"Once we complete the mission, do we go back the way we came?"

He shakes his head. "No need. You can leave through the same exit as everyone else. They only check people going in, not going out. When you return to this building, go to the eighth floor. We'll be in Suite 804."

"Okay," I say, turning to Patrick. "Are you ready?"

"Sure," he says.

"Wait," Apollo says. "You need this." He hands me a small plastic tube with a snap-top. Inside is some kind of tiny circuit.

Of course. The transmitter.

"You read the instructions on installing it?"

"Yes."

He nods. "Be careful."

I open the door and we step through.

Having worked in the tunnels under the cemetery, it's not unfamiliar—just a long concrete hallway without doors. It only takes us a few minutes to come across a series of doors, each a different color. Finding the purple X7 door is not a problem.

I open it and step inside. A single, dim light bulb shows a roughly ten-by-ten room. A tall box with a rope/pulley system stands in the corner. A sign on the wall says MAX WEIGHT 250 LBS.

"I guess only one of us at a time."

"This is a dumbwaiter?"

"Yeah. Usually they're smaller, just meant to haul items from one floor to another."

"You or me first?"

"Me. I'll wait for you up there."

He salutes, and I climb on the strange box. I consider the rope, grabbing ahold of the one nearest to me, then begin pulling. The box jerks upwards an inch or so. I pull harder, and it goes a few more inches.

This is going to take a while.

* * *

I finally make it to the top—or at least as high up as the thing will go. I step off onto a small ledge between the dumbwaiter and a door. I release the latch and lower the platform back down into the hole. It goes a lot quicker and soon hits the bottom. A few moments later, the rope starts moving, and I know Patrick is on his way up.

I turn towards the door and see there is no knob. I give it a slight push and it creaks open. I move it as slowly as possible until I can look through the opening—but there's nothing to see. It appears to be another room, and dark. I slowly open the door further, avoiding the creaking, until there's enough room for me to pass through. I step in, listening. A slight line of light shows beneath what appears to be another door. I approach carefully, putting my ear to the wood and listening.

A couple of muted voices.

Behind me, the dumbwaiter continues to rise with a *shush shush shush* sound.

I wait.

A few minutes later, the dumbwaiter clunks into place.

I listen again at the door, but hear nothing.

I turn to Patrick. *Once we're out, just walk as if we belong there.*

Okay.

I pull out my phone and check the map. *We should be in the kitchen. Out to the hall, turn left, then right, then straight.*

Got it.

I push the door open *extremely* slowly. I peek through the crack. It is the kitchen. I don't see anyone, but my field of view is too narrow.

I push it open more. Then a little more. Eventually, it's wide enough to poke my head through. My heart is beating hard, but not too hard.

I look around quickly and see the room is empty.

Let's go.

We step out, and head for the exit.

The hallway out goes around the back of the kitchen, then into a main hallway. I do my best to walk purposefully as we step out and hang a right. Not ten feet away is a man dressed just like us except with an earpiece. I have no doubt there's a gun under his buttoned-up jacket.

I keep walking and point down the hall. "Oval Office?" I say as we pass him.

"ID," he says, hand out.

We stop, and I sigh as I unclip the White House Pass from my pocket and hand it to him.

He takes it and stares at it, then takes Patrick and stares at that. "SSIT doesn't usually make house calls," he says, looking up to stare me in the eye.

I shrug. "New OS malware called Bluefinger, Priority Five." I leave it at that.

"What were you doing in the kitchen?"

"Wrong turn. Haven't been here before."

He reaches down to his belt and I try not to stiffen.

"Asphalt Ten," he says, apparently via radio.

I work at finding his flow.

Roger Asphalt Ten.

"Confirm SSIT visit to Silver Fox."

A pause. I slip my hands into my slacks, trying to look casual. Patrick stands next to me, hands clasped in front of him.

Stand by.

"May I see your weapons, please," he says.

I unbutton my jacket. "We're not authorized," I say, showing him the inside of my coat. Patrick does the same.

"Where are your tools?" the agent asks.

"None needed. It's an encrypted secure download from the SSIT server."

"Don't you need a computer?"

"It downloads directly onto the phone, which provides higher security since there's nothing to bring in or take out to compromise the device."

Asphalt Ten, SSIT is approved. Silver Fox has authorized.

The man still eyes us warily, but hands back our badges. "Asphalt Ten, acknowledged. I will provide escort."

Roger, Asphalt Ten.

"This way," he says, turning down the hall.

We march, not seeing another soul. We come to a door that leads outside, and step out into the chilly air. We walk around the outside to a door that leads back inside. If my map was correct, we just skirted around the Press Briefing Room.

Another hallway, a left turn and then into a small room featuring a woman behind a desk, typing on a computer. Our escort steps to the side.

"SSIT Congill and Cano to service the President's phone," I say to the woman.

She nods, gets up, and goes through a door. We wait.

"Does there really need to be two of you?" our escort says.

"Policy," I say. "He will verify what I do to make sure it follows protocol."

The woman returns. "Go right in," she says as she slips behind her desk.

I nod at both her and then our escort, and turn towards the door.

I step into the Oval Office to come face-to-face with President of the United States, and the man who is trying to help destroy the planet.

Chapter 14

"Accuracy of observation is the equivalent of accuracy of thinking."—
Wallace Stevens

We walk into the Oval Office and I see the President isn't alone.
There are five other people—four men and a woman—sitting on
the couches or chairs. I see Thomas Osborne, who does not
acknowledge if he recognizes me or not. He only makes a cursory
glance our way, then returns to reading the paper in his hand.

MacNeill Quinn is impressive on TV, but even more so in
person. He smiles warmly at us, looking us each in the eye, then
frowns seriously as he pulls his phone out of his pocket.

"Glad you're here," he says in his smooth, polished voice.
"The email stopped syncing. Haven't received anything since
last night."

I nod as I take the device and give him a reassuring look.
"We'll take a look at it."

"Thanks," he says with a smile, full of warmth. Then he
turns to the group. "Lex, you were saying the Russians are on
board, but . . . ?"

I look down at the phone and press the power button.
It comes right on, and, surprisingly, he doesn't use a passcode. I
power down the phone.

I am not a tech person. I had to study and re-study the instructions on my phone so I can get the micro and chip in the right place. Now I have to fix his email, and I'm not sure how to do that.

I pull the small vial out of my pocket, open it, and tap the tiny "bug" into my palm. I remove the back of the phone, take out the battery, then look for the small notch where I'm supposed to insert the chip.

Gold side-up, the instructions had said.

It's difficult to get the chip in correctly as it's about the size of a small drop of water. It takes a couple of attempts. Meanwhile, we're just standing there like dorks.

Finally, I get it into position and hope it's the right way. I slip the battery back in, replace the cover, and power it on.

Patrick has his phone out, texting Apollo.

Okay its in.

It takes a minute for the phone to boot up and find a signal. I take the time to look around the room. I look at each person in the meeting. Other than Osborne, I don't recognize any of them.

"Pietrev is upset he wasn't advised on Project Onyx," a man says.

"I wish I had been too," Osborne says.

"It was a top secret military experiment," the President says. "They do hundreds of these and don't mention it until they're sure it works."

Patrick's phone buzzes softly.

No signal, Apollo's text says. *Try again.*

I power down and pull the back off. Probably have it right-side up, but still upside-down.

"The operation devastated the Chechens, and while Pietrev is not losing any sleep over it, he's more hung up on the principle that Onyx was sent in without a heads-up, much less his blessing," the first man says.

"There are forty other countries that have . . . observed Onyx, friend and foe. None of the other friends have complained about 'blessings,'" the President says.

After the battery is out, I gently turn the phone over so the chip falls into my palm, but it doesn't as it's wedged in rather nicely. I try to ease it out with my fingernail, which works, but too well: The chip pops out and ends up somewhere on the carpet. Patrick immediately kneels to search for it.

I pretend to continue to work on the device.

"Well, the media has latched onto it," Osborne says.

"Yes," Quinn says. "I contacted Brighton in New York, and he's agreed to restraint, but some of the international channels are going nuts, making it hard to ignore. I should get an update shortly."

Patrick comes up with the chip and hands it to me.

"How's it going over there?"

"Almost done, I think," I say, having no idea.

I try again with the chip, and manage to get it in place quicker this time—and hopefully the right way.

Battery, back plate, power on.

"China's Channel Nine is just starting to run with it," the woman says. "A village near Lhasa has been wiped out."

The phone finishes booting. I notice the email icon starts showing numbers, increasing from *121* to *409* in a few seconds. Apparently, restarting the phone fixed the email problem.

Signal attained, Apollo texts.

"Sir," I say.

The President pops up out of his chair like a kid on Christmas morning. "Is it working?"

"It seems so." I hold the phone out for him to take it.

He beams as if he were Homecoming King just after winning the crown. "Fantastic." He looks at the screen, smiling, then looks up and pats me on the upper arm. "Good job."

Then the smile falters before disappearing. He's staring at me somewhat blankly.

"What happened to Doug?" he says, as if realizing for the first time that I'm not Doug.

"Nothing," I say. "Has the day off, I heard."

He looks at Patrick, the same odd look on his face, but then quickly turns back to me.

"You look familiar."

I give the slightest of smiles, but have no clue what I should say, if anything.

"Have you been here before?" Before I can answer, he looks away, shaking his head, frowning, as if trying to dredge up a memory. "Maybe during the campaign? Setting up the offices?" A pause. "No."

I wait several moments while he rummages through his memory. "Is there anything else we can do?" I ask.

"Huh? Oh, no. Thank you." Then, still frowning, he looks at me again for several second before he turns back to his "guests."

Patrick and I open the door, and step out, closing it behind us.

Asphalt Ten, or whatever his name was, is waiting for us.

"Thank you," I say to the woman, then nod at the Secret Service agent.

"I'll show you out," he says.

We head down the hallway, back the way we came. We end up on the east side of the building, and Asphalt Guy points to a door. "Have a nice day," he says.

We head out into the gray chill, down a long sidewalk, to what is basically a guard post, where a short line of people wait to get out.

I realize my heart is going about 1,000 miles an hour. Sweat trickles down the inside of my shirt as we get at the back of the line.

I look at Patrick who, on the surface, looks cool as a cucumber, but his eyes are watchful and not at all calm.

As we reach the guard, who scans our badges with an electronic gun, there's a shout from behind us.

"Wait!"

I don't turn to look, but instead, step away, out onto the public sidewalk.

"Stop or I'll shoot!"

And that's when I run.

I'm supposed to go east, to the next block over, then left to the building where Apollo and Leslie are waiting for us. But if someone is chasing me, I don't want to lead them there. So I cut right, onto another street, looking around, looking back, not seeing anyone following, and realizing Patrick isn't with me. I don't see him anywhere.

I cut across onto a short street that leads to another larger one.

From here, I walk. There are no other pedestrians, but some traffic from cars passing by. I turn left, heading in the direction I think I need to go.

Where is Patrick? Did they capture him? Did he run another direction? Where did he go? I feel frantic thinking of the possibilities.

I watch ahead for anyone who looks like Secret Service or police. None that I can see. I blend in with a small crowd on the corner, waiting for the light. I look towards my left, towards the White House and the gate where visitors go in and out. People are milling about, but nothing looks different.

I cross Pennsylvania Avenue, and walk down to the building, slipping inside as quickly as I can. In the elevator, I push the button for 8.

My mouth is dry, but my body is sweaty.

The elevator doors open, and I walk out and to the right. 800, 802, 804. I knock. Leslie opens it.

"Hey," she says.

"Is Patrick here?"

She blinks, confused. "No. He isn't with you?"

"As we were leaving, someone yelled 'Stop!' and I took off. I thought Patrick was behind me."

Apollo, sitting at a desk in front of a monitor, swivels around to face us. "We'll have to assume he's been captured."

"What do we do?"

He shakes his head, and turns back to the monitor.

* * *

On the phone, Sylvana sounds very calm.

"Do you have your personal cellphone with you?"

"No, I was instructed to leave it in my room."

I hear her telling someone to go fetch it.

"We will do what we can, but I think Apollo is correct in assuming he has been captured."

I think about the last time he was captured, and what they did to him. I doubt that this time they would leave him alive for long.

"I have your phone. It looks like you have a voice mail. May I listen to it?"

"Of course."

A few seconds later, I can hear it play:

"We have your friend 'Enrique,'" Henry Davis, a.k.a. Harod Dunraven says. *"Let's make a deal."* Then a long silence.

"That's it?" I ask.

"Yes," Sylvana says.

"Okay. Let's do it."

* * *

I dial Henry's number.

"That didn't take long," he says.

"You can have your men back in exchange for my friend," I tell him.

"No. I want you."

I pause, a little surprised. I try to think quickly. I realize there is only one answer, even though it kills me.

"No," I say, and hang up.

* * *

We sit and wait. An hour goes by. I try to think through all the angles. I even bounce some ideas off Apollo and Leslie.

"Maybe I should make the exchange," I say. "If I'm on the inside, I can probably do more damage to his operation than from the outside."

Apollo shakes his head. "No, you won't get a chance."

"He can lock me up, tie me down, but with my powers, I won't stay that long."

Apollo sighs but doesn't say anything for several long moments. It's kind of weird getting advice from an ancient man in an 8 year old's body. "The first thing he'll do is kill you."

"What? Stab me? Carve me up like he did to Patrick? I can *heal* myself."

"He'll cut off your head," Apollo says, flatly. "No healing that."

I let this sink in. But not for long. I can't give up.

"Maybe I can find where he is, break in, and figure out a way to get him out. I did it before." But even to my ears, what I'm saying doesn't sound plausible. "You could track his phone."

"I've already done that. The signal went dead half an hour ago. It was still at the White House. Quinn's phone also went invisible. They found the chip." He gets up and goes to the mini-fridge, pulling out a plastic bottle of orange juice. "No, you did the right thing. He needs his men more than he needs Patrick. In his mind, if you're willing to sacrifice your friend to defeat him, he'll get nervous. If you give yourself up to save your friend, he'll think you are weak."

I sit in silence for several minutes, thinking. I see his point. I just don't want to do nothing.

"If Patrick dies because of this, I'll never forgive myself."

Neither of them say anything.

* * *

It's nearly another hour until Apollo says:

"We should go."

"Go where?"

"Home."

I shake my head. "I can't leave Patrick here."

A long pause. "You must."

"We have people here," Leslie says. "They can continue to work on finding Patrick while we . . . move on."

I know she's making sense, but it's hard for me to accept.

Apollo gets off the chair and heads for the door. "The car is waiting," he says.

* * *

We don't go back to the airport where we arrived—Reagan National—instead driving an hour to Baltimore. "They'll be looking for you there," Apollo explains.

While waiting in line to buy tickets, my phone vibrates in my pocket. I pull it out to check the Caller ID.

Unknown caller.

I answer anyway. "Yes?"

"Last chance."

"No deal." As I say this, a little part of me dies.

"Too bad. But it doesn't matter. The kid has given us a lot of information already."

I don't believe a word of it, but I'm not going to play that game. "I'm going home, but I'm sure I'll see you soon."

"I have a nice stick which will fit his head quite nicely."

Apollo is standing just in front of me, frowning. I'm sure he's listening in.

"I'm sure you do," I say. "I've got to go."

And, again, I hang up.

It takes everything I have to not cry.

Chapter 15

"Our deepest fear is that we are powerful beyond measure. It is our light, not our darkness, that most frightens us . . . And as we let our own light shine, we unconsciously give other people permission to do the same. As we are liberated from our own fear, our presence automatically liberates others."—Marianne Williamson

By the time we land, it's dark, like my mood. Between myself, Leslie and Apollo, we haven't said a word to each other.

As we wait to get off the plane, I check my phone. 5 voice mails.

I listen to each, but there's only a few seconds of silence before being disconnected.

He's breaking.

I look at Apollo. Now what?

Call him.

I wait until we are in the terminal and I can find a semi-private place to call.

"What?" I say when Dunraven answers.

"Coffee shop on P Street, near 14th."

And he hangs up.

Apollo is on his phone, looking a bit odd with a big smart-phone up against his 8 year old head. To whoever he's talking to, he gives the coffee shop information.

We go out to the pickup area, and our familiar black car pulls up. We all climb in, Apollo taking the front passenger seat.

My hopes have risen, but I remain guarded.

I try to consider the possibilities. Patrick is found alive and well at the coffee shop. Or he's found alive, but not so well. Or he's found dead. Or there is no Patrick at all.

Ten minutes later, Apollo's phone rings. He answers, listens, then simply says: "Thanks."

He turns around.

"They have him. He's drugged, but fine."

A wave of relief washes over me, as well as confusion. Dunraven gave in pretty easily.

"Something's up," I say.

Leslie looks at me, with an expression of an unspoken question. Apollo says nothing, not disagreeing.

* * *

We reach Manor House without Patrick, who has stayed behind until he can be checked out. We don't bother trying to sneak in through the tunnel. Dunraven's Regulators are still in the backyard, and have all lined up, watching us.

I get out of the car and head for the house, not acknowledging them. Inside the large living room, Sylvana greets us, looking as stately as ever.

"The doctors will examine Patrick, but he seems to be fine."

I offer a weak smile, and nod.

Mr. B walks in, looking as troubled as I feel.

"That was too easy," I say. "No strings attached is hard to swallow."

"Just because we can't see the strings doesn't mean they're not there."

I nod. Satan is sneaky that way. "I guess I should keep my word and let those men go."

Both Sylvana and Mr. B looked troubled by this, but don't reply.

After several moments, Leslie says: "I'll arrange their release."

And she starts to leave, Apollo following.

"Wait," I say. "Wait until Patrick is here and safe."

She gives a small smile. "Okay."

"He'll be on a plane shortly with two of our men," Mr. B says. "He should be here in a couple of hours. In the meantime, you and I should catch up on some stuff."

I'm tired, drained, but I know he's right.

* * *

"Apollo usually gets what Apollo wants, but that's not always the best thing," Mr. B says as we walk down a corridor. "So, I should apologize for not voicing my reservations when he brought up this idea of planting a chip on the President's phone. Don't get me wrong, Apollo's intentions are pure, but sometimes he over-reaches."

"I don't blame him, and I don't blame you," I say. "We actually accomplished the mission."

"Yes, and you did a very good job. But my point is the mission wasn't necessary. We have microphones in the Oval Office. We were listening in while you and Patrick were in there. We pretty much know what's going on. And while Apollo is right that we have a blind spot when Quinn is not in the Oval Office, we've been extremely successful at filling in the blanks."

"So you heard about Project Onyx."

"Yes, the unleashing of the ravens. It's still technically in the testing phase, but it's obviously expanded."

"Who were those other people there?"

He rattles off names, but it was their titles that caught my attention: Secretary of State, Majority Leader of the U.S. House of Representatives, Majority Leader of the U.S. Senate, Chief Justice of the Supreme Court.

"So, the most powerful people in the country."

"Yes, as far as their titles go," Mr. B says. "But they're all under Quinn's thumb, for one reason or another. They're all contemptible, spineless cowards—and I'm not saying that because they're politicians and that's an easy thing to say. It's just a matter of following the money. Dunraven—through Quinn—has greatly supplemented their lifestyles both financially and through their proclivities. He knows their weak spots and knows how to use them."

"So, money and sex."

"Not always sex, but often yes. The Chief Justice, for example, doesn't seem to harbor any . . . deviancies. But there is an issue surrounding the death of his first wife. And the Senate Majority Leader doesn't seem to have any skeletons in her closet, but has an ego the size of Texas. It's remarkably easy to manipulate people like that."

We walk through a doorway, and I see it's like a small theater—several rows of seats all facing a small stage in front of a white screen.

"What's this?"

"Our meeting hall. It's time to bring everyone up to speed. Including you."

"You mean there's more?" I ask with a smile as we step down the stairs.

Mr. B doesn't return the smile, only looks more serious. "You have no idea."

"Should I be scared?"

"No, of course not. Fear is imagining the unknown, not living it."

I pause, thinking. "That reminds me of a saying I like—I'm not sure who said it: 'Fear can keep us up all night long, but faith makes one fine pillow.'"

Mr. B chuckles as we reach the bottom, and he takes a seat in the front row.

"Okay, so what's the bottom line?" I say, standing in front of him, my arms crossed. "What do I need to know?"

"We'll talk about that when the group gets here, which should be in a few minutes."

"I know I have a lot of support, but I still . . . well, I kind of feel that I'm a leader without a plan."

He sighs, pauses, frowns. It's several seconds before he answers.

"Apollo will be our greatest asset, as far as planning," Mr. B says. "He's recorded untold amounts of information, and remembers most—if not all—of it. His only problem—besides a bit of impulsiveness—is he has trouble with context. He'll know some piece of information he picked up weeks ago, but doesn't always apply it to current events. That's where we need to put it together. But he's great at organizing, and can help us plot out each move, as long as we don't play to his every whim."

"So does Apollo have plan of action?"

"He's more about what happened in the past, and what's happening now, but the context is not always there. Forward-thinking plans are not his strength, although once he's given a scenario, he works through it pretty well."

"I guess you and I will need to put it together."

"I would suggest taking the End Game and working backwards."

"So . . . finding the Ark."

"Not just finding it, but protecting it and using it when . . . needed."

There's the sound of chatter above us, and I look up to see people starting to file into the theater.

Mr. B gazes up at me. "Have a seat. It will take a few minutes for everyone to get here."

* * *

The lights dim, and a few stage lights come on. Sylvana glides onto the stage from somewhere in the back, and the low murmuring from the audience dies completely.

"Thank you for joining us," she says, her voice perfectly clear. "Before we begin, I would like to bring in a friend and special guest."

She turns, raises her arm to the back of the stage . . . and out steps Patrick.

I stand up, and jump on the stage, embracing him. He looks fine, still dressed in his suit and tie, looking impeccable. He pats me on the back as the crowd stands and offers a thundering applause.

I pull back, beaming, and look him in the eyes. Other than a slightly dazed look from either the lights or all the attention—probably both—he seems okay. I was worried about them beating him or even brainwashing him, but neither seems to have happened.

"Go ahead and take your seats," Sylvana says as the crowd quiets down.

"Good to see you, man," I whisper as we go down into the front row.

"Good to be seen."

Sylvana takes the center stage again, and looks solemnly out over the audience.

"I have called you here so we can get an update from Professor Burkfelt on what is happening, and what to expect. But before we do, I just have a few words to say."

She offers a slight, sweet smile as her eyes twinkle.

"I have known Collin since he was a little boy. I know his strengths, I know his weaknesses, I know his intellect, and I know his heart. I think you know it too."

She pauses, and looks over to me for a moment before looking back up at the people.

"I know there has been talk about him. I can feel the reverence. I am sure he has sensed it as well. You have all been not only welcoming, but perhaps a little too . . . in awe." She waits a moment. "I realize you are looking for a hero, and you have heard things that may or may not be correct.

"Collin is just a man. A special man, true. He has been given a special task, and with that task comes special powers, but he is no more special than you. You each have special powers and special gifts, different from his, but no less special. He will need your gifts and powers for his to succeed. There may be pain. There may be blood. Maybe even his blood. But that is the sacrifice we all must choose."

She waits to allow this to sink in.

"Collin will lead us against a terrible foe. We all know the foe's name. We all know the power of the adversary, and you may even be able to sense that there are powers that have yet to be imagined, much less witnessed. Ultimately, evil cannot survive on its own. It always collapses upon itself, but it often takes with it the innocent, the powerless, and the righteous."

Another pause.

"And that is the goal of this adversary, to destroy. To destroy you, to destroy us, to destroy itself."

A very long pause, where it appears as if she is looking into each person's eyes, one at a time.

"There have been many before you. Those who have been sold, tortured, abused, those who found death as the only relief. Yet we know, there is no such thing as death as His Love takes us to another level, another place, where there is no pain, no tears, no blood."

The lights dim even further, and the stage lights go dark. We sit in a kind of breathless silence as . . . well, it's hard to explain. I see things. Faint trails of glowing mist, swirling. I glance quickly around and realize everyone else sees it too.

The mist grows, and then begins to separate, re-forming, taking a new shape. Soon, I can make out faces, the faces of children, hundreds of them, smiling, laughing, waving. Out of the corner of my eye, I can see some in the audience waving back. There are gasps, there is crying, and tears fill my vision.

In the center of the sea of children's glowing, floating faces, I see Jill.

Chapter 16

"You are my angel / Come from way above / To bring me love."
—Massive Attack: "Angel"

What happens next is both amazing, and bizarre. The faces of the children disappear, leaving only Jill, large and looming, her face just like I last remember it, as I had seen it smiling across from me as we sat in a restaurant.

Her eyes scan the crowd, seemingly looking at each and every face, smiling warmly. As her gaze moves our way, her eyes lock on me, and she smiles even more broadly.

Her lips move.

I love you.

"I love you," I whisper. My heart suddenly feels both filled with joy, yet heavy and troubled.

I know, she mouths.

A single tear escapes, running down her cheek, as her eyes close, her head bows, and the image dissipates into nothing.

The auditorium goes dark.

There's silence, yet I hear many people sniffling. Then a glow comes from the center of the stage, a new mist that begins to materialize into a human shape. Once again, it is Jill, this time as she was as a child. She appears like a hologram, not quite real, yet extremely vivid. She's wearing a blue dress with yellow flowers, black shoes, and a yellow ribbon in her hair. She stands there, smiling at us, as if she's a young actress in play waiting for her cue.

"This is a true story," she says in her little-girl voice.

She doesn't move, but behind her, from the dark shadows comes a beam of a flashlight. Beds appear in two rows on either side of the stage, and Jill runs to the side of one bed, where she kneels.

The beam of light comes closer, scanning up and down the rows, checking the beds, each with a child beneath the covers.

"Oh dear Lord, please save my soul . . ." Jill's voice says from the side of her bed. *"Oh dear Lord, please save my soul . . . Oh dear Lord, please save my soul . . ."*

The beam of the flashlight stops on Jill's head as it is bowed in prayer.

She looks up, out to the audience as she stands and gets under the covers. Laying on her side, staring at us, just her head poking out of the top of the blanking, she starts to speak.

"I'll never forget this day. I could feel her sharp owl-eyes focus on me. I pretended to be asleep, but inside I shook, knowing. Her footsteps came closer and closer to my bed. Then, they stopped as her flashlight burned brightly on me."

The beam of light, held by a vague figure in a dark dress, hovers over Jill's head.

"The stillness was terrifying, realizing it was my time. On this night, I am to be the one wishing away the unknown. I know something happened to the others, but if they came back, they were too shocked and traumatized to ever say what it was. They only had an awful blank stare. They rarely spoke, and never again smiled. And now, it's my turn. I've never been so frightened."

The light suddenly goes out, and all is pitch black.

Everyone in the hall is holding their breath.

"Oh dear Lord, please save my soul . . ." the voice of Jill whispers in the dark.

Again, a soft glow appears showing Jill standing in the middle of the stage, this time in a plain white night dress. Instead of her pretty smile, she looks petrified.

The vague form in the black dress moves behind her, hands with long fingernail painted fire-engine red slip a hood over Jill's head. Then a black leather collar with a large silver ring is place around her neck, followed by the sound of a click as a leash is attached.

"Oh dear Lord . . ."

The hands disappear behind Jill for a moment, then slip the night dress off Jill's shoulders. The plain gown falls to the floor.

". . . please save my soul . . ."

Other than the hood and collar, Jill stands naked in the harsh white light.

Standing behind her, holding the leash, is a woman I've seen before: Unbelievably bright red hair, fishnet stockings, leather corset, her crotch and large breasts exposed. Her face is powdered white, making the ridiculously long black eyelashes and ruby red lipstick stand out.

Behind the woman, a half-circle of mirrored walls appears.

Jill's voice floats out to us:

"I can feel the lurking of anonymous eyes fall upon me from behind the glass."

The bizarre woman jerks on the leash, yanking Jill backwards a few steps.

"The overwhelming trapped feeling made my heart sink as she began to parade me around the room."

The hooded naked Jill is walked in front of the mirrors.

"She tugged on the leash, commanding me to heal."

They walk from the left to the right, then the right to the left.

"She is yours," the strange clown-like woman says, *"if you're the highest bidder!"*

Then Jill is led to the center. The woman's hand pushes the girl down into a sitting position, her back to us. Then with a red stiletto shoe, shoves her to lay flat on the floor.

The leash is dropped, and the woman squats, pulling Jill's arms up, over her head, and shackles her wrists into leather buckles that are bolted to the floor.

Gasps are heard throughout the audience. Even Patrick softly says "Oh my God."

At the back of the stage, one of the mirrors opens like a door, and a naked man walks out. I recognize him, too—Russ Zorbo, former TV news anchor.

The woman steps back and Zorbo approaches Jill, standing over her, straddling her. Then he squats down on Jill, rubbing against her gently. Jill squirms beneath him. Then he reaches for her head and removes the hood.

We cannot see Jill's face, but we hear her scream *"No!"* in her little girl voice and see her kick her legs.

Zorbo stands, and looks down.

Jill continues to kick her legs, squirming. The woman approaches again, squatting down and taking one of Jill's ankles, holding it down.

Zorbo steps back and kneels between the girl's legs, leans over, and begins licking her chest.

"Oh dear Lord, please save my soul!" Jill screams.

I close my eyes and look away. The screams continue.

When I open them, I look around at the crowd in the hall. Most have their eyes closed, or a hand over their face, many with heads bowed, praying. Others are staring, aghast, at the scene on the stage.

I close my eyes again, unable to watch.

A few moments later, there is a scream of unbearable pain.

And then all goes silent except for the echo of the scream, which seems to bounce around the hall.

Warily, I open my eyes and see the stage has gone dark.

We all wait, and I'm afraid of what we're going to see next.

Slowly, a new scene takes place, but with the same people. And one other: An old man lying on a couch. He is on his side, naked, and seems to be sleeping.

The red-haired woman is laying in an old-style bathtub, only her head showing.

"Sex is power. Money is power. Power is power," she says. *"Sex is power. Money is power. Power is power. Sex is power . . ."*

Zorbo, still naked but now sitting in a chair, is reading a newspaper. Behind him, Jill appears, holding a baseball bat. She is fully clothed, and the expression on her face is passive. No emotion there at all.

She swings the bat, connecting solidly with Zorbo's skull. His head explodes in an eruption of blood. He's not just decapitated, but his head has evaporated. For a few moments, his body remains as it was, sitting upright, holding up the newspaper. Then the paper lowers to his lap and his headless corpse slumps to the side.

Jill then turns to the man on the couch, approaching him. The baseball bat in her hand has changed—it is now a hammer. She raises it above her head, and the man's eye suddenly open. She brings the hammer down with such force that it is embedded deep in the man's skull. Jill tries to pull it out, but gives up, leaving the tool protruding from his head. Blood pours out like water, over his face, over the couch cushion and onto the floor.

Jill, now holding a white towel, turns to the woman in the tub.

". . . Money is power. Power is—"

Jill jams the towel down on the woman's face, pushing down hard, her head disappearing below the edge of the tub. An arm comes up and frantically grabs Jill's, but Jill keeps pressing down. After a minute, the woman's hand lets go, and slips down into the tub.

Again, all goes dark.

Kind of surprisingly, there is some applause from the audience, but it seems tentative and awkward.

Appearing on the stage again are the beds, two rows, one on each side, seemingly going back forever. A stocky woman in a gray matronly dress is standing with her back to us. She holds a whip in one hand and snaps it onto each bed as she walks down the aisle.

"Get up, you lazy weasels, get up!"

Boys and girls climb out of their beds, naked, and form a line behind the woman.

This scene fades, and a new one appears, outdoors in the snow.

The children are shivering in a holding pen. Around the outside, dogs appear, barking and growling at the kids.

"Again, gentlemen, the rules," a male voice says as if over a loudspeaker. *"Shoot to kill. Head shots are worth the most. Torso but still fatal is good as well. Anywhere else, not so much. Any wounded game must be dispatched manually."*

The door of the pen is opened, but the children don't move, they just stand there, looking scared.

The barking of the dogs increase, and one of them jumps into the pen, grabbing one boy on the calf of his leg, shaking the boy as the child screams in pain and terror.

The other children now run, scrambling across the white, empty field. And one by one, each is shot, falling into the snow.

Then, as the last of the children goes down, there is nothing but quiet. Only bodies lying in the snow. One of the children's legs move, but it is fleeting.

From the right, a man in a large brown coat and warm hat trudges out into the snow. He approaches the child whose leg moved, stands over the body, raises a machete in his right hand, and plunges it into the small body. He pulls it out, nods, then turns and heads back to where he came.

The scene fades away.

When it returns, it appears to be the same field. In the pen are dozens of senior citizens, naked, some crying.

There are no dogs this time. The pen is opened, and the adults begin to move, some trying to run, some walking, some shuffling. Once again, gunfire, and they are taken out, one by one.

Again, fade out.

After several moments, what appears is, again, a girl laying on the floor. It is not Jill, but a different girl, with blonde hair.

I'm wondering when this horror is going to end.

Standing towards the back is yet another naked man. He steps forward, and I realize it is the President of the United States, MacNeill Quinn. His hand is around his flaccid penis, tugging on it. He is licking his lips as he stands near the feet of the girl.

"Please, daddy, no . . ."

He continues to rub himself.

"It won't take long this time," he says.

Jill appears behind him and steps beside him. Her arms are at her side, a long, gleaming knife in one of her hands.

He turns and faces her. *"Would you like this, sweetie?"* he asks, removing his hand and showing her his erection.

She smiles. Her free hand reaches down. He leans his head back, closes his eyes and moans. She wraps her fingers around the sack and tugs down. His erection arches upward, pulsing. She brings the knife up and cleanly cuts off his scrotum.

His head snaps back, his mouth open, looking down at what she has done, shocked.

He stands, blood squirting from the wound between his legs. He sways slightly, and then collapses onto the floor.

Jill turns to us, still holding the knife. She begins to speak, but it is not hers. The voice is male, a strong, deep baritone.

"Finally, be strong in the Lord and in the strength of His might. Put on the full armor of God, so that you will be able to stand firm against the schemes of the devil. For our struggle is not against flesh and blood, but against the rulers, against the powers, against the world forces of this darkness, against the spiritual forces of wickedness in the heavenly places. Therefore, take up the full armor of God, so that you will be able to resist in the evil day, and having done everything, to stand firm."

The stage fills with mist, Jill disappearing in a fog . . . and then again, all goes dark.

Chapter 17

"Tell me and I forget. Teach me and I remember. Involve me and I learn."—Benjamin Franklin

The mist dissipates, the lights come up and the stage is empty.

Mr. B gets out of his seat and takes a series of steps up to the stage.

I am still a bit stunned, as is everyone else. Yet I am heartened by seeing Jill. She was even more beautiful than I remember. While watching her kill her tormentors was tough to watch, I have to remind myself that I've done something similar a few times. The blood on my hands still weighs on my conscience.

Mr. B walks to the center of the stage, behind a lectern, and gazes out at his "students." There is still the sound of sniffling here and there.

"Good evening. For those of you I have not met, I am Professor Burkfelt, and I am here to provide you with some historical background to give you some perspective on what we face. Our adversary would prefer you not know the truth, but as George Santayana said, 'Those who cannot remember the past are condemned to repeat it.' And as Sylvana implied, we are not condemned. You should not, however, worry about how much of this you retain—there will be no test."

Some laughter, and a spirited young man shouts "Praise the Lord!"—which brings more laughter.

"You, sir, are welcome to stay after for some personal tutoring," Mr. B says with a glint in his eye, followed by more laughter from his class.

"But in all seriousness, our adversary is quite strong, and very cunning. He knows each of us, but not out of love or sentiment. He knows your strengths, your weaknesses, and can devise plans to undermine our lives in ways both large and small."

"Can he read our minds?" a woman asks.

"Good question. Although I think he is able to whisper to us—perhaps some kind of spiritual telepathy—I don't believe he can know what you're thinking. He does, however, have a very strong power of observation, and acts upon it by 'suggesting' to you the things you find enjoyable, even if they are not worthy of your attention. He absolutely targets those things that both allure us and undermine us. It is the gift of discernment that we need to practice that will help keep him at arm's length."

On the white screen behind him appears the official portrait of the President of the United States.

"Throughout our nation's history, starting with George Washington, through Abraham Lincoln and beyond, there are citizens who have sincerely believed that whoever was President at that time was the most evil person on the planet—and in the case of Lincoln, was assassinated because of it. Wilson was vilified. Hoover condemned. Truman mocked. Nixon. Reagan. Clinton. Bush. Obama. All have had their detractors. Even our current Chief Executive, MacNeill Quinn, has both a broad swath of supporters and enemies.

"But there are aspects to Mr. Quinn's life which his supporters do not know, and his enemies wish they did. This, for example."

On the screen appears a censored image I had seen before, and wished I didn't: A naked Quinn and a little girl.

Gasps from the crowd.

"I apologize for the lewdness of this image," Mr. B says, "but this is one of the more modest ones. I sincerely debated showing you one of the other photographs, uncensored, exposing the reality of Mr. Quinn as he rapes that child."

"But that's his daughter!" a man from the back shouts.

"Yes. Yes it is. And she is not the only one."

"How do you know that wasn't doctored—altered—by one of the President's enemies?" another man asks.

"There are tests that can be done, such as pixel ratio, and putting it through an Image Error Analyzer, although nothing is foolproof. Truth is, this could be doctored, along with the other two hundred and fifty other images of the President we have showing him in this kind of . . . state with other children. Boys and girls." The images disappears. "But I think the source where we obtained these files would indicate they are real, and not altered, since we found them in the home of his father."

Murmurs of dismay and disgust from behind me.

"Yes, we should discuss a little bit of the Quinn family lineage. His father is this man—" the image appears of a man I recognize "—who has gone by many names over the years, but is currently known as Henry Davis. He is the companion, one might say, of our adversary, who also has gone by many names. Currently, the adversary likes the designation 'Dymortis.' So, to keep all these evil people straight, that's what I'll call him.

"Dymortis met the young Henry Davis many, many years ago, and they struck a deal—Davis would help do Dymortis' dirty work, and in return, Davis would become immortal. I have been able to trace them back to before the birth of Christ, and through many events, large and small, through authenticated history. And it is our friend here, Collin, who unearthed even more evidence of their treachery."

"So President Quinn is literally the spawn of the devil?" a woman asks.

Mr. B pauses for a moment, letting this question sink in. "Pretty much," he says.

* * *

He spends the next several minutes going over some of the malicious things these men did, up to President Quinn releasing

Project Onyx on unsuspecting people around the world, under-scoring it with a video of the giant ravens attacking what appears to be fans leaving a soccer game in England—hundreds of these monsters swooping down from the sky to injure, maim, and kill thousands of people. Some of the people can be seen being clutched by large talons, grabbed on the head and taken away.

"This is from yesterday. Sorry, again, for the gruesomeness, but it is reality, and what we are up against."

The video fades from view.

"There are other plans in place or underway, including restricting gun ownership, a takeover of the U.S. and foreign financial systems, and strategic deployment of both domestic and foreign military personnel. You may have seen in the news over the last eighteen months or so how the U.S. has successfully negotiated peace treaties with those countries and people that have been, traditionally, in conflict with one another, including the ground-breaking Middle East Unification Accord.

"This is not altruistic. It is part of the U.S. government's plan to unite the world under one government, one leadership, one financial system, and one military. However, recently, things have changed that have necessitated a speeding-up of the process in some areas. Dymortis now understands the strengthening of the Soulmadds and the inclusion of an individual—our friend Collin Graves—to the hierarchy."

He pauses to take a drink of water.

"We do not know God's intentions, but we can make an educated guess that the actions by Dymortis and his followers goes against God's plans. There are some theologians who believe that Jesus Christ would return after the 'One World' system is put into place. It appears Dymortis is attempting to accelerate the process, trying to force God's hand, in a way. This is just my interpretation, and not Biblical, but it appears to me that God is trying to tell us that now is not the time for the Second Coming."

He pauses, allowing us to consider this.

"But we, as mere mortals, cannot battle this successfully in the new time-frame Dymortis has decided upon. Again, this is just speculation on my part, but it explains why, now, the Soulmadds have been brought together and Collin has been blessed with both new gifts and a kind of spiritual ascendency to lead us against all of our adversaries."

"So, Collin is . . . the risen Christ?" someone asks.

"No, and I think Collin would be the first to admit this as he has no special insight or understanding of what he is or what he is doing here."

I feel myself blushing for no apparent reason, though I also feel many sets of eyes looking my way.

"While many of his powers seem Christ-like, Collin does not have the power to forgive sins, to offer eternal life, and he is not the Son of God. Although Collin may pray like you or I do, he has not been given any insight by God of what to do, nor how to do it."

He waits again, as if expecting a question, but there is none.

"Which brings us to what we expect Dymortis may be planning. It begins with something called 'Red Sky.'"

An image of ominous clouds appears behind him.

"Red Sky is quite complicated, basically wiping out humanity, but there's several steps to get there. The 'Red Sky' is just the first sign. And I suspect it may begin sooner than later."

The threatening clouds behind him turn a deep red.

"The initial plan was to enslave the people of the earth. That was to begin by the taking away of citizen rights. He has it fairly easy in many countries, but in the free world, it's been a struggle. It's difficult to take away something people have taken for granted. Christmas trees are obvious, and it's been badly handled. The cutting off the gun supply has been more well executed, and surprisingly effective. The Internet shutdown is equally impressive. They started with the outlying fringe sites, and slowly constricted it. Now only the most popular sites seem to work properly, and they're under Dunraven's thumb, quietly collecting information and keeping tabs on everyone who uses it."

"This 'Red Sky' sounds bad, but what, exactly, is it?" a woman asks.

Mr. B cocks his head. "I've done some research, although there's not much to go on. From what I can piece together, Red Sky is a precursor to decimation of everyone—and everything—on Earth."

"This year has been the coldest fall and winter in history," another woman says.

The Professor says nothing, only nods. Everyone in the room comes to the same realization: The Red Sky has already begun. And, as if to underscore this, the auditorium seems to drop ten degrees—although that might have been my mind playing tricks on me.

"So, what's he gonna do?" a young man asks. "Blow up the whole planet?"

"It would be humane if he did that. No, there will be much suffering before life on earth ends."

"Like what? What are we up against?"

"Red Sky will not just be red, it will soften the effects of the sun, lowering the temperature drastically. Crops will dwindle, livestock will die off due to lack of food, and that will lead to disease and starvation of the human race on a massive scale. There's not much I can find beyond that, but there are some hints that Dymortis is interested in basically knocking the earth either off its axis, or out of its orbit to kill the planet."

"How can he even do that?"

"It wouldn't take much. A well placed asteroid would do it."

"How does he have the kind of power where he can move asteroids around, or change the color of the sky?"

"How can he infiltrate your dreams, or get people to do what he wants? I mean, we can sit here all day wondering and questioning, but in the end, he can and will do it."

Another pause as he lets the people contemplate this.

"I know it is hard to grasp. We are all in search of 'Why?' What are we doing here? What is the meaning of life? We don't have concrete answers, and now, the balance of life, all perfectly arranged, is in jeopardy, with one little thing able to not just upset it, but throw it all into devastation on an unprecedented scale. If you think of all the horrible things that have happened to people and this planet—plagues, war, nuclear destruction, the Holocaust, slavery, sexual abuse—it can all be overshadowed by this one thing."

Several moments go by as Mr. B stands in silence, with his head bowed as if in prayer. Then he looks up and scans the audience.

"So what next?" he asks. "What do we do? We have a battle in front of us. A war. Our God is a loving God, who forbids us from hurting one another, where murder is a sin and life is precious. And yet we must now go into battle in a manner that will stop our enemy, using fatal techniques and weapons. Do we have God's permission? His blessing? Is He leading us? Or are we John Wilkes Booth, using our own demented beliefs to 'correct' a perceived evil?"

He lets this question hang for a minute.

"We think we know evil when we see it—"

The image of Quinn appears behind him again.

"—but what do we do about it? In the Bible it says to confront the sinner in private, but what do we do in this situation? We do know from our surveillance that the President has plans, and those plans will be put into place soon, and we have the opportunity to undermine them. Is it God's will, or our folly? Can we prevent evil from taking place, or are we going against God's plan?"

The image of the President disappears. "If we can stop it, we should," an older woman says.

"And I agree. That is why we're here. I would like your feedback, since we're all in this together. By a show of hands, how many believe we should take steps to stop the evil we know and can prove is happening?"

I raise my hand, and I look around, as does just about everyone else. As best I can tell, every hand is in the air.

"And who believes we should wait for a better understanding of God's will?"

Another look around, and I don't see any hands raised.

"Then so be it," Mr. B says.

Chapter 18

"The real voyage of discovery consists not in seeking new land-scape, but in having new eyes."—Marcel Proust

It's nearly midnight, way past dinner time, but in my worrying about Patrick, I didn't feel like eating. Now I'm starving.

We go to the empty cafeteria and take seats, me with my chicken piccata, Patrick with a double cheeseburger.

After I say Grace, I notice Patrick's head is still bowed, staring at his food.

"Were those graphic images of Jill the ones you saw in your dreams?"

I sigh. "Yeah."

"I never had a chance to meet her. I think I understand, even though it hurts."

I shake my head. "It's so hard to believe anyone would want to hurt anybody in that way."

Some of the others are preparing for the release of the Regulator prisoners. There seems to be a couple dozen of Regulators in the backyard, and we're going to release 24 or 25 more. It doesn't sit well with me, but I feel like I have to keep my word—even though, now that I think about it, I never actually promised to release the men. A loophole that I might be able to use.

"So what happened to you in DC?" I ask.

"Not much. When we went out the gate, I thought we needed to go right, but you went left. When I turned, there was an agent there with a gun. I just stopped. I didn't really think he would shoot, but didn't want to find out. And I figured it would give you a chance to get away."

Patrick plows into the burger, taking the biggest bite possible, not all of it making it into his mouth.

I take a bite of my meal, waiting for him to get some of the food down before asking my next question. "Then what? It doesn't look like they beat you up."

He shakes his head. "An SUV pulled up and we got in, and then they drove around, looking for you."

He takes another monster bite.

"You should slow down, dude. It's not going to disappear."

"Mmmm, furf nunn roff nerm."

"Where did they end up taking you?"

"Not sure," he finally answers. "I guess it was Secret Service headquarters. They put me in a room—like an interrogation room—and I just sat there. After a while, I just laid my head on the table and fell asleep. Then a guy comes in, wakes me up and says 'Let's go.' Him and another guy led me downstairs and into the lobby, outside and into an SUV. Then they drop me off at the coffee shop. As I get out, the passenger window rolls down, and the guy hands me a twenty. He says 'Have a nice day,' and they leave."

I'm frowning. It doesn't sound like something Dymortis or Dunraven would do. Just give in so easily? Without any strings attached? It doesn't make sense to me.

A door at the far end of the cafeteria opens, and a man walks in pushing a mop pail. Patrick turns his head to look and I glance at my friend, noticing an angry red bump behind his left ear.

"That looks like it hurts," I say. "Maybe you should see a doctor."

"What?"

"That thing behind your ear."

He shifts his burger to his right hand and touches irritated skin. "Damn. That does hurt. Is it a pimple? It feels gigantic."

"Maybe it's a boil. Let me see."

He drops his hand and turns his head so I can look.

It might be a large pimple or a small boil, except for the fact that it's perfectly square.

"That's not right," I tell him. "We should get it checked."

He nods, not concerned. I don't want to tell him what I really think it is.

* * *

Patrick sits in a chair in his room, and a guy not much older than us uses a penlight to examine behind Patrick's ear. Leslie, Sylvana and Mr. B are also present, waiting patiently.

"It . . . well, I don't know what it is," the young doctor says. "But I think it should be lanced."

"You mean cut it open?" Patrick asks, not sounding too keen on the idea.

"I don't think it should be left like that."

"Can't you put an ointment or something on it?"

"Like what?"

"I don't know, you're the doctor."

"Don't worry. I'll numb it first." The doctor opens a small backpack he brought with him and pulls out a small bottle, and sprays it on the area. Then, a needle stuck in another bottle, drawing out what I could only guess is Novocain or something. "Just a little pinprick."

The needle goes into the skin just above and below the affected area. Then out comes a small knife—a scalpel?—and the doctor neatly makes a couple of cuts. He holds a gauze pad to the wound with one hand while a pair of tweezers comes up in the other. He pokes at the cut and after a minute, holds up a small black square, which looks plastic.

"A tracking device?" I ask.

The doctor nods. "A sub-dermal microchip, I would guess."

"What?" Patrick says, sounding surprised. "They put a chip in me?"

"Looks like it," I say. "Probably when you were sleeping. They didn't give you a shot or anything?"

"No, they didn't touch me. Except I guess they did."

"Nothing to eat?"

"No, just a bottle of water."

I look at Mr. B, who is frowning.

"I've heard of drugs that are tasteless," the doctor says. "Basically untraceable."

"That one is kind of obvious," Leslie says. "I'm sure they would have put it under his scalp if he had any hair. They just inserted it in the most inconspicuous place possible."

I glance at both Sylvana—who just looks sad—and Mr. B, who is still frowning.

They're thinking what I'm thinking.

"You'll need to strip," I tell Patrick.

"What? Why?"

"Because I bet that's not the only one they put inside of you."

I watch his face, and it goes through a few different emotions, ending on disgusted.

The doctor dresses the excision with a small piece of gauze taped in place. Then Patrick stands and turns to face us.

"If you'll excuse me, ladies," he says.

Sylvana, Leslie and Mr. B all leave and Patrick removes his shirt. The doctor pulls out some latex gloves and hands me a pair. We put them on and check over every millimeter of his arms, shoulders, back and chest.

"This looks like an old scar," the doctor says, pointing at Patrick's abdomen.

"Yeah, that's from another encounter with these jerks," Patrick says.

The doctor nods, and Patrick steps out of his shoes, then removes his slacks. We look over his feet, ankles, calves and thighs. Nothing.

"Okay," I say. "I never thought I'd say this to you, but off with the boxers."

He does so, and remains expressionless. I won't go into graphic details, but let's just say I saw parts of Patrick I don't think he's seen. And, using his penlight, the doctor finds something else.

"Alright, there is another," the doctor says. "Not in a great place, but I don't think it'll be too bad."

* * *

The chips are wrapped in a tissue and I take them down to Apollo's lab.

"Hi," he says, like an eight-year-old would. "Guess what? I've been able to tap into the President's encrypted phone. I can now monitor *everything*."

"Well, that's great."

"And, since I've cracked the encryption, I can also tap into Dunraven's line."

"Even better."

"This is huge!" He sees I'm not as enthusiastic. "What?"

I hand him the tissue. "Can you check these out? They were implanted in Patrick's body."

"I'll do my best!"

* * *

Finally, time to sleep. Only one dream, a fairly pleasant one with just me and Jill. She was gorgeous. The only problem was she couldn't talk—she would say something, but no sound came out. Or maybe I was deaf. But I still enjoyed seeing her.

* * *

The smartphone I had used on my trip to Washington buzzes on the nightstand. Groggily, I reach for it and squint to look at the Caller ID.

Unknown Caller.

I press Answer.

"*We had a deal.*"

"Hello."

"*Where are my men?*"

"Right where I left them, I guess."

"*I held up my end of the bargain.*"

"You put a tracking device in Patrick," I say, not bothering to mention we also found a second one. "Not cool."

"*He illegally entered a government property and misrepresented himself. He also tried to tamper with the President's phone.*"

"Actually, I was the one who did that. Besides, your men illegally gained entrance to a home without a search warrant, did a lot of damage to the property, and tried to sexually assault a woman. Also not cool."

"*Release the men.*"

"I'll think about it," I say before I hang up.

* * *

After showering, dressing, and grabbing a quick breakfast, I go down to see if Apollo found anything interesting.

"It works great!" the little boy says.

"What? The microchips?"

"No, the phone tapping. Listen."

He taps some keys.

"*We had a deal.*"

"*Hello.*"

"*Where are my men?*"

"*Right where I left them, I guess.*"

"*I held up my end of the bargain.*"

"*You put a tracking device in Patrick. Not cool.*"

Apollo stops the recording. "Works like a charm. Right after he called you, he called Quinn. I recorded that too, but haven't listened yet. I'm waiting for the Professor so we can listen together. Hey, look what else I did!" He opens a drawer and pulls out a Drat. At least I think it's a Drat. It looks incredibly real. The previous one didn't quite look right, but this one is on the money. It sits motionless until Apollo picks up a tablet and begins controlling it, powering it on.

The Drat raises its head and looks in my direction, then scurries towards me. It movement is very life-like, and a bit spooky.

"I've got my assistants putting more together, now that I've got the right materials sorted out. I hope to have twenty-five or thirty by the end of the day. I call this one Cyril."

Cyril looks up at me, stands up on its hind legs, its front paws kind of clawing at the air while its nose twitches and whiskers flick.

"The eyes are cameras, and it has four dynamic noise-canceling microphones, GPS and a satellite uplink. Stainless steel teeth that can inject whatever we want—like that stuff that knocked Patrick out."

"Were you able to figure out what that stuff was?"

"Xylenomine. It's similar to ketamine, but without the side-effects. It was developed a few years ago, but hasn't completed testing with the FDA. Obviously, the government conducts their own experiments."

Sylvana and Mr. B walk in. "You've got something for us?" Mr. B asks.

"Yep. I haven't listened to it yet, but it's a conversation between Dunraven's cell phone and Quinn's, and clocks in at forty-two minutes."

They take seats as Apollo clicks away on the keyboard. Then we can hear ringing through the speakers of the sound system.

"*Hello.*"

"*I just got off the phone with Graves. He is not releasing the men.*"

"*Okay. Let me get to a secure location.*"

"*They found one of the transmitters on Williams, but apparently not the other. That is good. It will allow us to continue to monitor them.*"

"*Okay, good. Just a sec.*" A long pause. "*Alright, I'm good. Do you still want to take them out at the first opportunity?*"

"*Yes, but it would have to be a shot to the head, at least for Graves. He has apparently gained the power of self-healing.*

Williams should be easier, but no sense in taking chances since he slipped by us once before."

I look over at Sylvana, who is only gazing down at the table. I'm glad Patrick isn't here to hear this.

"Can you bring me up to date on the banking situation?" Dunraven asks.

"It is mostly in place. I had to personally call the CEO's of the two biggest institutions to persuade them. When I brought up the subject of their . . . indiscretions, it didn't take long for them to change their minds."

"Long prison terms can do that."

"That, and the safety of their children. It was kind of odd— though not really a surprise—that their spouses weren't held at as high a value."

A chuckle from Dunraven.

"Other than that, the oil companies have agreed to the increases. The mythical shortages due to the refineries either going offline or experiencing technical issues should have gas prices double within a week. The farm subsidies being revoked last summer has started to have its effect -- bread, milk and eggs have all skyrocketed in the last month, beef and chicken shortages are making for slim pickings at the markets, and the supposed insect infestation has devastated the produce supplies. Once we start locking down canned goods and other pre-packaged groceries, I think the panic will start to set in."

"What's the situation with trade?"

"The labor dispute at the ports has effectively shut down shipping. There are over three hundred ship floating out in the ocean with nowhere to dock."

"And the electrical grid?"

"The computer viruses are almost complete, and should be deployed within a few weeks. They're actually going to conduct a test tonight in Western Canada."

"Good. Dymortis is getting anxious. He wants everything in place by Christmas. Is that still possible?"

"Yes, if all the tests go well, which it looks like they should."

"What about the Internet?"

"We plan to knock it offline tomorrow for about an hour to see how the ISP's respond. If they can figure out what's happening in that time, we'll go with the backup plan, but I think once we take out the major providers, it will be difficult for them to react in a timely manner. Then we'll put everything back online before they can troubleshoot it."

"And the satellites?"

"We'll do a test run over the weekend. Turns out it's a little more complicated than we thought to jam all of them at once."

"What is the cover story for that?"

"Solar flares. The sun has been relatively inactive for the last month in regards to the flares, so it's time to use that as an excuse."

They then talk about the Ravens—a.k.a. Project Onyx—and the President explains that he has 10,000 more birds to release, but needs to do it soon as they're running out of "slurry."

"Can you use prisoners?"

"Already have, but almost tapped out there. Hospitals are being looked at next, but that won't last long."

They talk about the faked satellite images of the polar ice caps, and how playing into the fears of global warming has begun a round of finger-pointing with little talk of solution.

"It's ironic that it's a totally made-up dilemma causing so much hand-wringing," Quinn says. "Even the doomsday preppers are getting in on the act."

"What is going on with the other governments? Are they still on board?"

"For the most part. Russia is, of course, being stand-offish, but I have intelligence indicating that behind the scenes, they're falling in line. China has kept to themselves, but all this stuff is right up their alley. Pakistan and India were the lone hold-outs, since neither wanted to blink first, but after the monsoons hit, the devastation has made them more amenable to our way of thinking."

"They need the aid too badly. How long will it take for the infrastructure to be all tied together?"

"Once they sign off, it will be just a matter of days. They, and the other countries involved, won't know what hit them."

"And it will all be handed over?"

"You'll have complete power before the ink is dry."

"And where will you go?"

"Cheyenne Mountain is being prepared as we speak. I've got three Generals to run things. The others will be removed one way or another."

"Do not take Air Force One. It will be too easy to track. See if you can get a military transport arranged. It might not be the most comfortable, but it will be more secure."

"Good idea. The more my staff is out of the loop, the better."

Chapter 19

"Grace, who haunted my thoughts when I couldn't Dream."—Maggie Stifvater

Sylvana suggested taking the rest of the day off to recharge, pray, rest. I didn't argue since I had a lot running around my mind that I needed to work through.

"But before you go," she said softly, "I do need to consult with you."

"Sure."

"I don't think we should keep the men in the holding area."

"We should let them go?"

"With a caveat. I can . . . help them forget."

I blink a few times. "Erase their memory?"

"Temporary amnesia. The telepathy we are able to access can be used to short circuit their memories, in a way."

"How long will it last?"

"Two to four weeks."

"Would you like me to help?"

"If you could. I've asked the other Soulmadds to assist as well. Even one can be quite tiring, mentally."

"Okay, let's do it."

"It will be a few minutes. We need to put the men to sleep.

In the meantime, I can teach you what to do."

* * *

Standing outside the metal doors, there's myself, Sylvana and six other Soulmadds, all of us dressed in the brown robes. We're just waiting for the gas to dissipate.

"*Clear,*" says Apollo's little-boy voice over a handheld radio I was holding, which I slip into one of the robe's pockets.

Two of the Soulmadds unlatch and unlock the steel doors, and open them carefully. We see the fourteen or fifteen men lying on the concrete.

We file in and each take a Regulator. I kneel over a man, older, salt-and-pepper hair, dressed all in black. His eyes are closed, and though he's frowning, he's breathing smoothly.

Even while he's "asleep" I can find his flow, a light dream sequence which, in his case, appears to be nothing more than him lying on a beach, watching women in bathing suits walk by.

I place my fingers as Sylvana showed me—left hand on his right temple, right hand on his forehead. It takes me a minute or so, but I find his memory center, and start to sort through them. I need to find some point before he was dispatched to enter the Manor House. It's kind of a jumble, and come across a scene of him and some buddies in a bar. Good enough.

"The memories are like cards," Sylvana had said. "Just find the ones you want and flick them away."

There seemed to be about a dozen. Him in the van, running up to the house, entering the hallway, going into the entertainment room, breaking things, falling, waking up in the holding room. I understood what Sylvana said about "flicking." Push them too hard, and it could burn a hole in the memory, taking with it much more than just the last week. I practiced, going too gently at first, then figuring out the right amount of mental "spring" needed to eliminate the particular memory. It took a lot of concentration.

* * *

I ended up working on the memories of three of the men. I understand what Sylvana meant by it being tiring—but I had the added element of a throbbing headache. Actually it's closer to a migraine.

I'll let the others move the men out of the room, and up to the street level. I don't know how they're going to do it, and frankly don't care. All I want to do is lie down and close my eyes. It's making me sick to my stomach.

* * *

I end up in the spa, naked and soaking in a hot tub. If there are other people enjoying the facilities, I don't notice them. I close my eyes and try to turn my brain off. I need to think of something soothing, relaxing. It doesn't take long.

The hot tub I'm in becomes a spring pool at the edge of a grassy meadow. A small, pleasant waterfall is at the far end, churning up the water just enough to be calming. Birds chirp and the sun bears down with a warm reassurance.

I look to my right, and sitting a few feet away is Jill, her head leaning back, her eyes closed.

"It's so good to see you," I say. "I've missed you."

Her head turns and she looks at me, smiling. "I am always with you, Collin."

I scoot closer, and under the water, my hand finds hers. She squeezes gently.

"I've kind of felt alone and lost without seeing you."

"You've done great. And I know you'll be brave."

I pause as this sinks in.

"I'm not even sure what it is I need to do. I mean, what's next?"

She doesn't answer for a minute or two. Then, all she says is: "Just relax. Find your peace."

So, I try. I take a deep breath, close my eyes, and tilt my head back, feeling the sun soak into my face.

Soon, I am asleep, yet still cognizant and aware. And in a dream-within-a-dream, I float in a gray type of suspended animation, bathed in calmness, and quiet.

My migraine is beginning to unloosen, like a tight knot slowly unraveling.

I can still feel Jill's hand in mine, though I can no longer see her—a metaphor of her being with me even though she's not there.

I am relaxing, feeling myself drift and unwind. Then a voice, male, firm, yet gentle.

"Well done, good and faithful servant."

The gray opens up like a hole in the clouds, a flawless blue sky behind it.

"Therefore rejoice, you heavens and you who dwell in them! But woe to the earth and the sea, because the devil has gone down to you! He is filled with fury, because he knows that his time is short."

In the sky, dots appear, slowly growing bigger. I soon see they are the giant ravens, circling, coming down to earth. In the middle is a much bigger bird, only I begin to realize it's not a bird. As it nears the ground, it belches fire, devastating what looks like a small village. It swerves back up into the sky, bellowing in triumph.

Then the blue is swallowed up by the gray again.

I know well enough not to ask how to defeat the dragon —that will come in its own time. Instead I ask a more pragmatic question:

"How should the ravens be abolished?"

Several minutes pass, and I begin to think maybe I have been too presumptuous, when again the gray parts. The scene behind it is a farm, green pastures, a few brilliant trees dotting the landscape. Off to the side is an enormous building, something like a metal barn, only extremely long. The view zooms in to show the large water tower next to the building. Then the gray returns.

I understand.

I have about a thousand questions, but none of them seem . . . worthy. Part of it is my self-consciousness not wanting to sound like a blabbering idiot. I finally decide to leave it at that, for now, when again the gray dissolves showing a large ornate box.

Slowly the lid is opened, and a pure white light shines from it, consuming all there is to see.

The Ark of The Covenant.

The lid falls shut, the light is extinguished, and the gray returns.

Okay, the Ark is a priority. I get it. I wish I could remember the setting—what kind of room was it in? All I recall is concrete, plain and whitish-gray. Nothing else.

The gray begins to completely dissipate, returning me to the spring water, cool air, and warm sunshine.

Jill is sitting across from me, on the edge of the pool, feet dangling in the water. She is naked, but all I can see is her beautiful face, smiling at me.

"You're going to get all pruney," she says.

"Like when I'm old and gray," I say with a grin.

A brief frown passes over her face like a cloud, then is gone. I could read different things into that expression, but the one that sticks is *You won't live that long.*

"Come," she says, "let's lay in the sun."

I climb out and walk up to her, taking her hand. We go to the middle of the field where the grass is low, and we sit. I lean over to kiss her, and as our lips meet, her hand caresses my face.

This, to me, is a glimpse into heaven. Warm sun, cool breeze and—

"No bugs," a voice says.

I break away from Jill and turn my head towards the voice.

"What are you doing here?" I ask.

"No clue," Patrick says. "Sylvana asked me to lie down so she could help with my headaches, and here I am." He pauses, looking down. "Not even a pair of shorts?"

I lay down on the grass and close my eyes. "No one cares, dude."

"Says the guy who is—"

"No need to go there," another voice says.

I lift my head to look and see Leslie standing just behind Patrick.

"Let's go in the pool," Leslie says, turning and walking away without waiting for a reply.

* * *

I wake to find myself in bed. So soft, so warm. I don't think I've ever been so comfortable.

I turn my head, half-expecting to see Jill lying next to me, but I am alone.

Although there is a twinge of disappointment, I close my eyes, wanting so badly to go back to sleep, dreaming of lying next to her, the cool spring water drying on our skin. No need for talk or questions or even touching—though I long to feel her skin beneath my fingers, her warm breath against my neck.

The dream does not come, though sleep does. A calm, restful sleep.

And then, another dream, a different dream comes. It whispers. It reveals. It tells me what is to come, and that I must pass it on.

Are you willing to do this for Me?

Yes, I whisper.

A long pause. *Carry on, good and faithful servant.*

* * *

When I finally wake up, I feel really good. No headache, no worries, no burdens. There is a calm and peace that I can't say I've felt before.

I get up, clean up, get dressed and head out. I realize I'm starving. I walk across the hall and knock on Patrick's door.

"Come in," he says.

I open the door, and he's sitting in a chair, putting on his shoes.

"Did you sleep well?"

"Like a baby."

"Me too." I pause, considering how to approach this. "I had a great dream at a spring pool, laying in a meadow."

He stopped in the middle of tying a sneaker. "That was real?"

I shrug. "I have no idea."

"But if we share a dream . . . what does that mean?"

Again, I shrug. "No clue."

He goes back to tying his shoe.

I try something. Just thinking a thought. Not broadcasting it, just letting it lie there.

Your scars are healing nicely.

Patrick sits straight up in the chair. "Whoa."

"What?"

"Did you just . . ." He shakes his head. "Nevermind."

"Are you hungry?"

"Is the President a pervert?"

* * *

We take our trays piled with food to the cafeteria, which is packed. We wander around, trying to find a place to sit, with several people offering their seats.

"Sit," I tell them, "enjoy your meal."

Finally, we see Leslie sitting with three others and she waves us over.

"Good morning," she says, introducing the others.

We all shake hands before Patrick and I take our seats.

"Excuse me, ladies and gentlemen," a voice says over a PA system. I look up and see Sylvana standing on a podium at the far end of the cafeteria.

Everyone hushes quickly.

"I wanted to bring you up to date on a program we've been working on," she said in her smooth, almost Shakespearean voice. "Some of you may have heard about the Fosai, and wondered if they were just a conspiracy theory, or a real, but secret underground group." She paused. "And some of you are members of the Fosai, and have kept the secret. As you may know, there is also a unit among us known as the Challengers, the counterpart to our adversary's group called the Regulators. The Challengers are a military-esque subset of the Fosai, much like the Army Rangers or Navy SEALS."

I stuff some sausage in my mouth, very interested in what she is saying, but also just as hungry.

"There has been speculation that the Fosai are similar to other powerful groups, either real or imagined—The Illuminati, the Freemasons, the Bilderberg Conference, the Trilateral Commission, to name a few. But the Fosai are like none of those. It is a grassroots movement that began several years ago, comprised mainly of lower-to-middle class working people. Farmers, construction workers, clerks, bus drivers, waitresses, and thousands of other occupations that, in reality, make this world function. They have the same goals, principles and intentions that we do. And through our connections, incentives and guidance, the Fosai have grown exponentially."

She pauses to take a sip of water. I shovel scrambled eggs into my mouth.

"The Fosai are us. We are Fosai."

"*Laus deo!*" the diners shout out. I would have as well, but I had just taken a big bite of hash browns.

"Laus deo," Sylvana says. "Collin, I apologize for interrupting your breakfast, but could you come up here, please?"

I look up, just about to eat a piece of toast. I put it down, use my napkin, and get up to go to the podium.

Sylvana is stepping down.

"What do you need me to do?" I ask.

"I don't know," she says. "I understand you were blessed with a vision, and were asked to pass it along."

I blink at her, confused. And then something drifts up from my subconscious. The dream. The whispers. The words begin to come.

I step up onto the podium and in front of the microphone.

We battle a strong, fierce enemy.

"We battle a strong, fierce enemy," I say, repeating the words that were whispered to me.

The Adversary uses not only their own evil ones . . .

"The Adversary uses not only their own evil ones, but also the lost, the proud and those who believe they are uncommitted. For many, we have no influence. For others, our only encouragement can be by example. Now, however, there is little time. We must soon begin to act. We must act together as one, yet we are millions."

I pause. The whispering has stopped.

I wait, willing the words to bubble to the surface.

It seems to take a very long time, but it was probably only ten seconds.

God has supplied us all with gifts . . .

"God has supplied us all with gifts, some which we know, some which have yet to be revealed. I have been blessed with skills and talents that I am still mastering, and, so, you will be as well. In order for us to act together as one, as Fosai, God shall bless most of you with a powerful ability, one that is potent and formidable, but which can also be horribly misused. Others will be given different gifts, equally as powerful. God knows your heart. He knows what you can handle, how strong you can be, even if you do not feel it or believe it. And He also knows your weakness. He knows who will be tempted to abuse or exploit His gift, and He knows who will actually do it."

Another pause. Everyone is watching me intently. I'm not sure what comes next, so I wait.

I take a sip of water.

Eternity stretches out in front of me.

I wait.

Finally:

You be notified soon . . .

"You will be notified soon, and you will be given instructions. Your faith, love and perseverance will be rewarded. Laus deo."

"Laus deo!"

Chapter 20

It happened while they slept.

Sleep, as I've known too well, is not a time for the brain to shut down, but in many ways to open up. I spent the time with Sylvana, walking through the dorms as they snoozed. It was easy for me to take a look at each person and immediately know whether they were red or purple.

Like the Jews and the Gentiles, Sylvana said telepathically, there are two types of people which God wishes to bring together in unity under Him. But the truth was there are dependable Fosai, and trustworthy Fosai. Although they are not mutually exclusive in God's eyes, the individuals choose what they will be.

It is important to not let one group think they are of greater or lesser value than the other. They are two different groups, with different tasks. When you look into them, you will see their color. The red are trustworthy, completely faithful and true to God's word, even if they occasionally slip and fail. They are to be known as Infrared. The purple are dependable, but not sure if they should be fully committed. They will do what they are asked, to a point. They are Ultraviolet.

I nod, understanding without knowing.

God will bless each with their own traits. The Infrared will be vital to your quest to defeat the Adversary—and they are not only here, in this building, but worldwide. You will have at your disposal millions of Infrared, who will be able to answer the call.

The Ultraviolet will also be important, but on a different scale. You will know who you can depend on, and who you can trust.

As we walk quietly, I keep count in a small notebook. I can see many of the sleeping faces, some I recognize. I can find their flow, and see immediately whether they are red or purple, Infrared or Ultraviolet. Some haven't received their colors yet. They are just a gray. While standing next to a man who was gray, he suddenly flipped to white, then phased into a maroon. It was like watching dozens of computers downloading new software.

What does maroon mean? I ask Sylvana.

In-between.

Not trustworthy?

Almost.

We move along. Soon we come upon an orange.

Deceptive, she tells me. *We may need to relocate her.*

When we reach the last dorm room, I check my numbers. 406 total, 195 red, 5 orange, 2 maroon, 204 purple.

So, I'll be in contact with all the reds?

You'll be in contact with all of them. But the reds will be networked with each other. The purples will not have access to the network.

I still don't fully get it, but I guess I'll figure it out when the time comes.

* * *

A couple hours of sleep, and then a morning meeting with Apollo, Mr. B and Sylvana.

"It looks like we'll have a while until Quinn tries to make his escape," Apollo says.

"What is 'a while'?" Mr. B asks.

"Five to seven days. Maybe up to fourteen. In accessing his phone, I noticed an entry on his calendar for 'AF1' on Friday, and 'Cheyenne' on Saturday."

"AF1?" I ask.

"Air Force One."

"Do we stop him?" I ask, looking at each face. "We should stop him."

"Not we," Mr. B says. "You."

"Okay. Yeah. But . . . how? I can't arrest him."

"Basically, you need to bring him here," Apollo says.

I think about this for a few moments. "Kidnap him? Kidnap the President?"

"Unless you prefer to kill him," Apollo says. Coming from the body of an 8 year old, it sounds quite strange.

"Okay. So I go to Washington, sneak into the White House, and . . . what? Stick a gun in his face and order him down the dumbwaiter? That thing can only hold one person at a time."

"It will take some persuasion," Sylvana says. "We are not coming at this without a plan. I will need to provide you with some training. We can start this afternoon."

"Your training will also help you with the other task at hand," Mr. B says.

"What would that be? Tying up the Pope? Terrorizing the Queen?"

I sound more angry than I feel. But it isn't really anger. It's fear.

The others stay silent for a while, either waiting for me to calm down or have another little outburst.

Mr. B clears his throat, and takes a sip of water.

"We need to take care of the Cravens."

"We?"

"Yes, in this case. Us. The Soulmadds and the Infrareds. There are thousands of them, and thousands of us. Until they are immobilized, the Cravens will prevent us from achieving our goal."

"And how do we eliminate the Cravens?"

They all look at me like I'm dumb, which maybe I am.

"Guns," Apollo says.

"It will be like the biggest bird hunt in history," Mr. B adds.

"Okay, that might help me blow off some steam," I say. "Where do we go, and when?"

* * *

Like when Patrick, Leslie, Apollo and I went to Washington DC, we come up through the stairway into the men's room at the park, only this time Sylvana joins us. It's a brutally cold day, and there is no one to be seen.

"We let the Regulators out here," Apollo says, "after you erased their memories. It was kind of funny seeing all those guys wandering around, not knowing where they were or what they were doing."

"Yes," Sylvana says without a trace of humor, "it was quite funny."

"At least they all went away," Patrick says.

"Physically, yes. But you can be assured they are still watching the house. Which is why we have come this way, to avoid being seen."

We are here so I can practice my Orb transport, which I am both interested in refining and leery of ending up in another Target parking lot.

"You will first need to learn to control yourself," Sylvana says. "Absorb your surroundings. Keep your mind open to all that's around you—particularly what is in front of you. Since you will be traveling at the speed of light, you need to practice instantaneous maneuvers to avoid collisions. Obviously, the higher in altitude you are, the fewer objects can impact your journey."

"So, go up and then out."

She nods in approval. "It's a learned trick, but once you master it, it will be as easy as tying your shoes in the dark. Do you have your telephone?"

I nod and pull it out of my pocket.

"Very well. Your first assignment is to transport yourself to downtown Chicago. There is a Marriott hotel. Land on the roof and take a photo. Then, return."

"I have no idea where the Marriott is."

She offers the slightest of smiles and points at my hand. "Look it up on the map."

Feeling slightly dumb, I do as she says, and come up with the address.

"The application includes a button to determine latitude and longitude," Apollo says. "Memorize it, concentrate on it, and when you are ready, that's where you'll go."

"Memorize it? It's a bunch of numbers."

Apollo shrugs. "That's how it works."

I stare at the numbers.

41.8881720000. -87.6234100000.

41.8881720000. -87.6234100000.

41.8881720000. -87.6234100000. Over and over and over.

"Okay," I say, sounding as uncertain as I feel. I step several feet away, staring at the map, making sure I'm pointed in the right direction.

"Remember, up and over," Patrick says, as if he knows what he's talking about.

I glance at him, nod, and take a deep breath. How do I access it? I don't—and then it comes to me. Draw the power in, towards the core, then—

Half a second later, I crash into the side of the huge air conditioning unit, then fall down the side, ending up between some pipes. I consider myself lucky. With the cold and ice, I could have slid right off the side of the building, plummeting some 50 floors to Michigan Avenue. At least I held onto my phone.

I get up and make my way out of the tangle of pipes and onto the roof. It's flat, and doesn't have much of a wall along the edge, so I play it safe, stand in the middle and snap a photo towards Lake Michigan.

I turn around, facing the way I came and wonder if I need to look up the coordinates of the park. Or can I just go—

Back, I think, and an instant later, I'm plowing head-first into the snow, pretty much where I had started.

I lift my head up and look around. The other four are staring at me warily, probably wondering if I'm okay. I'm kind of wondering the same thing.

"Dude," Patrick says, "you have got to work on your landings."

I get myself up on my knees. "Says the guy who is scared of flying."

"Hey, those things crash."

"Yeah, well, apparently, so do I."

"This is all very amusing," Sylvana says as I get to my feet, "but it is your turn, Patrick."

"Uh . . . what?"

"I suggest Soldier Field."

"But . . ." He looks white as a sheet. "I . . . heights are . . . oh, man. I don't even like roller coasters."

"I'll go with you," she says, holding out her hand for him to take.

He looks to each of us, hoping someone will rescue him. He becomes sickly yellow, shakes his head and mutters:

"Shit."

* * *

Half an hour later, after we all made trips to various locations —Leslie included—we head back down into the tunnels.

"It was like 85 in L.A.," Patrick says, trying not to sound excited. "I probably looked like a dork in my parka and ski hat."

"Don't worry," Apollo says. "You look like a dork without them."

"Look at this beach," Patrick says, pretending to ignore him and handing me his phone. "Just like the movies."

"Did you eat sand?" I ask, looking at an image of a pristine white beach and a guy in the distance, walking his dog.

"No, I landed on my feet. I've got the balance thing down."

"Miami was nice too," Leslie says. "And I landed on my feet

—although it was right in front of this woman just coming out of the water. I scared the daylights out of her."

She passes around her phone, and there's an image of a slightly overweight mom in a too-small bikini walking away, dragging her five-year-old by the hand, looking over her shoulder at Leslie with an expression something like horror.

"You leave tonight," Sylvana says as we get into the golf carts.

"For where?" I ask.

"Texas."

Chapter 21

"No man chooses evil because it is evil; he only mistakes it for happiness, the good he seeks."—Mary Wollstonecraft Shelley

West Texas—at least where we ended up—is a whole lot of nothing. According to the map coordinates, we're 80 miles from the nearest town, and 40 from the closest ranch. Except for La Granja, or The Farm. We're two miles from that. It's cold, and it's bleak.

Sylvana told us what to expect: 850 Citizen Challengers, fully armed. And I could hear them in the darkness, roughly 100 yards away. They didn't need to be quiet, since there was no one out here to hear them.

Me, Patrick, Leslie and Apollo trudge through the desolate brush and approach the edge of the group, all chatting with each other, all with shotguns either slung over their shoulders or in cases. All are bundled up in thick coats and warm hats.

I turn to Patrick. "Can you whistle?"

"You mean like this?" And he lets loose with an ear-piercing shriek that pretty much cuts the chatter to nothing.

I take a deep breath and tap into what Apollo calls the Neural Network. Although I could speak, I'd have to yell to have everyone hear me.

Good morning. I'm Collin, and I'll be heading up this adventure.

I go through the details, marching to La Granja, arriving an hour before dawn, encircling the property while Apollo—the only one without a weapon—sneaks onto the property, into the Haven —a large building housing the Cravens, and opens the roof.

Once the birds take flight, open fire. Are you ready?

A verbal murmur of "Yes!" "Let's go!" and "Rock and roll!" fill the air.

Follow me.

* * *

Finding the property was easy. A few lights are on, but not enough to illuminate everything.

The Challengers split off, half going to the left, the others to the right. We lay in the dirt and quietly wait.

* * *

Dawn begins to come, and within fifteen minutes, we begin to see the buildings more clearly. The "Haven" is a gigantic oval building about the size of a football stadium. And, as dawn turns lighter, the occupants are waking up. The squawking is mild at first, then becomes louder until it sounds like a roar of noise.

"Here I go," Apollo says. He gets up off the dirt, brushes himself off, then, in an instant, becomes an Orb and zaps himself to the side of the huge building.

He disappears through a door.

We wait, listening to the cacophony of hungry birds.

It's a couple of minutes before roof begins to open, and the noise seems to get even louder. It takes at least a full minute for the roof to completely open, and when it's finished . . . nothing happens.

I see Apollo come outside, and just as he does, the first of the birds take flight. And then another. And then a dozen more.

Apollo zaps his way back to where Patrick and I wait. He lays down.

Fire when ready.

The birds, at first, circle the building, as more pour out. It doesn't take long until there are hundreds, if not thousands, flying. It is a large oval of teeming blackness, cawing and squawking. But they are still too far out of range.

I look towards a building off to my right, which looks like the quarters for the staff, and I see a man exit. He just stands on the small porch and stares up at the mass of birds.

Then, a section of the flock breaks off and heads in our general direction. It's only moments before they come streaming at us.

Although we had a quick lesson in firing and using our shotguns, this is the first time I've actually shot a gun—as it is with Leslie and Patrick.

We're not the first to open fire, though. That comes from somewhere off to my right, a loud crack, and even through the din of cawing, I can hear the squeal of a Craven as it is hit and begins a fall to Earth.

I line up and pull the trigger at the same instant Patrick does. More squealing, and there is an explosion of gunshots erupting around us.

The torrent of birds turns in unison and head to our left. More gunfire, and more birds going down.

I have my shells sitting in a plastic grocery bag next to me, and quickly reload and fire again. It's hard not to hit a Craven or three. Some are taken down, others wounded but still flying.

Several of the birds break off and dive-bomb a row of Challengers, most of whom open fire. Most of them go down, a couple landing on people, one still flapping and attacking a man, who swats at it with his gun barrel.

Another swarm launches directly at us, and I manage to pull off a shot, making direct contact. For a moment after, I see nothing except a wide maw and black beady eyes as it zooms inches over me before crashing to earth just behind me. I glance back to see it tumbling into the brush.

More come at us. I'm loading and shooting, loading and shooting, not even bothering to aim. I didn't need to since there were so many.

The surrounding air becomes filled with the cracks of gunfire, the sight of floating feathers, and the scent of burnt gunpowder.

One of the Cravens swoops down and grabs at Leslie's coat, getting enough of a grasp to lift her a few feet in the air. Patrick immediately rolls over and blasts the creature, and both fall to the ground with a thump.

"Are you okay?" Patrick yells as he scrambles to Leslie and another Craven launches at him. I, and another hunter several yards away, open fire and hit the giant bird from two different angles.

It lands on top of Patrick, flapping. Patrick shields Leslie's body as the Craven goes through its death throes.

Gunfire is relentless, as are the birds. They are launching themselves at the Challengers with abandon, most of the monsters being taken out before doing any damage. But I see at least one bird grab a Challenger and lurch off with him. There are others from what I can see, but not many. Someone shoots at the Craven, and both man and bird fall. I wonder if the Challenger sustained a gunshot wound, but think it's probably preferable to being eaten alive.

Load and shoot, load and shoot.

Patrick has flung the now dead bird off of him, and I can hear him asking Leslie if she was all right. She is wheezing and doesn't try to speak.

Fine. Wind knocked out of me.

I keep shooting, looking to the skies as I reload. There are noticeably fewer birds, but still a lot.

Another one zooms in on me, and I pull off a shot just a couple of yards away, moments from its claws clamping down on my chest. It nearly explodes from the gun blast, but crashes into me, and bounces off. The weight of it was like a large boulder trying to crush me.

I do my best to shake it off.

Load and shoot, load and shoot.

* * *

I'm not sure how many Cravens got away. Maybe a dozen —not many considering how many there were.

The man who had come out of the house was joined by four others, and the Challengers who were closest got into a gun battle with them. None of the five men survived.

I made my way around the perimeter with Patrick, Leslie and Apollo. We took care of the more severely injured as best we could. A rancher who lived a couple of hundred miles away had arrived near our meeting site with a helicopter, and he volunteered to take the three very hurt folks to the nearest hospital. The others we treated as best we could.

All told, 42 injured, 11 dead, 5 missing and presumed dead. I look over the dense landscape, now littered with thousands of empty shotgun shells, their colorful skins in stark contrast to the sea of dead black ravens. The remaining Challengers pick up their casings, while leaving the birds to rot.

We burn down the buildings on the property before we go back to Chicago. I don't think a word is spoken.

* * *

We had four more sites around the world to destroy. Southwest Russia, Northern Vietnam, Western Brazil, and Southern Chad.

Although I wouldn't say it got easier, it did seem to go smoother, with fewer injuries and fatalities on our side, and almost all the birds killed.

Even though each operation took less than an hour and a half, it was extremely exhausting. When we returned from Africa, all we could do was eat a quiet meal, and go to bed.

I slept for 12 hours.

If I dreamt, I don't remember it.

* * *

Sitting in the cafeteria, Patrick, Leslie and I eat in silence. I'm sure they're as drained and groggy as I am.

Apollo comes skipping in like an eight year old, making me feel close to ancient.

"Hi," he says around a big wad of gum.

"Hey," Patrick says.

"I've got over two hundred Drats, and almost a thousand Flones."

"That's cool," Patrick says.

"What are you going to use them for?" I ask.

"Well," he says taking the seat across from me and next to Leslie, "I think that's what they want to talk about."

I nod, warily. All I can think is that Sylvana and Mr. B have another mission up their sleeve. Hopefully, it doesn't involve birds.

"Why do you smell like bubblegum?" Leslie asks.

He pulls the pink wad of goo out of his mouth and holds it up for us to see. "I'm testing a new device. It's infused with a titanium polymer that can be tracked by satellites." He pauses. "I'm thinking of calling it 'Navigum.'"

"Clever," I say. "But what if whoever you're trying to track doesn't like gum?"

He looks at me as if that's the silliest question he's ever heard. "They don't have to chew it. Just stick it on their luggage or car or whatever."

"How do you come up with these ideas?" Leslie asks. "Drone flies and rats. GPS gum. What else do you have up your sleeve?"

"All kinds of things! Basically, it's just identifying a problem and adapting a solution. Like before we blew away all the Cravens, I was working on a solution that could be introduced into their feed—that slurry—that would poison them. But, I didn't have enough time to refine it. It took too long to take effect, and it didn't kill them. Just kind of made them lethargic."

I received a telepathic message: *Collin, could you meet us in the conference room.*

* * *

"Did Apollo tell you?" Mr. B asks.

"Tell me what?"

"I got sidetracked," Apollo says, climbing up on a stool.

A brief expression of annoyance crosses Mr. B's face. "It looks like Quinn is looking to leave early. The destruction of the raven sanctuaries probably got him to move a little more quickly than he intended."

"So it's time to intervene," I say, my mind starting to race. Patrick and I take seats.

Mr. B nods solemnly. "It's late morning here, almost noon in DC. I would suspect he'll attempt to escape under cover of night, so we have some time."

Kidnapping the President. I've done and gone through a lot over the last several months, but this would certainly be the most newsworthy.

"We'll have some support teams in place, but for the actual breach of the White House, it will just be you and Patrick. The Secret Service is already on high alert and they've doubled the personnel on patrol and making rounds."

"How will we get around them?" Patrick asks.

"I would suggest using the Orb transport in short bursts," Mr. B says. "Zap yourself down halls from one end to the other in quick successions. Even if they see you, they can't stop you."

"Don't forget the Drats and Flones," Apollo says.

"Yes, there will be some of those available for your use."

"They'll transmit to your smartphone!" Apollo adds.

"Yes, well, let's go over the plans," Mr. B says.

* * *

We didn't get very far before an alarm went off—a siren.

All three of our heads jerked up at the harsh, alien sound.

Looking out of the conference room, we can see people running.

"What's happening?" I say.

Mr. B looks confused. Apparently, the sound of the alarm is new to him as well.

"I don't know, but it can't be good."

Patrick and I jump up and hurry over to the control center. Apollo is sitting in the Captain Kirk chair holding a big keyboard with a joystick attached. Under any other circumstance, I'd think he was playing a video game.

On the monitors, the tanks are back, and more than before. They are crawling down the unplowed street, through heavy drifts of snow, over the front yard, lumbering through the backyard. I can see men running, holding large bulky weapons.

"What are those?"

"Rocket launchers," Apollo says, not taking his eyes off the screen.

Sylvana glides into the room, Mr. B following. Their faces are very solemn.

I return my attention to the screens. I can see little dots in the gray sky, moving closer.

Fighter jets.

They swoop down low and strafe the Manor House -- although where we are underground, we can't hear them. I can only imagine the thundering noise they made.

Standing next to me, Patrick's head is swiveling back and forth, looking at each monitor.

"Holy crap," he says, nervously. "This isn't good."

"Notice how the temperatures have gotten much colder since you got back from the raven kill?" Mr. B asks. "I doubt that's a coincidence."

"Yes," Sylvana says. "I suspect Dymortis is quite displeased, and probably trying to throw as many tricks at us as he can."

The phone in my pocket vibrates.

I pull it out. *Unknown Caller.*

Except I know who it is.

I press *Answer*.

"If you're trying scare us, it's not working."

"I don't need to scare you—just destroy you."

"Good luck with that. We're pretty good at destroying things ourselves."

"The President has asked that every resource of the U.S. Government be used to capture you—dead or alive."

"I'm on the Ten Most Wanted List? What else do you have up

your sleeve? There's a CIA spy who's infiltrated our inner sanctum?"

A pause. Either he's surprised that I'm onto him, or he's boiling mad and trying to not explode.

"I give the word, and your precious Manor House is gone. I will wipe you off the face of the Earth."

"If you could do that," I tell Lord Harod Dunraven, "you would have already done it."

Sylvana appears in the doorway, looking more concerned than ever.

You need to leave. Now.

Dunraven has gone quiet again, so I take advantage of it.

"Good night, and good luck," I say before hanging up.

Chapter 22

"Don't fight forces, use them."—*R. Buckminster Fuller*

"I can't leave," I tell Sylvana.

"He will kill everyone here in order to destroy you."

"I understand that's his intent, but—"

Above comes what sounds like thunder just before the house above us shakes.

"That was a mortar," Apollo says.

"Is the shield holding up?" Mr. B asks.

"Without sounding too much like a Star Trek episode, yes, but it was activated after some of the Regulators made their way onto the grounds."

"How many?" I ask.

"A few dozen." He swivels around to look at us. "They will break into the building—it's just a matter of when."

"Have you sealed off the lower level?"

"Of course. That should hold almost indefinitely."

"Almost?"

He tilts his head as if thinking. "Nothing is completely impenetrable."

My mind is racing. All I can picture is hundreds of troops crawling through the building like ants.

I turn to Sylvana. "You taught me how to access The Flow and get inside people's heads. Is there a way to use it . . . as a weapon?"

They all look at me like I'm speaking Swahili.

"You mean a reverse Flow that scrambles their thought process?" Mr. B asks.

"Yeah, something to debilitate them."

He looks at Sylvana, who looks at Apollo, who shrugs.

"I suppose it might work. We've never tried it," the little boy says.

"What do you think the range might be? How close do I have to be to them?"

Apollo cocks his head in the other direction, thinking. "A person's internal electrical field is really only a few feet. But that's emitting outward. Sending a focused beam of energy is a different matter. I have picked up thoughts from a hundred yards, as long as the subject was within my line of sight—but it required a large amount of energy on my part to pick it up. *Sending* the energy . . ." He drifts off, his gaze turning to a frown. He shrugs. "It's worth a try."

"So you think that as long as I'm in the line of sight, I might be able to do it."

He sighs, still frowning. "I can't think of a reason why not. I'm just not sure what amount of telepathic energy would be needed."

"What's your plan?" Patrick asks. "Peek out the windows and zap them with your mind?"

"It does sound weird, but other than evacuate this place, what can we do?"

"Both," Sylvana says without hesitation. "But instead of evacuating through the park, it would have to be farther away."

"The tunnels extend to a warehouse in a business park near O'Hare," Mr. B says. "But it will have to be on foot—we don't have enough vehicles for everyone."

"It will need to start now," I say. "Can you begin the process of getting everyone out?"

He nods, then pats me on the shoulder. "Be careful, okay?"

"I will."

* * *

People are already heading for the tunnels as I make my way upstairs. After a brief argument with Patrick—who insisted, with Apollo, he was going to tag along—we're on the first floor of the house and meet Leslie in the hallway.

"You need to get out of here with the others," I tell her.

"What's the plan?" she asks as if ignoring me.

"Evacuate, now."

"We're a team. I can help."

I'm a little annoyed but other than picking her up and taking her downstairs, I don't see an option. "How do I get on the roof?" I ask Apollo.

He turns and leads us up the stairs—second floor, third floor, then a final flight to the roof. We climb out of the hatch and stay low so as not to be spotted by anyone on the ground. The mid-afternoon sun is hidden behind dense clouds and we sneak our way to the edge of the building, peeking our heads over the small wall for a few moments to have a look.

There are more than a few dozen men with rocket launchers and machine guns scattered about the inside perimeter. I estimate it's close to 75. The electronic voice of someone on a bullhorn drifts up at us.

"Come out now, and you won't be hurt. We have you surrounded."

In the near distance are half a dozen tanks and another dozen military trucks sit as a light snow swirls in the -18 degree wind-chill cold.

We duck down. This is going to be harder than I thought—as easily as I can see them, they could as easily see me.

I sit for several moments while the other three watch me. I'm considering how I'm going to do this. It's a kind of experiment that I have no idea whether it will work or not. I basically need to pop my head up, pick a target, find his Flow, and channel energy at him that will scramble his brain. All in a couple of seconds. At least I have a general idea where my first victim is.

I close my eyes, take a deep breath, then pop my head up over. I feel the energy well up inside of me, and I train it on the first man I see—a guy with a machine gun laying on the ground, pointing it at the side of the Manor House. As my eyes find him, I see there's a whole line of them, spaced about six feet apart. This makes me pause for a second in confusion and I forget to lock onto a Flow. I mentally unleash a burst of energy aimed in the general direction of the first guy I see, and I'm stunned when he literally explodes. The seven men laying next to him are victims of collateral damage, four exploding and the other three bursting into flames.

I fall back as if the wind has been knocked out of me, staring up at the gray sky. as if the wind has been knocked out of me.

"Are you okay?" Patrick asks.

I open my mouth to reply, but find it hard to breathe.

"Jiminy," Apollo says, carefully looking over the wall. "You blew them up!"

My chest has a hard, painful lump in the middle of it, my head is throbbing and even my testicles ache as if I'd been kicked by a mule.

From below, from inside the shield, I hear gunfire erupt, and more than one projectile fired from a rocket launcher explodes into the side of the building. Everything shakes.

There's also yelling and screaming from below, as if chaos has broken out.

A tank from outside fires a missile at the shield, and there's a loud crackling sound as it ricochets off.

I raise my head, fighting a brief bout of dizziness and nausea.

"That didn't sound good," Apollo says, looking off in the distance.

"What do you mean?" Leslie asks.

"The shield didn't take that very well. A couple more like that and—"

Another one erupts, and this time the crackling sound is more like a gigantic wall of glass shattering.

"So much for that," Apollo says.

I get into a sitting position and make my way back to the wall. The pain subsided as quickly as it came, and I pop my head up again, seeing a line of fifteen or twenty men in two rows facing the side of the house. They see me, and their rifles all rise up to point in my direction. Without a moment to spare, I let loose another burst, and the entire group explodes in a ball of flame.

I took this blast much better than the first, only closing my eyes for a second as the lump in my chest returns, then dies away.

There's a scream of panic below as the men who hadn't blown up scramble to run and hide.

Someone in the distance takes a shot at me, and I hear the bullet whiz by my head.

I turn my head in that direction and draw up all the energy I can. It leaps from me and takes out another squad—another twenty men. The fireball rises into the air. I've managed to take out more than half the men on the lawn.

"*Cease fire,*" the voice over the bullhorn says.

Apollo stands up next to me, looking to the sky. "The shield seems to be holding, but barely."

"Can you reinforce it?"

He shakes his head. "I'm not sure how. I would need to power it down, and add a layer of Element 79 dust. We don't have any of that here."

"Can you get some?" I ask.

"I wouldn't know where to get enough. It would take at least two bars, maybe three."

"What's Element 79?" Patrick asks.

"Gold," Apollo says.

Patrick and I look at each other.

"The key is downstairs, in my nightstand drawer," I tell him.

Patrick nods and takes Leslie by the hand. "I'll need your help."

* * *

Apparently, I've literally scared the hell out of them. Seeing soldiers explode has seemingly made Dunraven re-think his position

—and my power. He doesn't know that one good missile from a tank would knock the shield into uselessness, and I'm not going to tell him.

Apollo is babbling, explaining how the reflective properties of the gold dust . . . blah, blah, blah. I don't want to tell him that a C- in science was the best that I could do, but I comprehend enough to know that *he* knows what he's talking about, even if I don't.

The soldiers on the lawn have retreated as far back as they can, still trapped inside the shield. Those outside have congregated around the tanks, most keeping a wary eye on the house and probably wondering if they're the next victims of spontaneous human combustion.

Leslie and Patrick left around 2:45. I figure it would take them a minimum of an hour to get out of the house through the underground tunnels, drive to the storage unit, get the gold, and come back.

In the distance, I can see residents of the neighborhood packing their cars and pulling out of driveways. They're being evacuated.

" . . . and at some point we'll need to turn off the shield and figure out a way to move Dunraven's men out and away so I can add the Element 79 to the particle transit."

"How long will that take?"

"I should probably flush and replenish the whole system."

I look at him with a blank expression. He gets the drift.

"Half an hour."

Okay, so if Leslie and Patrick make it back by 3:45, and Apollo gets right to work, we're looking at 4:15. I pull my phone out and check the time. 3:02. How am I going to hold them off for more than an hour? Just then the phone vibrates and the screen changes. *Unknown Caller.*

"Yes?" I say in as pleasant a voice as possible.

"*You cannot escape.*"

"I beg to differ. Besides, this is a lot more fun. Which tank are you in?"

"*This isn't a video game, Jacob. We have more power at our disposal than you can even imagine.*"

"So . . . you've ordered a nuclear weapon, but it's not here yet. Might take a while. Thanks for tipping your hand."

Dunraven chuckles. *"You may think you understand, but you have no idea. However, if you surrender now, this can all end peacefully. I'll even let your friends go."* He pauses. *"All I want is you."*

"And yet, I belong to another. The Lord is my shepherd, I shall not want. He maketh me to lie down in green pastures, He leadeth me beside the still waters. He restoreth my soul, He leadeth me in the paths of righteousness for His name's sake. Yea, though I walk through the valley of the shadow of death, I will fear no evil, for thou art with me. Thy rod and Thy staff, they comfort me. Thou preparest a table before me in the presence of my enemies. Thou anointest my head with oil -- my cup runneth over. Surely goodness and mercy shall follow me all the days of my life, and I will dwell in the house of the Lord for ever."

"Bravo," Dunraven says. *"And in the King James version, too —or at least close enough. But your Lord cannot save you here, Jacob. He will not swoop in from the sky and whisk you away to a safe haven. Even you are aware of that."*

"So you know the words, but miss the point. I hope you're watching."

I move the phone away from my ear and extend my arms away from my body. I raise myself off the roof and levitate twenty or thirty feet in the air above the house.

"You are correct in saying my Lord and Savior will not swoop in, for he is already here."

I look out over the landscape, watch some of the men gape at me in wonder, while others scurry behind tanks and trees.

I lower myself and stand on the roof. I see an old man in what looks like a thick wool coat step out from behind a tank, holding a phone to his ear. From a distance of fifty yards, we stare at each other.

"I am not afraid," I say into the phone.

"Good for you. I hope your Lord is merciful, because I won't be."

Chapter 23

"Politics is war without bloodshed, while war is politics with bloodshed"—Mao Zedong

Patrick's head pokes out of the hatch. "We put the gold in the conference room."

I check the time. 3:15. "Wow, that was fast."

"It would have been faster, but we had to take more than one trip. Those bars are frickin' *heavy*."

I understand—they used the instant Orb transport to go back and forth.

"How many bars did you bring?" I ask as Apollo makes his way to the hatch.

"All of them." He backs down, and Apollo follows him.

I remain on the roof, and wait, though I'm not sure for what.

A couple of minutes pass, and I hear a faint clink sound, and the low, barely audible hum of the shield goes quiet. Apollo has shut it down.

I peek over the wall. It's difficult to see the shield in the daytime, but apparently the soldiers knew it was turned off. I would have expected the men outside the shield to rush forward, perhaps storm the building, but instead, the roughly thirty soldiers that had been trapped inside the shield—and were still alive—

made a hasty retreat back to the tanks down the street.

I wait and watch for a few more minutes. They seem content to wait and watch as well. I decide to go back downstairs.

I find Mr. B and Sylvana in the conference room.

"Apollo is delighted," Mr. Burkfelt says. "It's going to take a little time for him to get enough of the gold into the form he needs for the shield reinforcement."

"I had no idea gold was anything but a valuable metal."

"It's true gold has been an element that has been fought over for centuries. Both in war and monetarily. Even in this country the Gold Standard has been both a top priority and a sore subject among the ultra-wealthy and influential. Many of the rich oil barons and bankers were bitterly against the Gold Standard."

"Did it threaten their fortunes?"

"The Gold Standard evens the playing field in the world of financing and banking, and doesn't give power to individuals. Ironically, there was believed to be a large stash of gold aboard the Titanic, brought aboard by John Astor and placed in a large valet. It has been said this gold was his seed money to invest into the United States."

"I vaguely recall that name—Astor."

"Probably from one of Dunraven's journals. Of course, if the story is true, there's still a lot of gold at the bottom of the Atlantic. President Franklin D. Roosevelt's first day in office—and his first Executive Order he ever wrote—was to abolish the Gold Standard. J.P. Pinepoint heavily invested in his presidency and it was payback for the campaign financing during his Roosevelt's election run. World War ll and the Holocaust plans had been in motion for years prior to it happening. Pinepoint needed Roosevelt badly, and landed him. He spent a lot of money on FDR. Pinepoint was on a mission to control the U.S. and the world, as well as laying the groundwork for all future Presidents. You might say a thick, dark line was drawn in the financial sand. Conspiracy and wealth was at the heart of it and was intended to control the American economy. From President Wilson on, all who took the Oval Office sat under Dunraven's control. John Kennedy was the only oddball in the bunch, resisting

Dunraven's ploys. And we know what happened to him."

"Dunraven had him assassinated."

"JFK stood up against the monetary system. He wanted to be responsible for America's growing debt by implementing the Silver Certificate—a means to pay off that debt. Just like Abraham Lincoln with his greenback dollars, to make them a means to ease the U.S. debt created by the Civil war. And, look what happened to him."

I think of the skull with the bullet hole sitting on Dunraven's desk.

"The good news, if you want to call it that, is you've completely pissed off President Quinn. You and the Citizen Challengers taking out the Ravens has him both incensed and scared. Dunraven is even more pissed! So you can imagine that Dymortis must be furious!" Mr. B laughs in delight. "It's hard to tick them off, but you managed to do it."

"Well, it's obvious he's not going to sit around and mope."

Mr. B turned serious. "No. They're regrouping, trying to figure out what you did to their men, and what you might do to their armored vehicles. They'll redouble their efforts once reinforcements come in."

"So, they'll just storm the house like a bunch of Nazis."

He shakes his head. "More than that. They know we have a lot of computing and monitoring equipment here. They know about the shield—they don't know how it works, but they're trying to figure it out."

"So we need to abandon this place."

"Not right away. Once the shield is up, and Apollo gets it fine-tuned, they will have a very difficult time breaching it."

"They're considering a nuclear weapon."

Mr. B's eyebrows go up. "I guess Apollo knows his stuff."

"Of course I do," the boy says from behind us.

We turn, seeing him holding a box of juice.

"Since the Manor House is in a rural area of Chicago, the weapon of choice to eliminate it and the Soulmadds is Electronic Warfare. They'll try several other means before resorting to atomic weapons, but I guess it's inevitable."

"Will the shield withstand a nuclear bomb?"

Apollo shrugs. "I doubt it. Gold is a good reflector of electromagnetic radiation such as infrared and visible light as well as radio waves. It is used for the protective coating on many satellites, in infrared protective face plates, in thermal protective suits and astronauts. It's also used in electronic warfare planes like the EA-6B Prowler, and it produces a high output of secondary electrons when irradiated by an electron beam. Gold's very high electrical conductivity drains electrical charge to the earth, and its very high density provides stopping power for electrons in the electron beam, helping to limit the depth to which the electron beam penetrates. Gold also makes a good heat shielding." He pauses as if we understood any of that. "But could a few pounds of gold flakes in a manipulated electrical power dome bear up under a one-ton thermonuclear weapon?"

"Dunraven wouldn't really drop a bomb on Chicago, though, would he? He'd kill a couple of million people, including his own."

"Are you kidding? He burned Chicago down once. He couldn't care less. But, I seriously doubt he'd actually do it this time."

"Why not?"

"Because if he drops a bomb and evaporates us all, he'll never know if he actually killed you or not. He wants to have you in custody so he can kill you himself."

I look at Mr. B, who nods.

"I'm afraid he's right," the Professor says. "He won't take any chances."

"I would think this place was designed like a bomb shelter, to take the impact of an atomic bomb."

"It is," Apollo says. "But do you really want to sit here and find out?"

* * *

It's almost 4:30, and Apollo is still tinkering with his super-secret shield.

Sylvana is in another room, praying. I had joined her for a

while, but my curiosity of what Dunraven's next move might be made me leave. I sit in the conference room with Mr. B, Leslie and Patrick watching the monitors. The tanks are repositioning—closer, but still outside the reach of the shield.

Mr. B is on a laptop, typing in little bursts occasionally. "Okay, so the Challengers we evacuated from here have finally made it to the alternate site. I've requested that they be split between the Infrared and Ultraviolet. I've also put a call out to other Citizen Challengers in the Chicago area to meet at the site, and I ordered a small fleet of buses."

"Buses? For what?"

"We've built a small armory in the warehouse, and we'll arm the Challengers for a mission." His eyes are twinkling.

Before I can ask what the mission might be, he starts to explain:

"Nationwide, the Citizen Challengers are on alert, waiting for instructions. We've been communicating mainly by encrypted email, but we suspect the NSA has cracked that. So, the idea is to have the Ultraviolets head to downtown Chicago and infiltrate and take over the radio and TV studios to broadcast our message."

I think about this a moment. "But the broadcast would only cover the Chicago Metro area. How will it reach the rest of the country?"

He points to the monitors. "The networks are getting the feeds from their affiliates and broadcasting them on their over-the-air and cable networks. You can see the NBC, Fox and CNN feeds right there. Radio, particularly the network news and talk stations, are doing the same thing."

All three news networks have blazing red banners either saying *BREAKING NEWS* or *NEWS ALERT,* and either *Stand-off in Chicago* or *Chicago Showdown*. And each is showing long-distance helicopter shots of the scene outside.

"The Challengers are already watching this, coast-to-coast, and know something is coming."

"Okay. But if Dunraven controls the networks, they'll just kill the feed."

"Absolutely, but that could take several minutes, if not longer, for the word to come down. It will give us enough time to get our message out and mobilize the Challengers into action. We only need one shot."

"And what about the Infrareds?"

"They'll be armed as well, along with as many Citizen Challengers we can mobilize. While Dunraven is busy focusing on Manor House, the Infrareds will be in his backyard."

"The Meadows?"

Mr. B nods. "An eye for an eye."

"And the rest of the Citizen Challengers around the country?"

Mr. B's eyes twinkle again. "They'll have their orders."

We hear a *fwoomp* sound, and we all look around. The shield has come back on, and it sounds more ominous than before.

"The buses are arriving at the warehouse. It will take at least half an hour for them to reach their destinations, probably longer considering traffic. So, let's say an hour." Mr. B stares at his laptop as Apollo enters the room.

"Done, and done," the little boy says.

"We should prepare for Operation Courier," Mr. B says.

* * *

Dunraven has gotten up the nerve to unleash a full-scale attack—rifles, machine guns, rocket-propelled missiles, grenades, and even flash-bombs—all of which did absolutely nothing, but looked great on TV. The shield is working so well, the booms and crackles and explosions soon become background noise as we work out our next move.

It all seems straightforward—go to Washington DC and kidnap the President of the United States. Apollo has come up with a great idea—if he can get it to work. He runs off to his lab to try it out while we sketch out the escape plan.

"Once you get the President into the underground tunnels, transport him across the street to the office building, and make your way to the curb. A car will be waiting," Mr. B says. "It will drive you to Andrews Air Force Base, where Air Force One will be ready to taxi. The pilots will probably not have the flight plan as Quinn wants to wait until they take off to tell them where they're going. He's planning on Denver, then a car to Cheyenne Mountain, but we'll just bring him here."

"And what about his wife and daughter?"

"I would think his plan is to kill them. If you can get to him before he gets to them, then he won't be able to blame their murders on the Challengers. Or on you."

He taps on his laptop and points at one of the monitors where his screen is projected.

FBI Ten Most Wanted.

And there is a picture of me. My high school senior yearbook photo.

Unlawful flight to avoid prosecution. Possession and distribution of child pornography. First degree murder. Government espionage. Breaking into government property. Hacking government electronic property. The FBI is offering a reward of up to $10 million dollars for information directly leading to the arrest of Jacob Collin Davis.

I'm kind of impressed. Most of the others on the list are topping out at $100,000.

The building above us shakes as another mortar tries to blast away the shield.

"Do you really think it's wise to bring the President here?"

"Where else would you suggest?"

I look at Patrick, and he nods.

"I have an idea."

* * *

After sandwiches and a change of clothes—the all-black Secret Service garb—Patrick and I head for the tunnels.

"Wait, wait!" Apollo says, chasing after us. "You forgot the supplies."

"What supplies?"

"Secret weapons. I can't carry the bag—you'll have to."

So we go back and see a satchel sitting in the corner.

"Don't open it until you get there. I'll give you instructions on how to use them when you're ready."

"Them?"

"You'll see," he says with an impish grin. "Stay true and pay attention!"

I pick up the bag as he skips away. It seems to weigh 40 pounds.

We take a golf cart to the exit, go up the stairs, and through the park men's room, which is deserted.

Outside, it is dark. No car waits for us. We're on our own.

Chapter 24

"The ultimate tragedy is not the oppression and cruelty by the bad people but the silence over that by the good people."—
Martin Luther King, Jr.

We sit in the White House, in the area behind the pantry, listening to the kitchen staff finishing their clean-up for the night. Apollo occasionally texts, giving us updates on the President's whereabouts.

Library.

Oval Office.

Moving down hall.

First lady's bedroom.

Patrick, reading the texts over my shoulder, mentally whispers: *She has her own bedroom? They don't sleep together?*

Apparently, I reply.

Based on Apollo's previous monitoring, he believes Quinn will soon be in his own bedroom. Unlike other evenings, though, he'll pack for a trip. Our goal is to intercept him before he leaves —preferably before he connects with his Secret Service escorts.

The kitchen, finally, goes quiet.

I crack open the hidden door and peek. The lights seem to be out. We can make our move.

Let's go.

We've already gone through what we're going to do and how we're going to do it several times. It seems easy when it's laid out in my head.

I pull open the door slowly, listening in case there are any creaks that might give us away. We step into the pantry, and move to that door, replicating the slow open.

The lights are out and all is eerily quiet, the only sound coming from the refrigerator, which is big enough and suitable for a restaurant.

I step out into the kitchen and Patrick follows, carrying the satchel. He sets it on a counter and opens it. Apollo showed us what to do, and Patrick spent time while we waited in the hidden passage activating each unit. Now he pulls them out, one by one, setting the larger ones on the floor, and the smaller ones on the counter. I move to the door that leads out of the kitchen and open it, again, slowly. I peek and see the dimly lit, short hallway that connects to the main one. The short one is empty.

I text Apollo: *Bots are ready.*

Several of the Flones rise from the counter and zip their way towards me, through the doorway and into the hall. They split directions, some going left, the rest going right.

The Drats come to life and scurry the same way.

Soon all of the robotic creatures have left for their part of the mission.

Patrick put the satchel back in the pantry, and then we wait.

Hallway is clear, Apollo texts. *Agent in next hallway, about halfway.*

He's using the cameras in the Flones and Drats to feed us info.

No others seen.

We step out into the hall and look both ways. No one.

We quietly make our way to the next hallway and pause. This, of course, is the tricky part. Sylvana taught me a trick called The Tap. After hearing how I'd used my internal power to literally blow up the soldiers on the lawn, she thought it might be wise to help me harness it in more subtle ways. Nervously, I tried it out on Patrick and Leslie, worried I still might push too hard and scramble their brains. But other than a brief headache, it worked.

Standing by the corner where the hallways intersected, I carefully sneak a quick peek, sticking my head out for a second to take a momentary glimpse down the hall. The man is standing across from the stairway that we needed to use to go up to the Presidential residence.

Ready? I ask Patrick.

Ready.

I need to time this well as I only have a few seconds.

I pop my head out again and quickly sent a Tap.

Go.

We step out, and using the Orb transport, instantaneously zip to the base of the stairs, then zip up to the next landing.

The Tap managed to blind the agent with a light amount of power that short-circuited his brain—but only long enough for us to zip by.

I text to Apollo: *On the stairs.*

Several seconds before I receive his reply.

All clear.

We zip up to the next landing, and step out into the hallway. We walk down past a few closed doors and I figure out which one we need to enter. Pick the wrong one, and we could be in for trouble.

I select what I hope is the right one and try the knob.

From down below, down the stairs where we had just come, I hear voices. I don't understand what they're saying, but I have a good idea what's going on.

Apollo warned us there would cameras on the lower level for security to monitor. He said he would program some of the Flones to land on the camera lenses to block the view so we could sneak by.

"They probably don't have any on the residential level," he had told us.

Probably.

So, I guess the security guys had come in to find out what was blocking the lenses. If they were half as good as they should be, they would suspect an intruder set up something to distort their view.

Now they're checking it out.

I pull open the door, and we slip inside, Patrick closing it.

The bedroom is dim, with just a low-watt nightstand lamp acting as a nightlight. It takes several seconds for my eyes to adjust, and I make out a bed just to my right. I also hear a slight buzzing and realize a couple of Flones have followed us into the room. I see one land on the lampshade.

Outside, we hear muted voices, coming closer. One of the voices sounds like it's just on the other side of the door.

"*No, I haven't seen anything,*" the male voice says. "*No one else is up here. Go back to your posts.*"

Another voice says something unintelligible in reply, but I know we can't just stand here. I grab Patrick's forearm and pull him with me to the closed curtains. We slip behind them with only a moment to spare before the door opens.

"See? Empty."

I only hope the curtains aren't moving, giving us away.

"Yes, sir," another male says.

"I'm just going to say goodnight to my daughter. Go back to your posts."

"Yes, sir."

A few seconds later, the sound of the door clicking shut.

A whisper.

"Tabby."

Silence.

"It's daddy. I have to go on a trip and want to say goodbye."

"No. Please, no."

A long pause. The sound of fabric rustling. I'm guessing the bedspread and sheets are being pulled away from the 10 year old.

"Don't you want to say goodbye? I'll be gone for a while."

No reply.

I decide to peek out between the break in the curtains. I see a figure standing next to the bed, leaning over the child. He straightens up, and his hands move to his waist. One hand moves down in a motion I recognize. He's unzipping his pants.

"Just say goodbye, and I won't have to tell mommy what you did."

I see Quinn flail his hand in the air, and I guess the Flones were making buzz-dives at his head. He swats at his crotch, which means one of the robot flies landed on his weiner. Then he slaps his ear. I wonder if Apollo programmed them to bite.

I can see Quinn's face sour as his head follows the Flones flying away from him and into the middle of the room before turning and landing on the lampshade.

Then his head jerks as if he's seen something out of the corner of his eye. I look in the same direction of the floor and see a Drat dart, running over his shoe, then under the bed.

He jumps back and then looks wildly around.

The Drat runs along the baseboard, behind a dresser, then out the other side. I lose sight of it, but realize it has come behind the curtains. I feel it scurry over my shoes.

Quinn's eyes go from the bottom of the curtain and up, as if he's looking right at me. He tilts his head and his eyes narrow.

The Drat suddenly jumps out from behind the curtains and does something no rat can do: It launches itself at the President, practically flying a distance of eight feet, landing on the man's trouser leg.

This is our cue.

We both step out from behind the curtains, and Patrick walks up to the President, pressing the muzzle of his handgun against the man's temple.

President Quinn's mouth opens in surprise.

"What—"

"Zip up your fucking pants," Patrick says, "or I'll shoot that thing off of you."

"You can't talk to me that way. I'm the President of the United States."

"Okay, Mr. President, my apologies," Patrick says, then clicks the hammer back on his gun. "Sir, please zip up your fucking pants, *NOW*."

He straights up slowly and zips up.

"You're going to come with us," I tell him. "We're going to walk out that door, and if we come across any agents, you tell them we're taking you to the kitchen for a snack."

The little girl is staring at us with wide eyes.

I walk around to the left side of the bed and gently touch her forehead. "Go back to sleep," I say softly, and her eyes close. She is out. I hold my hand there and "flick away" the last five minutes of her memory.

Patrick walks to the door and puts his ear against it.

It's quiet.

"You can't get out of here," Quinn says, trying to sound slightly threatening.

"Yes we can. And you're going with us."

He licks his lips, eyes going a bit wild as he tries to think of something.

"I'll help you get out of here. I've got some money downstairs. You can have it. All of it."

"I have more money than you can ever imagine."

His eyes narrow as recognition rises on his face. "You're Jacob. You tried to hack my phone. Your father is—"

"Close. My name is Collin, and we don't have time for genealogy. Now we're going to go to the kitchen. You will not say anything unless we encounter someone else, and then only to say good evening. If they ask where you're going, just say for a snack. Got it?"

He nods, but his eyes are still narrow, taking me in.

Patrick opens the door, sticks his head out and looks around. "Clear."

"Let's go," I say waving the gun.

We step out into the hall, slipping our weapons into the pockets of our slacks. We go down the stairs, and my ears are on high alert, listening. But, nothing. We step out into the hall, and again, nothing. Down to the next one, and once more, surprisingly, no one is there. I'm partially relieved, but also suspicious. They obviously know we are here, somewhere. Unless they're on a wild goose chase on the front lawn, I can't believe they'd just go back to their posts—and since at least one agent isn't at his post, it makes me even more suspicious.

We slip down the hall, then into the kitchen. Patrick steps into the pantry, scoops up the satchel and I gently push Quinn to follow him. Patrick is through the "hidden" panel and I close the pantry door behind me when I hear a shout. It's not very clear, probably coming from the hallway outside the kitchen.

I shove Quinn through the panel, get past it myself, then shut the door into place.

There, we're in front of the old-fashioned dumbwaiter, the one with the sign that says MAX WEIGHT 250 LBS.

"Get in," I tell Quinn.

Patrick frowns at me.

Quinn picks up on this and says: "I'm not getting on that thing."

Patrick reacts quickly by reaching down and grabbing Quinn's crotch and squeezing. "It should take about ten seconds to castrate you," Patrick says through clenched teeth.

Quinn lets out a little squeal.

Patrick grabs Quinn's arm and pushes him into the small box. It's going to be a tight squeeze. I figure that if the dumbwaiter can't handle our combined weight, we'll just get to the bottom quicker.

Then I wonder if I could do it a little differently.

"I'll just orb my way down," I say.

"Oh great. So you want me ride down next to this pervert alone," Patrick says.

"He doesn't like grown men," I say. "He prefers the small and helpless."

They step into the box, and just as the door begins to close, a Drat dashes in with them, quickly racing up the President's leg, over his chest, perching itself on Quinn's left shoulder. Its snout begins to nuzzle his neck as if looking for a place to bite. Then door closes completely to the sound of the President's screams of panic.

The box begins to laboriously descend and I feel my phone vibrate. I pull it out and look.

A text from Apollo.

LOL

I can hear voices on the other side of the hidden panel. Just as someone begins tapping on it, as if to test it solidness. They're getting the idea.

Once the box clears the first floor to the basement, I zip down and wait for the box to reach bottom. When it does, I pull open the door and the two men tumble out, the Drat hopping off the President and scampering away.

Patrick looks up at me, a mixture of horror and being pissed on his face. "That wasn't funny you guys!"

I try not to smile.

Quinn lays in a heap, dazed and confused. Patrick gets to his knees and grabs Quinn by the collar, yanking him up into a sitting position.

"Now we run," he says as we hear a crash above us, followed by excited voices. "And I mean run."

They get up, and I lead the way, out of the little 10 by 10 room, into the next, and then down the long hallway.

* * *

We come out of the elevator, Patrick and I on either side of the President of the United States, walking through the lobby of the office building across the street from the White House.

I pull both of them to a stop. I stick out my hand. "Give me your phone."

"I left it in my bedroom."

"Give me your phone," I repeat.

Quinn opens his mouth to argue, and Patrick shoves his hand in Quinn's front slacks pockets—first the right, then the left. He comes up with a square plastic rectangle that looks familiar.

Patrick hands the phone to me, and I turn it off before putting it in my pocket.

We step out into the cold midnight night air, a couple bundled up walk past us on the sidewalk, a taxi drives by, but otherwise the street is empty.

Patrick looks over at me and I look back.

A car was supposed to be here, I tell him.

I believe you.

"I'm a little cold here," Quinn says.

"Oh, shut up you baby," Patrick says.

As he says that, a limo glides around the corner at the intersection and pulls up to the curb. Without waiting for the driver, I pull open the back door we practically throw MacNeill Quinn into the back.

* * *

"We have him, we're safe," I tell Apollo on the phone.

"Take him to Andrews Air Force Base. Air Force One is ready. The usual pilots have been replaced with our people. They'll fly you to where you need to go."

"Where's that?"

"You'll see."

"Andrews," I tell the driver, and he nods.

"They'll find you there," Quinn says.

"Not if they find you first," I say. "Remember, Agent Williams, behind the left ear, once."

Patrick nods, and even in the bad light of the limousine, Quinn seems to go five shades whiter.

* * *

On the tarmac at Andrews Air Force base, we exit the vehicle, bathed in the glow of a pair of harsh lights apparently set up for this departure. A pair of Marines stand at the base of the stairs, along with another military official, his stern hat giving him away as someone important.

I'm a little nervous as we flank President Quinn to Air Force One. Will the soldiers get word the President has been kidnapped and stop our mission right here? Maybe they already have. They could just be waiting for us to get close enough to take us out.

The older man bundled in a nice, thick parka approaches

with a warm smile. His hand comes out and the President, perhaps out of habit, sticks his hand out as well. I glance at Quinn, who is smiling like meeting an old friend.

"Agent Graves, Agent Williams," the military man says, his friendly hand reaching out to me. "General DiCarlo, here to assist you to your destination."

We shake. "Thank you for your help."

The General looks at President Quinn for a moment, an unmistakable expression of disdain on his face. "Mr. Quinn, I hereby declare you a prisoner of war. You will be afforded the privileges of the Geneva Convention." He turns to the two men flanking the stairway up to the plane. "Please take Mr. Quinn into custody."

The two men move forward, and one of the men pulls out a pair of handcuffs while the other begins to shackle the President's ankles together. After each taking an arm of the President, they slowly escort him up the stairs to Air Force One.

The General turns to us. "The pilots of Air Force One and of the fighter jets who will be accompanying you are members the Challengers and will assist you in any way they can. Is there anything you need right now?"

"Not that I can think of, General. Thank you, again."

"We received word as you pulled up that the Secret Service radioed they've found the President safe inside the White House and the alert is called off."

I frown. "How? He's right there." I point at the stairway as the shackled Leader of the Free World takes each step one at a time, very slowly.

The General shrugs. "I don't know but it's some kind of ploy. It might be a way to fool us into relaxing. Or it could be just to keep the media from hitting the panic button, since they monitor the White House. Either way, we won't let our guard down."

"Yes," I say. "We won't either."

He nods and smiles. "This mission will be classified as . . . well let's just say as if it never happened. You should get going."

"I hope you don't get in trouble," I tell him.

"Don't you worry about me—there's more of us than you think. Thank you for helping to remove this walking venereal disease from our country." DiCarlo then salutes us.

Awkwardly, we salute him back, then hurry up the stairs.

Chapter 25

"Ideas are more powerful than guns. We would not let our enemies have guns, why should we let them have ideas?"—Josef Stalin

To his credit, Quinn stayed quiet the entire flight, but I could see the gears churning in his head. I was tempted to sneak in there and get a glimpse of what he was thinking, but decided to stay away, at least for my own peace of mind.

Watching out the window, I see a city come into view, and as it grows closer, I realize we have come back to Chicago. But we seem to bypass O'Hare and Midway and begin to descend into a more suburban area. It's more like a long landing strip than an airport.

The touchdown is smooth, and we come to a gentle stop. There are no lights or military officials here to greet us. A staircase is wheeled into place, and Patrick and I step down the stairs, followed by the two military men with the shackled MacNeill Quinn between them.

A car with its lights off pulls up and Patrick gets in the backseat with Quinn while I take the front passenger seat.

"Gentlemen," our driver says. I see it's Derek, the guy who drove us around when we were followed by a white van of Regulators.

"You know where we're going?" I ask.

"Of course. Seat belts, please. And I recommend you find

something to hold onto." He winks at me just as he floors it.

As makes an arc around Air Force One, I see the outline of a fuel truck making its way towards the airliner. It will refuel and take off for elsewhere.

We speed through the darkness, lights still off, and I see ahead what looks like a tunnel. We race inside, enveloped in total black. For a few seconds, I'm terrified, unable to see my hand in front of me, much less whatever we might crash into. As I open my mouth to tell Derek to turn on the headlights, they come on, bathing the cement tunnel in a harsh whiteness that makes me flinch.

I glance over at the Derek's side of the dashboard and see we're doing 82 miles per hour.

I'm sure Derek knows what he's doing, but I take his advice and place my palm on the dashboard in front of me.

* * *

Eventually, we arrive at a familiar sight: The long corridor just off the Control Center at Manor House. Apollo and Mr. B are waiting for us. We climb out, and I pretend that my knees aren't wobbly from the joy ride we just were on. None of us say anything, perhaps because we don't want Quinn to hear.

Patrick leads the President into the conference room, seating him in a chair. Quinn leans forward, resting his hands on the table, the metal of the handcuffs making a clinking sound.

"Can we get you anything? Something to drink?" Mr. B asks.

"A scotch and soda would be nice," Quinn says.

We all look at him to see if he's joking, but he just stares at the table, frowning.

Mr. B looks at me and shrugs, then leaves.

I pull Quinn's phone out of my pocket and power it on as I take the seat directly across from him.

"Would you like to talk with your father?"

Quinn's head snaps up as if I he couldn't believe what he was hearing. "Seriously?" He licks his lips, staring at me intently to see if I'm playing a trick. I can read his mind clear as day, and he's scared spitless. Outwardly, he's doing a phenomenal job of hiding it.

I scroll through the list of contacts on his phone and see a who's who of the powerful, the famous, and the infamous. On a hunch, I go to the letter "D" and the first entry is "Dad." But I pause.

I reconsider what I'm about to do. On the plane, it seemed like a good idea. Now, the consequences start to rise up. Quinn calls, and Dunraven will know. He knows, or at the very least suspects, we have kidnapped his son, the President of the United States. He would expect us to listen in. I know Dunraven well enough to know he won't grovel or beg. He may listen, perhaps negotiate, but it will be tough to tell how far he is willing to go to get the centerpiece of his plan back into the fold. He knows we won't kill Quinn, though we may have every right to. Dunraven won't back down. We have his son, but what could we possibly ask in return? Dunraven wouldn't keep a promise if his own life depended upon it. What could we possibly ask that Dunraven would even momentarily consider?

Our goal is to cut off the head of the snake, and he's sitting right across from me. Without him, the military has no leader, the financial maneuvering and deceit is stopped, the string-pulling is over. Sure, the Vice President is as far up Dunraven's butt as Quinn, but he has all the nuance of a circus clown at a funeral. The military hates the VP, and his knowledge of the financial system would fit under the fingernail of his pinkie, with room to spare. Plus, it would take a while for them to even figure out what they're supposed to do when the President is missing. Do they wait? Do they swear the VP in? Do they tell the American public the President is missing? Kidnapped? Would anyone even believe that?

The other reason I pause is because I want Mr. B to witness this. He would have invaluable insights.

As I consider and reconsider, Mr. B walks in with a tall clear glass of a light amber liquid in ice cubes. He sets it in front Quinn, then looks at me.

It might loosen his tongue.

I thought as much. I'm going to let him call Dunraven.

Mr. B frowns for a second, then nods as Quinn takes a healthy sip of his drink, using both shackled hands to raise the glass..

I press "Call" on the phone and set it in the middle of the table. Quinn sticks both hands out, reaching for it, and I hold my hand up.

"No, it stays there, on speakerphone," I tell him as the first ring comes through the tinny speaker.

"*Where are you?*"

"I have no idea."

"*I will assume they are listening.*"

Quinn looks at me, and I stare back. He can say whatever he wants. The USA may soon no longer be a free country, but we can pretend. Oddly, he stays quiet.

"*Why are you calling?*"

I thought that was a weird question, and apparently, Quinn did as well. He frowns.

"I need your help to get out of here."

"*I cannot imagine what ransom they would expect. I doubt they want money.*"

I roll my eyes. But I'm beginning to see the futility of this. I have no intention of letting Quinn go under any circumstances, so this isn't a negotiation.

I shoot Quinn a thought: What's the plan?

He flinches, then parrots what I sent him. "What's the plan?"

"*Nothing has changed.*"

Nothing more. I don't need to ask the next question.

"What about me?"

Something that sounds like a chuckle. "*Enjoy your vacation.*"

The line goes dead.

Quinn looks like he's in shock. I let him stew in it for a while. He takes a big slug from his drink.

"So, he's dumping you," I say.

He nods, takes another two-fisted drink, finishing it.

"What did he mean 'Nothing has changed'?"

Quinn sighs. "What kind of deal can we make?"

"What do you mean by 'deal'?"

"I give you something, what do you give me?"

I look to Patrick who is not bothering to hide his disgust, and then Mr. B who is keeping his expression passive.

I shrug. "I got nothing."

"Then me too."

I sit back and study him. I'm in his Flow and know he's scared out of his mind, but his politician experience has allowed him to keep his exterior silky smooth.

"You understand," I tell him, "that you've done some pretty horrible things. You're not going to walk out of here."

His eyes narrow, and his stream of thoughts take what I said as a threat—first, literally, as if he's not going to be walking; then figuratively, that we will execute him.

I add a finishing touch: "And your father has left you to swing alone."

He begins to stutter. "I . . . you know . . . I was . . . um . . . under orders. It's not like I . . . you know . . . I didn't make the . . . uh . . ."

"You raped your daughter," Patrick says.

I shoot him a look. *Stop.* But the look on his face shows his venom. If given the choice, Patrick *would* execute him. I can't say I blame him, but it's not option right now.

There's a long silence.

Quinn is beginning to sweat. His gears are turning, mind racing. I wait him out.

"Osborne's dead."

I blink, trying to remember who Osborne is, and it comes to me. His National Security Advisor. The guy who tipped us to some of the President's plans and actions.

"Dad—"

"Dunraven."

"Yeah, he suspected you were talking with him. I had him checked out, and found a link to a video feed."

"And you killed him?"

"I didn't," he says, a little too defensively.

"Well, of course, not *you*. You have people for that."

I glance at Mr. B, and I he looks both sad and surprised. I guess he was closer to Thomas Osborne than I knew.

"What else?" I ask.

"Can . . . I have another drink? Please?"

Before Mr. B can get up, Patrick snatches the glass and is heading for the exit.

Don't put anything in it, I tell him. I don't want him poisoning the President.

He disappears without replying. As horrible as child molestation is, the issue between Quinn and his daughter seems to be affecting Patrick more than anyone else. I'll see if I can talk to him later.

"So, what else?" I ask again.

He's trying to think, but nothing is bubbling to the surface. I'm beginning to think the term "figurehead" applies all too well. He may not know much of what's going on, just signing the papers put in front of him and standing on a mark for the TV cameras.

"I'm really tired," he finally says.

Patrick returns with the glass refilled with scotch, sets it on the table, then turns and walks out again.

Quinn takes a big slug. "Can I get some sleep? I'll be glad to talk to you after that."

I look over at Mr. B, who shrugs.

* * *

With Quinn safely locked away in a concrete room, Mr. B and I watch the video feeds from the news networks. Morning has arrived, and the top story is the death of National Security Advisor Thomas Osborne. They don't tell us anything we don't already know, but at least it confirms Quinn's story.

The other news is about three airline incidents—one shot down over a war zone, another crashing upon take off, and the third simply disappearing. In all, over 700 people dead or unaccounted for.

And then there's the weather—temperatures nose-diving in many parts of the country, with some of the northern states sinking to -15, -20, even a -38 in Minneapolis. At least three dozen people have been found frozen to death inside their own homes, and who knows how many others there are that just haven't been found yet.

Mr. B switches one of the monitors to a view outside Manor House as dawn begins to break. The sky looks cloudless as the first rays of sun sneak over the horizon. But instead of the usual yellow-white harshness of a clear December morning, there's a pinkish hue to the sky.

"Is something wrong with the monitor?" I ask. "It's like the color has gone out of whack."

Mr. B stares at the screen, frowning. "The monitor is fine," he says solemnly. "I'm afraid the Red Sky has begun."

Chapter 26

"False words are not only evil in themselves, but they infect the soul with evil."—Socrates

I get in a shower and have a brief nap before I'm awoken by Leslie. "They need you."

I meet them again in the Conference Room, which is becoming much too familiar.

"What's up?"

Mr. B points at a screen. "The news channels are waiting for the President to speak in the Press Room."

"They might have a long time to wait."

"That's why I thought you might want to watch. Who knows what they're going to pull."

"I'm sure the Press Secretary or the Vice President will come out and say the President has to attend to some pressing matter, and they'll speak on his behalf."

"How long will they be able to keep that up?"

"Not just that, but it could bring questions as to what this 'other pressing matter' might be."

"So what is this speech supposed to be about?"

He shakes his head. "A lot of speculation, but the notice sent to the media said to expect the President to speak at nine A.M.

eastern time on an important issue involving the health and welfare of the American people."

I smirk. "You mean like he's trying to kill everyone?"

"I'm thinking it's about the NERV scare. A couple of days ago, CNN picked up an article from an alternative news website and began airing reports about NERV. There has been a mini-panic going on, mostly in the suburbs among parents trying to protect their children since they're most susceptible."

"They're only susceptible because the government is targeting them. So now they're going to come in and save everyone?"

"I'm not sure what tact they're going to take, but it should be interesting."

I pick up the remote control and raise the volume on one of the monitors. A couple of talking heads are conjecturing and hypothesizing the same as we were, only in more political terms. One side of the screen shows an older man in suit and tie is reasoning that the President just wants to use the time to calm people down and not get them all worked up. On the other side of the screen is a shot of an empty lectern with a microphone in front of a blue backdrop—the familiar White House Press Briefing Room.

"I'm sorry to interrupt," the anchor says, *"but we're going to switch live to the White House."*

The full screen is showing the small stage, and off to the left we see a couple of people enter—aides or staffers—and then a gray-haired man steps up to the lectern.

"Good morning, ladies and gentlemen," he says. The caption at the bottom of the screen says he's DUNCAN PRABST, WHITE HOUSE SPOKESMAN. *"As you know, there are several concerns affecting the American people at the moment, and the President would like to take a few moments to address these. He will speak for approximately ten minutes, and there will be no questions. I will be available shortly after the speech to take questions. Will you please stand for the President of the United States."*

I look at Mr. B, who shakes his head and shrugs.

And on the screen, MacNeill Quinn enters the picture and steps up to the lectern.

I blink, trying to figure out how this is remotely possible.

Mr. B looks as puzzled as I do.

"*Good morning,*" the President says. "*I would like to thank, again, Duncan for his loyal service. His retirement day is just around the corner, and I for one am looking forward not to his leaving, but only for a piece of that cake which will be served at his party this afternoon.*"

Sprinkled laughter from the assembled members of the press.

"What is this?" I ask.

"Well," Mr. B says, not sounding very certain, "since we know Quinn was planning to secretly leave the White House for Cheyenne Mountain in Colorado, I would guess this is a pre-taped press conference. If we hadn't gotten to him first, he'd be hiding out right now at the military facility there."

"Ah, so that explains why the Secret Service sent the radio message saying they had found the President after we kidnapped him—so they could continue with the charade."

"They might have half a dozen of these pre-recorded things lined up and ready to go."

The President formally launches into the meat of his speech, which is indeed on the subject of NERV—New England Respiratory Virus, which is, of course, no longer cornered in New England.

"*The amazing scientists and doctors at the Centers for Disease Control have managed to create an antidote to NERV, not only curing the virus in those already suffering, but also as an antivirus to the public at large. Because of the urgency of this matter, we have tapped into the National Guard and military branches to get this cure into as many hospitals, doctor's offices and pharmacies as possible, transporting it overnight and delivering it as I speak. We have also dispersed thousands of military medics to every corner of this nation to help inject this life-saving serum to every man, woman and child who requests it.*"

"Did he just allow the military to roam the streets and infect people with a drug that will probably kill them faster than the virus they're scared of?"

Mr. B nods. "I'll see if I can get Dr. Jarminsky on the phone after this is over."

"Okay, let me know when that happens. I'm going to talk to our friend, the President."

* * *

Quinn is sitting in a corner, knees up, the chain of the leg shackles laying on the floor. His forearms are on his knees, wrists linked by the handcuffs. He looks at me warily, eyes bloodshot and watery.

"You know, we're technically brothers," I say. "Not natural, of course, since I was adopted."

He only stares blankly. I'm not even sure he heard me.

"I'm all you've got," I add.

He nods in understanding, but says nothing. He avoids looking at me.

"What's it like being under his thumb?"

It's several moments before he answers. "It had its perks."

"I'm sure it wasn't easy to do his bidding."

He nods. "It had its challenges."

"It must be difficult to not be yourself, but always play this . . . role. Always pretending. Fake smiles. Do this thing, do that thing. Sit here. Appear concerned."

His eyes look at me. They seem . . . sad.

"It was easy, mostly. Read the scripts. Sign a document. Shake hands. Kiss babies."

I am silent for a minute. I let the quiet sink in.

"Why did you do it? I mean, you signed off on people losing their homes, their children, even their lives. You knew it was wrong. So . . . why?"

"Money. Sex. Power. But to be honest with you, I was fed misinformation. I was told that certain things were happening, and they had some plan to take care of it."

I nod. I'm sure he was misled. But he also didn't ask questions, or challenge his advisors, or stand up to his father.

"Were you afraid he would kill you?"

"Of course," he says immediately.

I say nothing for a while. Quinn obviously didn't care about his wife. Or his daughter. Or anyone else. In return, no one cared about him. He used people, and they used him. It was what he knew. Now he's stuck in this concrete room, handcuffed and shackled, and no one cares. No one will come to rescue him, or even negotiate for his release. He has no friends, no one loves him—in fact, many people will be glad he's gone.

While I don't really feel sympathy for him, I get it. I understand what he did and why he did it, but I still feel disgust that he chose the route of hurt and pain for his own satisfaction and gain. I think of the scene in his daughter's bedroom, his penis hanging out of his pants, asking her to do something no little girl should do. That was not something he was asked to do. That was something he created on his own.

I could sit back all day and pass judgment or play armchair psychologist, but it would take me nowhere. Neither one of us had a positive father figure growing up. A mother. Friends. Sure, I had Sylvana, and he probably had countless nannies, but we still ended up worlds apart in our choices.

"I just saw you on TV. How is that possible?"

He closes his eyes and leans his head back, nestling it into the corner. "I taped some scenes over the weekend. Pain in the ass. Had to change clothes every five minutes."

"How many scenes?"

He shrugs. "I don't know. Eight, nine."

"Are they all press conferences?"

"No. Only three or four. Some are staged press events. I give a Medal of Honor to a wounded soldier. Eat a burger at a diner. Give a speech at a black church."

"What are the topics of the press conferences?"

He looks at the handcuffs, then at me. "Any chance for some *quid pro quo?*"

"Sure. I don't have the key, but I'll have it arranged. I'm sure you're hungry too. I'll have something brought in."

He seems to relax a little. "One press conference was about

the NERV virus and some cure they came up with. Another was on the problems with the financial system."

"What kind of problems?"

"Bank failures. Insurance company collapses. Stocks and investments disappearing."

"Where did they go?"

He smirks. "Where do you think?"

"So you basically announced a government bailout."

"Yeah, but since the government is basically broke and in debt beyond comprehension—at least on paper—the bailout is limited. People will be lucky to get a dime on the dollar."

"And when will this happen?"

"The collapse is already underway. Not sure when they're going to air the press conference."

"Okay. What other ones were staged?"

He leans his head back again, eyes looking off in the distance. "About a raven attack in Atlanta that killed almost four hundred, and the failure of the electrical grid in some parts of the country."

"Wait. A raven attack?"

He looks at me. "You seriously didn't think you destroyed all the bases, did you?"

I shake my head. I'm sure I look thoroughly confused.

"The sites you guys took out were just staging and training areas. The main ones are still fully operational."

My stomach sinks. "Do you know where they are?"

"*Quid pro quo?*"

"Depends on what the *quid* is."

He smirks.

* * *

"Dr. Jarminsky is on the line," Mr. B says, pointing at the screen as I return to the Conference Room.

"*Hello.*"

"Hi. What's up?"

Through the video feed, Jarminsky looks uncomfortable,

like he's going to tell me I have a terminal illness. *"Have you heard of 'sepsis'?"*

"No. Is this another new disease like NERV?"

"Not new, but much, much worse. It can literally kill you in a day."

"Okay. I can't say I'm completely surprised."

"I'm sure you saw the press conference."

A few minutes ago, my stomach sank as Quinn revealed the return of the Cravens. Now my heart sinks. "The antidote is this sepsis."

"Is there anything we can do?" Mr. B asks.

"Not really. The only way to stop it is to stop the injections of the 'antidote.' I'd suggest an information campaign."

"I'm not sure we have enough time for that," Mr. B says. "We can leak it to alternative websites, but the mainstream media won't pick it up."

Dr. Jarminsky looks distressed. *"You have to try. This could decimate entire swaths of the population."*

"That's not the only thing," I say. "I've learned the financial system is going down, and the ravens are back."

Even through the video monitor, I see Jarminsky go even more pale. *"I'm safe with my wife and kids here,"* he says, without adding where "here" is. The last time we talked with him, he indicated he would be going away and would not be in touch, yet here he was. *"I worry about the rest of my family. My brother. My sisters. Their kids. My parents."*

"We'll do what we can," I tell him, and I mean it. I just don't know what that would be.

Chapter 27

"Judge a man by his questions rather than by his answers."—*Voltaire*

I got Quinn out of the handcuffs and shackles, got him a meal, a change of clothes, and a shower. Sure, his living arrangements were still rudimentary—his bed was a thin mattress on the concrete floor of his cell and he showered in a large gym-style area where two guards stood by—but he didn't complain.

It's easy to judge, and I do it all the time. It's usually in my head and I try to keep it to myself. And passing judgment on Quinn is almost too easy since it's hard to find anything good about the man. But stripped away of his sex, money and power, he's just a shell, and a pretty pathetic one.

Judge not lest ye be judged.

We're not to judge anyone since we have as many or more sins than those we feel superior to. Sure, Quinn is a rapist and child molester—no getting around that—and it would probably be impossible to see him in any other light, yet I do see aspects to him that are less monster-like and more human. He was conceived and raised as nothing more than a tool for Dunraven and Dymortis to use. To Quinn, love is at best a concept that he's heard of, a word for which he has no basis to give, receive or feel. It is as alien to him as nuclear physics is to me.

I imagine the people—all guys, I'm sure—he considered as friends are as warped or worse than him. He only knew to use people because they used him. It's the only point of reference he has.

But I don't feel sorry for him.

We leave him to sleep while we try to figure out what to do next. Mr. B, Sylvana, Patrick, Apollo and I sit in the Conference Room, all of us frustrated—but not necessarily for the same reasons.

"We literally kidnapped the President of the United States, and it literally does not matter," Patrick says. "He's still on TV, and everyone thinks he's still in Washington."

"Is there a way we can reveal the truth to the public?" Sylvana asks.

We sit in silence for several moments.

"Do you mean like a public appearance?" Mr. B asks. He's in front of a laptop, moving the mouse around. "Trot him out at a media event?"

"Can we even risk that?" Patrick asks. "I mean, would he say what needs to be said?"

"Make it a control situation. A pre-recorded video," Apollo says.

"No one will air it," I say. "The media would never be allowed."

More silence as we consider possibilities.

"What if it were possible to hijack the network signals?" Apollo asks.

"Is it possible?" I ask.

"Anything is possible. Making it possible is the hard part."

"So, you're thinking we cut into the broadcast signal and air a video of Quinn telling the story of what's really going on?"

"Yes."

"Can we cut into the broadcast signals?"

"Sure. Just not all at once."

"What do you mean?"

"I can cut into one signal and get the video aired before they figure out how to cut it off. I don't think I can cut into multiple signals all at the same time."

"That is assuming Quinn will do it," Patrick says.

"So I guess the first question is *if* we should do it," I say. "Is it something that would work?"

A brief silence before Sylvana says: "It might not be the best use of our time. There are so many other pressing matters we need to consider. But it is good to have that option."

"What other pressing matters are there?" Patrick asks.

"That's right, you've been out of the loop," I say. I take a few minutes to fill him in on the sepsis, the financial breakdown, the coming electrical grid issue—which I still need to get more info on—and, finally, the return of the Cravens.

"Are you kidding me? Do you know how many of those monsters we killed? *And there's more of them?*"

All I could do was nod. What could I say? Don't worry, everything will be okay? It will all work out in the end?

Mr. B clears his throat. "Well, I hate to pile on the bad news, but . . ."

We all look at him. He's clicking, staring at the screen. Bad news from a bad news website, no doubt. He looks up.

". . . the Internet went down. Apollo, could you restart the server?"

"Sure." The little boy slides off the chair and scampers out of the room.

"It happens once in a while," Mr. B says. "Sometimes the Wi-Fi goes wacky too."

A minute later, Apollo re-enters. "The Internet is not down, it's *off.*"

"So, it's beginning," Sylvan says. "I am not surprised."

"It might take me a few minutes, but let me try something," Apollo says, dashing off again.

"What about this electrical grid thing?" I ask. "How do you think they'll spin that?"

"Solar flares," Mr. B says, giving up on using the computer. "I expect they'll simultaneously take the broadcast satellites offline, and the cellular phone system, and blame it all on the sun. That's another reason why a cut-in to the news networks might not work—the local cable systems won't be able to pick up the feed.

We could hijack their broadcast, but no one would see it."

"The electrical grid alone would probably do a number on life in the United States," I say.

"It could result in panic," Mr. B says flatly. "When there's word of a financial failure, what's the first thing people will do?"

"Run to an ATM."

He nods. "And with the power out, it won't work. Looting, burglary, robbery, murder will follow just so people can get their hands on the essentials. Without power, gas stations can't operate. Hospitals may have generators, but once the fuel for those runs out, then what? Traffic lights being out will be a minor annoyance, but what about air traffic control? Radios don't work without electricity, and the computer system that keeps track of all those planes will just stop working. With the cold snap—certainly a Dymortis creation—people will start to panic, or they'll die in their homes waiting for help to come."

"Wow," Patrick says, "you're just full of happy news."

"Yeah, I know. My job has always been on the glass-is-almost-empty side of things." He winks at Sylvana, who gives him a wry smirk.

Apollo enters and walks up to Mr. B. "I'll need to reconfigure the IP setting," he says, and Mr. B pushes the laptop to the child. "I've re-routed our access to the ShadowNet. We'll get messages out to the Citizen Challengers to switch to the ShadowNet, and we'll be able to keep everything up and running."

"But if their Internet is turned off, how will you get a message to them?" Patrick asks.

"Some may still have email access, but we also can use an MTM—mass text messaging system to get the word out."

"And if that doesn't work?"

Apollo looks at Patrick with a blank expression. "They have instructions on how to access the ShadowNet. They'll figure it out." He pushes the laptop back to Mr. B. "It should work now."

The Professor clicks, then shrugs. "Technically it works, but if the website on the other end isn't working, then it doesn't matter." He clicks some more.

"You should try the SWEN website," Apollo says. "It should survive the shutdown."

"SWEN?" I ask.

"It stands for Southwest Existential Network, but it's really just the word 'news' backwards."

Mr. B types on the keyboard. "Ah, yes. It seems to have all the—"

He stops, mouth open.

"What?" I ask.

"Unbelievable."

"*What?*" Patrick asks, a bit louder.

"The air traffic control has officially gone down, and apparently, all GPS with it. There are reports of at least two hundred aircraft crashing into each other, exploding, falling out of the sky, crashing on landing."

"Two hundred? That would be tens of thousands of deaths."

Mr. B nods solemnly. "As many as forty thousand."

A long pause.

"So, if the GPS is down, the satellites are going offline," I say.

"Looks like it." He turns to Apollo. "Is there a way you can check?"

"Sure." And off he runs, almost skipping.

"According to SWEN, there are reports of the electrical grid going down in the Northwest—Washington, Oregon, Idaho, Northern California. Also, Western Australia, parts of Southeast Asia, South Africa. As I recall, often when one parts of the grid goes down, it creates a cascading effect since it overloads other parts, and they become overwhelmed. It should—"

The lights flicker. The monitors around the room go black.

Then all goes dark.

* * *

It's an eerie silence. No one says anything. With the electricity out, the electronics have all gone silent, and the air system is shut down. Only the light of the laptop screen casts Mr. B in a ghostly glow.

All I can hear is the whisper of the laptop fan, and my own breathing.

From down the hall, we hear Apollo's faint voice: "Give me just a minute!"

"This is kind of spooky," Patrick says, looking out towards the hallway, which is black as night.

We wait.

"I'm concerned about the shield," Mr. B says. "I'm sure it is offline."

"They could make a move," I say.

"What about the security locks on the doors?" Patrick asks.

"I would say they are questionable," Mr. B says. "I don't know what the fail-safe is."

"You mean if the power goes out, they auto-lock?" I ask.

"Or unlock," he replies.

There's a loud *clunk* sound, and the lights come on. We don't move. It's as if we're waiting for the next shoe to drop.

I'm listening for the sound of crashing, of the Regulators breaking down doors.

Patrick picks up the remote control and begins turning the monitors back on.

A guy I've seen around walks into the doorway. "Everyone okay in here?"

"Just fine, thanks," I say.

He waves and leaves.

The monitors come on and Patrick tries to switch them to the right channel, but they're all stuck on a blue screen with the words *Searching for signal* in the middle.

"Apollo may need to reset all the equipment," I say.

After pressing a myriad of buttons, Patrick succeeds with one of the screens finally turning on. It shows the closed circuit feed from the front of the house. No one is in the yard.

He tries another, and it loads up the feed from the side of the house. In the distance, we can see the tanks, and a lot of people milling about.

"I would guess they were not prepared for the outage either,"

Mr. B says. "In the confusion of their GPS and communications going down, it looks like they just stayed put."

"I had to reset the reactor, but the shield is back up," Apollo says, holding a popsicle. He takes a small bite. "I doubt the satellite links will work, but we can try."

"Reactor?" I say. "You have a nuclear reactor here?"

"Of course," the little boy says. "You didn't think we could operate all this on gasoline, did you?" Then he giggles.

Patrick presses more buttons, looking from the remote up to the screen and back. Finally, an image appears—but it's just colored rectangles with the words CNN PATH 1 ONE in block letters.

"Looks like that satellite is working," Apollo says. "But there's no signal coming from New York."

"So, the grid is down there too," I say.

"Can you imagine the panic?" Patrick says. "Subway out of commission, elevators stuck, heaters not working."

"At least it's daytime," Mr. B says. "Wait until night."

"I'll see if I can get any other feeds," Apollo says, wandering back out of the room with his purple popsicle.

"What do we do next?" I ask. "We have the President. Do we go after Dunraven?"

"That will be tricky," Mr. B says. "We have to assume whatever powers you have, he has as well."

"You mean he can zip his way from here to Buenos Aires?" Patrick asks.

Mr. B shrugs. "I don't know. We just have to assume he can."

We fall silent for several moments.

"It may be time for an assembly," Sylvana says.

"An assembly of what?" Patrick asks.

"Of whom."

Chapter 28

"The Lord has promised good to me / His word my hope secures / He will my shield and portion be / as long as life endures."—John Newton, *Amazing Grace*

Mr. B read us a list of news from SWEN of all the other events taking place.

Gasoline and milk, a couple of barometers of the U.S. economy, were now over $20 a gallon—if you could find them.

The ISP, International Service Patrol, had taken over control of Europe, Asia, Russia, Australia, and most of the rest of the world. Martial law was declared basically everywhere.

The Mid-East erupted in all-out war, and there were reports a nuclear weapon was used, though all sides involved claimed someone else did it. It made me wonder if that might be true, and Dunraven was behind it.

President Quinn was scheduled to make a speech, declaring martial law across the country. No doubt the spin would be that it was necessary to "protect" the citizens.

More than 5 million Americans had rushed to get vaccinated against NERV, and reports were coming in that an "adverse reaction" to the antidote was leaving many, if not most, dead or dying.

Due to the electrical grid shutdown, most folks were without heat during the coldest month in recorded history, and water was not accessible due to the loss of power to the pumping stations. And that drastic cold extended beyond the upper Mid-West and East Coast, spreading into the South and West, dropping typically warm L.A. and Miami into the mid-20's. Residents not used to such temperatures have begun to panic, raiding sporting good and department stores for warmer clothing.

The ravens have made their comeback, and in the most gruesome way possible, with tens of thousands, if not hundreds of thousands, attacking those people not just unfortunate to be outside, but inside their cars and homes. There are reports of the beasts crashing into office buildings to break the windows to get at the workers inside. A video of looters ransacking a mall shows them being taken into the skies as they exited, some still holding onto their loot.

Trucks and trains transporting goods—food, diapers, toilet paper, bottled water, batteries, clothes, over-the-counter and prescription medications—are stranded in truck stops and depots due to lack of fuel.

Doctors and nurses are reporting they are taking care of patients as best they can, operating on generator power, but surgeries are limited. To add insult to injury, thieves have managed to siphon off fuel from the generators for some hospitals, killing their power.

Livestock that hasn't been picked off by the Cravens are dying of starvation.

Ham radio operator—those with sufficient batteries or generators—are about the only means of mass communication. I had no idea what a ham radio was—it didn't exactly sound edible—until Mr. B took me into a room full of what look like ancient electronics. He sat down and began fiddling with some of it, trying to explain how it worked. I didn't understand much of it, but I was just glad it came on and began making noise.

"I think I'll try listening to the police scanner," he said. "Should be interesting."

I got a quick bite to eat with Patrick before meeting Sylvana down in the tunnel.

"So, what's this trip about?" he asked.

"A gathering of the Soulmadds is all I know. I'm not sure Sylvana knows, or she would have told me."

"Do you all sit around and sing 'Kumbaya'?"

"Something like that," I said with a smile. "I'm sure it's more like a prayer vigil."

"Couldn't you do that here?"

"I guess. But there's a lot of distractions here."

He stared at me for several moments. "Do you want me to go with you?"

I sense something important from his question, a need to belong, to be part of something bigger, something life-changing. He's been my partner, my rock, doing things with me and for me that no one else on the planet would consider. But within him there was also a fear of the unknown, whisking off to a jungle to take part in some mysterious ritual that he may or may not be a part of.

"Where do you think you should be?"

He spent a minute thinking how to answer. "Here. I think they need me here."

I nodded. "You should oversee things, make sure everything is okay."

He smirked. "Are you putting me in charge?"

I pretended to think about this. "I don't know. You have an uncontrollable ego—things might go to your head!"

We laugh as we pick up our plates and silverware. Then he becomes serious as we put the dishes in a basket for cleaning.

"You'll be careful, right?"

"Of course. But only if you will. Besides, I'll be back in the blink of an eye."

"Literally," he says, smiling.

Sylvana is waiting in the golf cart. She looks as calm and controlled as ever. Gizzi, on the other hand, is almost out of control with joy when she sees us. Sylvana hands the dog over to Patrick. "Please take care of her—and no human food. The chefs know what to feed her."

"She's in good hands," he says as the wiggly animal tries to lick his face.

I get behind the wheel, wave at Patrick and get the cart moving to the exit.

"Wait!"

I stop the cart, looking around. I see Apollo running for us.

"You can't forget me!" he says, jumping on the back of the cart.

* * *

The trip to Nicaragua without the tortuous travel was a blessing since it only took a few seconds. No nine hour flights, no bumpy ride through the jungle, no bugs to try to eat me alive. Besides, with the air traffic control system down and all flights grounded, it would have taken days, if not weeks by any other series of methods.

We stand in the lush, green field, the pool of water nearby with its waterfall cascading gently. On the stumps surrounding the fire pit are the familiar brown robes. Without hesitation, Apollo and Sylvana begin undressing, and I do the same.

I have to say that standing naked in the warm, calming sunshine is a treat, and I remain still as the rays soak into my skin. I look up and see five balls of light streaking through the sky and landing just to my right. The Orbs transform into figures, and for the first time I get a good look at my fellow Soulmadds. Unsurprisingly, they look like a cross-section of people from around the world: An elderly Asian man in khakis and a polo shirt, a young Scandinavian woman in a black skirt and sweater, a middle-aged Black woman in shorts and a tank top, a Filipino teenage boy in beaten-up jeans and a Metallica t-shirt. They each nod and smile at me as they walk to the stumps and begin to get undressed.

"Laus Deo," I say, and they say the same to me.

I put on the robe, pull up the hood, and wait.

A few minutes later, two more Orbs appear, turning into a late-20's Latino man and a late-30's White woman, possibly from Britain or Australia. Then the last pair arrive—an Arabic woman and a Hassidic Jewish man. I greet them with "Laus Deo" and they quietly get undressed before putting on the robes.

We take our places, standing on top of our stools. One of the Soulmadds—it was impossible to tell who was who in the hooded robes, except for Apollo who is considerably shorter than everyone else—lit the fire, and we all gazed into it.

"Dear Father," Sylvana says in that silky voice of hers, "we come before You acknowledging our sins, and asking once again for Your loving forgiveness . . ."

Her prayer is not long, requesting guidance in battling the enemy, one that has become so powerful and perplexing.

There is then an extended silence. I close my eyes and quietly pray for both forgiveness and direction, offering up my soul for His use.

I raise my arms and feel myself being lifted, much like I had been the last time I was here. I feel a calmness come over me, and a peace. In the darkness of my silent prayer, I begin to see a light, not unlike the rays of the sun breaking through the clouds.

Within the rays, I begin to see a form, human in shape, but not well-defined.

"*Well done, good and faithful servant,*" a voice says. It is not loud nor booming, yet calm and clear. "*You have had many trials and tribulations, and have reacted admirably. But I regret that there is more to come. The fate of the human race and the planet Earth is in the balance, and you have been chosen.*"

The thought "*Why?*" crossed my mind before I pushed it away.

"*I know you are curious, and it is not a choice I have made easily. But you are of Royal blood from the ancient times, and despite your shortcomings, you have remained pure in all ways. There are many who follow, many who are sworn to allegiance, but who, in times of turmoil, have turned to their own needs. This I understand and accept, but you have acted and reacted often without question, showing your loyalty even when you were unaware you were being tested.*"

"Laus Deo."

"*The adversary is strong—more powerful than you think—and will literally stop at nothing to destroy my confused and beaten children.*"

"Why?"

"*His hatred of Me overwhelms him, and he has already hurt me in deep ways that you can never comprehend.*"

"Why don't you destroy him?"

"*To destroy him would require destroying all of humanity with him, destroying my children. He knows this, and is daring me. I cannot yet bring myself to vanquish a single soul. The blood is on his hands, and he knows in his defilement of the human race and the creatures I created, he pains me. He is but a wayward child which I love, and agonize over.*"

"Dymortis is your child?"

"*I am the Lord of all creation.*"

I am speechless, having never considered this before.

"*Contrary to worldly thought, I do not kill. Death is a human concept, which I reject. There is only different states of being.*"

"What can I do? I cannot vanquish him."

"*Perhaps not. But he can be defeated.*"

"I can't see how. I mean, he has the power to create monsters and change the weather. I can't kill him."

"*You speak the truth. It is not in your power to end his life. But it is possible to demote his power structure . . . and rob him of the power he currently controls.*"

"I don't mean to sound argumentative, but how? I mean, *how?*"

There is a long silence.

"I'm not backing down, I'm just . . . clueless."

Still, no response.

"I know you want me to think outside of the box, but I don't even know where the box is."

"*You will.*"

I admit, I feel a little frustrated. And it seems disrespectful. But I feel this great responsibility, and I don't have an idea where to begin.

"*You have my blessings, Collin. Use them well.*"

The vague figure begins to dissipate, and the light fades. All is gray.

I begin to become reacquainted with my surroundings and feel my body return to the Earth.

I open my eyes, and find myself once again on the stump, arms still spread. The other Soulmadds are standing in the same position, arms out, heads bowed.

"Laus Deo," I say.

"*Laus Deo*," they repeat.

"Thank you, Lord, for your blessings. I will do all I can, for Your will to be done."

"*Laus Deo.*"

* * *

We all disrobe and Sylvana leads us to the pool, where, one by one, we each step in.

There is no talk for a while. At first, I believe it is because some people are from different countries, different continents, and may not know English. I certainly don't know any other languages.

We soak in the crystal clear water, allowing it to cleanse and purify our body, minds and souls. I lay my head back, against the edge, and breathe deeply.

"Were you able to commune with God?" a male voice asks.

I open my eyes and see everyone is looking at me. I'm not sure which guy asked the question.

"Yes."

"Did you see His face?" the Black woman asks. She has an expression of hopefulness.

"No. But He spoke with me."

"I've spoken with Him," she says, "but He did not reveal himself."

No one asked what we spoke of, which is just as well. I'd feel uncomfortable relating the conversation.

"Will we be able to help?" the Latino man said.

"Yes."

"There are others," the Scandinavian woman says.

"Others?" I ask, looking to Sylvana.

She nods slowly. "Like Patrick and Leslie. They have been elevated, but are not Soulmadds."

"That's great," I say, feeling some relief. The more help I can get, the better. "How many of these 'elevated others' are there?"

There is a pause of several seconds.

"How many do you want?" Sylvana asks.

Chapter 29

"The first step toward change is awareness. The second is acceptance."—*Nathaniel Branden*

Before leaving Nicaragua, I tell Sylvana and Apollo I would like to see first-hand what might be going on in parts of the world.

Sylvana nods, and Apollo asks: "Where?"

"Why don't we go to Mexico City? See what's happening."

"Okay," he says. "I haven't been there in decades." He holds out his little-boy hand. "Let's go!"

Sylvana takes his other hand, and the three of us take the Orb transport to Mexico's capital.

* * *

We land on the top level of a parking garage. Immediately, we see several columns of black smoke rising into the hazy, early evening air. There are dozens of fires burning. The sound of shouting and distant machine gun fire is mostly what I hear, but also the sound of a helicopter hovering a few blocks away, a voice saying something in Spanish over the loudspeaker.

We walk to the side and look over the edge, into the street. It is filled with thousands of people, all moving in one direction or the other. It is like a controlled panic, mothers holding babies, children holding each other's hands, young men coming out of stores carrying items that they probably have no use for now. I see a pair of men carrying a big-screen TV, others with arms laden with small household appliances—irons, toasters, other devices that won't work without electricity.

I see a young father holding his three or four year old daughter get shoved to the ground, and immediately two men are on him, one taking his wallet before standing up and disappearing into the crowd. An old woman stands on the sidewalk, crying, as people push past her, going who knows where.

Then I see the bodies, twelve, maybe fifteen of them, piled in a doorway of what looks like a travel agency directly across the street. I look up and down the street and see it's not the only pile.

A car tries to make a left turn out of an alley, inching out into the horde. It honks several times, and people shout what are probably profanities at the driver. Someone with a metal bar walks up to the driver's side and swings at it, smashing the glass into a thousand bits. The driver panics and floors the accelerator, plowing into the crowd, knocking down and running over a dozen people before it gets stuck on the bodies, front wheels off the ground, back tires spinning uselessly. People are screaming and someone pulls open the driver's door and drags him out. Four or five men begin beating him to death.

"This is much worse than I thought," I say, needing to look away.

I watch the hovering helicopter a couple of streets away, still spouting some incomprehensible orders. Rapid-fire gunshots erupt, and the helicopter starts to wobble, then tilts to its side before crashing into the street below. A huge fireball balloons into the sky.

Off to the left, in the corner is a staircase, and I see three guys not much older than me step onto the concrete. They see us and begin a slow walk our way.

"Hey, we have company."

Apollo and Sylvana turn and we face the men as they slowly approach. One of them says something in Spanish.

"They're asking what we're doing here," Apollo says.

We don't reply. One of the men has a rifle slung over his shoulder. Another pulls out a knife that's big enough to gut a pig.

Still, we don't say anything or move. My heart is beating hard as I try to think. I'm not so concerned for myself as I am for Sylvana and Apollo, but I also know they can take care of themselves.

The man who spoke the first time says something, and Apollo translates: "Give us your money."

Again, we don't move or reply, we just stand there waiting as they draw closer.

"Where to next?" Apollo says, taking my hand.

* * *

We land at the airport, in the middle of a runway. No fear of getting run over by a plane. The sun is preparing to set behind the mountains, and it's eerily quiet. Like Mexico City, there are plumes of smoke, mostly off in the distance.

We begin walking. I'm not sure where to go, so we head for the terminal, climbing a stairway to a door. It's locked. We go back down and to the next, with the same results. Through the glass, we see no one. It's deserted.

We walk around to the end of the building, and come to a fence. We look at each other, and I shrug. We zip over the fence, and end up on the street in front of the terminal.

"Looks like a long walk," I say.

Apollo takes my hand. "Let's try Slow Mode."

It turns out "Slow Mode" is a modified version of the Orb transport, but instead of us turning into balls of light and zipping through the sky, we rise a foot or so off the ground and are propelled forward at what seems to be a scary speed, but is probably only 20 miles per hour.

Apollo leads us out of the airport and into the city streets. In minutes, we're on the main drag, a place I've seen many times in pictures and on TV but have never been to.

This evening, however, the Las Vegas Strip is dark. The neon lights, flashing bulbs, and video screens are all dark. Like Mexico

City, there are people in the streets, walking, most heading south. Unlike Mexico City, it seems calm and orderly, but the expressions on the people's faces are mostly filled with concern and fear. Most are walking, dragging their wheeled suitcases by the handles, trudging steadily along.

Of course, we get quite a few looks of surprise as we appear, floating down the street, but no one says anything as we stop on an empty piece of sidewalk. There is no shouting, no talking at all, really. No gunfire, and no helicopters.

We're in front of one of the resorts, a sprawling compound made up mostly of green-tinted windows. I lead Apollo and Sylvana to the entrance, an electronic sliding door that has been pried open. We walk inside to gloomy darkness. Rows of slot machines sit dead. I see movement towards the back and off to the side, a few people doing something. It's difficult to know what they're doing, but I'm guessing it's a restaurant and they're getting food. We go back out the way we came.

While the majority of people are in the street going one way, we go the other, on the sidewalk.

Off to the north, in the distance, Apollo points, though he doesn't say anything.

I see what he's seeing, and I stop dead in my tracks.

They look like just a bunch of dots in the sky, not easy to see in the approaching night, but they become bigger, closer. Technically, it may be a flock, but there are so many that it looks more like a swarm.

Cravens.

Within 15, 20 seconds, they're swooping down out of the sky, and grabbing people. Screams fills the air, both from the victims and the predators. Several dozen are close enough that I am able to hold up my hands and generate enough power to blow them out of the sky. Apollo and Sylvana do this as well, and the sky is raining pieces and chunks of exploded bird-monsters, as well as some of their victims.

I'm at once horrified that my power is not only killing the creatures, but the people as well. I know that they would have died anyway, and in more painful and tortuous ways, but it still sickens me.

The birds keep coming. We do our best to take out as many as we can, but they continue to fly in, seemingly as many of them as there are people on the streets.

Suddenly, maybe ten yards away, a man says "Hey!" very loudly. He has stopped in the northbound lanes of Las Vegas Boulevard and is pointing at us.

Then, the most bizarre thing happens.

His body begins to morph, first by growing bigger—it seems to double in size. The man's clothes begin to split and rip, and for a moment, I think of the Incredible Hulk when his body balloons and grows massive muscle.

But this isn't just muscle.

The face begins to lengthen, the nose becoming beak-like, sharp and pointed. The eyes shift both shape and color, becoming like those of a cat. The mouth has broadened, becoming an immense maw filled with teeth similar to what I imagine a tiger has. The ears have shifted to the top of the head, becoming pointed, like a bat. The neck elongates, and the skin turns to scales, dark and moist. The hair on his head becomes thin and wiry, and his arms turn into something like a T-Rex dinosaur, clawed, short and stubby. The legs, though, become long, angular and muscular, reminding me of a kangaroo. Wings unfold from its back, both leathery and rubbery. The span is . . . I don't know . . . 25, 30 feet. It has grown a long, thick pointy tail, and between its legs . . .

I have no idea what this thing is, but it's worse than any horror movie monster ever made.

It sort of hisses/growls at us, and I find myself taking several steps back.

"A Black Soul," Apollo says. "I haven't seen one in centuries."

Suddenly, several other people on the street begin to transform as well, turning into exact replicas of the creature in front of us.

They then turn and begin attacking the people around them, grabbing them with their jaws and biting through them like a marshmallow. I see one woman literally split in half, her torso falling to the asphalt as the beast begins to munch on her legs. Some of the creatures are hopping while others use their powerful legs to bound 50, 60 feet.

The one standing ten yards away from us takes a halting step, and I get the sense that he's not just appraising us, but he's a bit leery—as if he knows we're not like the others.

"How . . . how do you . . . handle them?" I ask.

"You don't."

He takes my hand, and I take Sylvana's, and we instantly zip away.

* * *

We're somewhere in the middle of the desert, only the glow of the sun behind the mountains in the west.

I know I'm shaken up, my hands and arms trembling. Sylvana takes a seat on the ground, looking shell shocked, while Apollo just stands still, looking off in the distance, as if watching.

"Excuse my language, but what the fuck?"

Apollo doesn't move, just keeps looking. "A Dymortis creation from the middle ages," he says in his little-boy voice. "Many think the Plague, the Black Death killed millions, but it was them."

"Did Dymortis send them into hiding and just decide to pull them out of his bag of tricks now? Just for us?"

"Wicked fast, and completely evil. Once they transform, there's no trace of humanity left in them. Their jaws can break steel. They're faster than any creature on Earth, and their appetite is unending."

"I thought they were extinct," Sylvana says.

"I would have thought that too," Apollo says, still staring out at the landscape.

"What are you looking at?" I ask.

He points. I don't see what he sees—and then I do, sort of. It's a plume of dust in the distance, miles away.

"They found us," he says.

"What? How could they possibly do that?"

"Their eyesight is unbelievable, and they can smell blood for miles."

My eyes are locked on the dust cloud, and I notice it seems to lessen. Maybe it's the night playing tricks on my eyes, but then I see the cloud has really gotten smaller, almost gone.

"Maybe they lost us," I say. "It looks like—"

And then I see why the dust cloud is dissipating.

They have taken flight, coming straight at us. Fifty, a hundred, I don't know.

Sylvana stands, and once again we hold hands.

* * *

When we arrive back in Chicago, it takes several moments for our eyes to adjust, but it's quickly clear this is not familiar territory. Everything has changed.

We stand, eyes wide, mouths open, not believing what we're seeing. I know I don't.

The landscape hasn't just changed, it's been obliterated. Buildings that had once been homes are now piles of rubble. Large chunks of stone and brick are scattered around with other bits of debris. Every single structure has been leveled.

There are several areas where fires are burning casting eerie glows in the night sky.

"What happened?" I ask, already knowing the answer.

"I did not think he would do it," Sylvana says. "I underestimated him."

"You underestimated his hatred and his fear," Apollo says. "He's now consumed with it, and has lost his reason."

"He *bombed* it?" I ask.

"A highly concentrated nuclear weapon, I would guess" Apollo says. "His will to kill you is overwhelming him."

Chapter 30

"Thinking is hard work. One can't bear burdens and ideas at the same time."—Remy de Gourmont

It takes us a while to find the entrance to the underground tunnels since the men's room that hid it was destroyed. Once we located the opening, it took us—mostly me—close to an hour to clear the passage and the stairway down. In the tunnel, things were better, but only by degrees.

The golf cart was still there, its roof crushed by part of the collapsed ceiling. We skirted around it and began walking. Most of the lights were out, a couple flickering, but there was enough to help us find our way. Some of the concrete lining the walls and ceiling had broken off, leaving big chunks littering the ground, and exposing major cracks created by the bomb. But it had held.

As we get closer to the control center, we begin seeing a few people, some standing, some sitting, all looking shocked. I would ask each if they're okay, and they nod, numbly.

We reach the entrance to the Control Center and begin to see some casualties, bodies laid out in the tunnel. I count eleven. Several more wounded are inside, one man sitting with his back to the wall, holding a towel to his bleeding head. The area itself is in fairly good shape, all things considered. There are some big cracks snaking through the concrete walls, and some light fixtures are dangling precariously, but overall, it held.

We make it to the conference room, which is empty. Apollo hurries off to his lab.

I walk around, checking the other rooms, and find Patrick and another man attending to a woman whose shoulder is bleeding.

"How many casualties?" I ask.

Patrick's head snaps around at the sound of my voice. "Wow, I'm glad you're back. Several dozen wounded, but mostly minor. I think sixteen dead." He continues to wrap what looks like an elastic bandage under her arm and over her shoulder while the woman grimaces in pain.

"Is everything down?" I ask as Sylvana leaves to check other rooms.

"I don't know, haven't had time to check."

Apollo comes up behind me. "It fried the circuitry," he says. "Shield's down, all the electronic equipment is out." He pauses. "I guess we'll have to reevaluate what a bomb shelter can take with a direct hit."

I try to think. I know we have to leave, but I'm not sure where to go.

"He took out his own men," Patrick said. "We were watching the monitors when it went off. All his men, tanks and weapons were sitting out there when . . . *ka-boom.*"

"He'll be back," I say. "Maybe at daybreak."

"Why?" Patrick asks, having finished bandaging the woman and turning towards me. "Is he going to gloat over what he did? Take pictures? Put them in his fucking journal?"

I take a deep breath before I answer.

"He wants to claim my dead body."

* * *

Sylvana returns with Mr. B, and the five of us head to the conference room. The monitor screens are all black, and half of

252

the lights are out, but it's enough.

"So," Mr. B says in an attempt at a light-hearted voice, "how was your trip?"

I consider several answers, then give up. Instead, I have a question:

"What would it take to destroy Dymortis?"

He frowns, pondering this for a few seconds. "I'm not entirely sure it's possible. Marginalize him, maybe. Knock him down a few pegs. Scare him off, possibly. But destroy him?" He shakes his head.

"What about the Ark?"

"The Ark of the Covenant? That would certainly paralyze him."

"But not destroy him? I thought you said anyone who opens it would be immediately killed."

"Humans, yes. Dymortis is a fallen angel, cast out by God." He pauses. "How do you kill an angel?"

I think of my conversation in Nicaragua, levitating, seeing the vague figure in the clouds. *"He is but a wayward child which I love, and agonize over."*

"We need to find the Ark."

He nods.

"Who has it?" Patrick asks.

"I am sure Dymortis found it, took it, and Dunraven has it hidden away for him," Sylvana says. "He knows it is his Achilles' heel, and the only way he can ensure it is not used against him is if he controls it."

"Okay," Patrick says, "so where would he hide it?"

We sit in a long silence, thinking. I'm praying. God knows where it is. If He wanted us to find it, to use it, He would reveal it.

"I believe it might be closer than we think," Apollo says.

We all look at him, but he says nothing further.

Then a thought comes to me. Something, again, that was said in Nicaragua. But not said by God. Something I said to him.

"I know you want me to think outside of the box, but I don't even know where the box is."

But now, I think I do.

* * *

Figuring Dunraven would be back—and maybe toss another bomb our way—we decide to evacuate. We gather as many Challengers as we can and tell them where to go, and how to get there. They'll have to carry the wounded out, but they seem relieved to be getting out of this place.

The five of us find our way back to the exit and go above ground. Not wanting to hold us back, Sylvana tells me, Patrick and Apollo to go on ahead while she keeps pace with the slower Mr. B.

"We might take the Orb, but we will see you there," Sylvana says. "Just remember—"

"Stay true and pay attention," I say.

She smiles, and the three of us head off.

Walking through the streets and avoiding rubble is a whole new experience. Nothing is the same. The asphalt is cracked and buckled, but for the most part, it's an easy walk. A few fires are burning, but there is no sign of life. I debated about just zipping over, using the Orb transport, but I wanted to take in what happened. It's disheartening, but it also strengthens my resolve. Dunraven, in his attempt to kill me, slaughtered thousands and thousands of innocent people sitting in their homes, while they sat in the dark, maybe eating dinner. With the Cravens back, and now the Black Souls let loose, I'm not sure how much of humanity will be left in the next few days.

As we walk further away from the epicenter of the bomb, the damage lessens. Buildings are damaged, but haven't collapsed. Street lights and power poles lie useless in the street, and there is not as much debris.

I suddenly stop. "I have to go back."

"Why?" Patrick asks.

"We left the President at the Manor House. Dunraven will find him and may use him again."

Patrick looks at me curiously. "Dunraven may find him, but won't be able to use him."

"What . . . what did you do to him?"

"I didn't do anything."

"Patrick. No games. What happened?"

"Well . . . I was busy watching over the monitors, so I sent a couple of the Challengers down to feed him."

"Okay," I said, thinking that made Quinn sound like a caged animal . . . which, I guess, he was. "Then what happened?"

"They said he tried escaping from his cell and they had to use fatal force against him."

"Do you believe them?"

"I played the video back of them walking into his cell, and he definitely tried to escape. The guy had some . . . well, I would normally have called it super-human strength, but based on some of the stuff we've seen in the last year, I guess it's not unusual. Quinn attacked, knocked one Challenger flat out. He came after the other two, but they managed to subdue him, and the next thing I see is them just punching and kicking the Quinn, over and over and over. I think all his child molesting finally caught up to him."

"Do you think he was dead?"

"Yes. The Challengers did their job."

I think this over. I had kind of hoped Quinn could have "seen the light" and changed his ways, but apparently not. "Well, he deserved what he got, and now he can rot in hell."

It takes us an hour to reach our destination. In this area, there is no damage, and we pass the ornate entrance to the Meadows. The gates are closed and locked. We walk past, and as the cemetery comes up on our right, I feel this dread come upon me, remnants of my old life.

We stop and look through the chain link fence, out over the dead grass blotted with snow, some graves marked with headstones, others with just markers placed in the earth. I recall all the times I walked through there, reading the names and dates, and thinking about what their lives might have been like. A man of 93, a woman of 61, a 3 year old girl.

"Look," Apollo says, pointing through the chain link.

There's a mist that has formed, a mist I had seen before when

I lived here, though it was fairly rare. But now the mist was different. Instead of being spread out somewhat evenly over the ground, this was almost like small groups of clouds. Then, to my surprise, I realized they were shapes.

And they were coming towards us.

Apollo takes several steps back, ending up in the middle of the street. We step back with him, keeping our eyes on the strange globs of fog.

Eight, nine, ten of them came up to the fence, rose, and hovered above it. They were human forms, but not really human at all. Their faces were gaunt, elongated. The eyes were large ovals that glowed a faint red. It was if they wore hooded robes, but unlike the one I wore in Nicaragua, these were long and flowing. The hands were skeletonized, with bony fingers. One opened its mouth, showing rows of razor teeth and a forked tongue. It hissed at us.

"Shadow People," Apollo says. "They can't hurt you physically, but they'll mess with your soul."

"*Chosen One*," the middle ghost says in an unearthly whisper, "*you shall not pass.*"

"Get behind me Satan." I say this calmly, without fear. "You are not welcome here."

It hisses again, its head jutting out for a moment like a jack-in-the-box. The others hiss with it, floating in mid-air. But they make no move.

We turn and begin walking again, moving towards the staging area where we can go into the tunnels. I keep an eye on the Shadow People, and they follow our progression, move along with us, but stay on the inside of the fence.

We reach the entrance and scramble inside. I'm not sure they're going to follow, so I keep watch behind us.

In the darkness of the staging area, where Patrick and the crew had brought in coffin for refurbishing, Patrick and I hunt around the work table blindly for the flashlights. I eventually find one, turn it on, and that helps Patrick find two others. He hands one to Apollo.

"Wait," a voice says behind us, and we turn to see Sylvana and Mr. B. "We will come with you," she says.

"You're welcome to," I tell them, "but it's a long walk, and we can't use the Orb down here."

They look at each other.

"Maybe we will wait here, in case there's trouble," Mr. B says.

"Did you see the Shadow People?" Patrick asks.

"Yes. More remnants of the evil past."

"More?" Patrick asks.

"Yeah," I say, hoping to explain. "There's these things called the Black Souls that . . . well, you never want to meet one."

Patrick looks at me warily. "Good. Cravens, Shadow People, Black Souls. I can't wait to see who shows up next."

"Can the Shadow People follow us down here?" I ask. "Because they didn't seem to want to go over the fence."

"They can go anywhere," Apollo says. "That's just their way of making you think they have boundaries." He pauses. "Usually, they're invisible."

"Man," Patrick says. "This just keeps getting better and better."

"Don't worry," Apollo adds. "They can only inhabit your soul when they're visible. Otherwise, they just watch."

"Yeah, that helps."

* * *

We wave to Sylvana and the Professor, then begin to make our way through the tunnels beneath the cemetery, flashlights leading the way.

"How did you guys meet?" Apollo asks.

"We worked at the same place."

"Yeah, Collin was known as Jake and was the biggest dweeb you've ever seen."

"More of a dweeb than Greg?" I ask.

"Greg wasn't a dweeb, he was more of a schlub."

"But at least I was a cool dweeb."

"There's no such thing. Only other dweebs think dweebs are cool."

"Well, maybe one day, you'll graduate to 'cool dweeb' status."

Apollo giggles.

"Which were you," Patrick asks the boy, "a dweeb, a geek or a nerd?"

A pause as Apollo thinks about it. "Maybe I'm all three."

"No, that's a cop-out. You have to be more of one than the others."

"Perhaps. But then maybe it is not for me to decide. Often, people like to define themselves, even if they are delusional—such as the male who believes they are a 'ladies' man' when in reality, they have quite a poor record with females."

"That sounds like someone I know," I say.

"You're talking about Greg, right?" Patrick asks.

I glance at him and can see his smirk in the dim light behind the flashlight. "Yeah, Greg was the delusional ladies' man," I say.

"So, which category would you place me in?" Apollo asks.

"Nerd," Patrick and I say in unison.

Apollo thinks this over. "Yes, I think that may be correct. I do tend to exhibit more attributes of a nerd than a geek. I know that—"

An unearthly scream wails from somewhere deep in the tunnels, in the direction we're heading.

We stop dead in our tracks.

"What the hell was that?" Patrick asks. "It's not another creation from the fallen world, is it?"

We wait, and listen. Nothing.

"Most likely, the Shadow People," Apollo says.

As if on cue, another wail. This time, closer. More distinct.

Apollo looks to his left at Patrick, then to me. "Are we going to stand here and wait for them, or go back?"

I put my hand on his shoulder. "Funny thing. I'm not scared. At all."

Apollo looks from me, over to Patrick.

"Me too," Patrick says, not very convincingly, as another scream comes at us.

Chapter 31

"Change your thoughts and you change your world."—*Norman Vincent Peale*

They come from both directions—the front and the back. Wispy tendrils of mist snake their way along the walls, the floor, the ceiling. Forms take shape, still a distance off, just within the far range of our flashlights. I'm turned, facing the way we came, watching the ghosts of the Shadow People begin to group behind us.

I sense Patrick's fear, though he would never admit it, and I would never ask him to. I need him to be cool and focus.

"What should we do?" I ask Apollo calmly.

"Nothing."

I glance at him, and he seems very much at peace. "Care to elaborate on that?"

The mist draws closer. Several of the forms are now full-body apparitions, with legs and arms jutting out from their capes. One has hair like dreadlocks, floating in the air. The only thing more menacing than the glowing red eyes are the razor-like teeth that seem to glisten even though they're not real.

"It's like Satan, Dymortis, Beelzebub, whatever name he chooses . . . He may whisper, talk to you, get inside your head, imitate your own voice, try to convince you . . . but if you just disregard him, think about something else, block him from your mind . . . nothing happens."

One of the forms draws closer, bony skeleton fingers reaching out to me. Something like a smile crosses its face.

"So you're saying if we just ignore these things, act like they're not there, they'll go away?"

The skeleton-finger comes within an inch of my nose, and I feel a cold chill coming off it.

"I doubt they'll go away," the little boy says. "But if you show them that they don't matter, they can't hurt you. They don't have the ability to physically interact with the corporeal world."

"*You are missssstaaaken, ssssmall one,*" a Shadow Being says from behind me. "*We have been ssssupplied with new powerssss ssssinccccce our lasssst encounter with yoooouuuu.*"

I take my eyes off the floating finger and peek at Apollo. He has no reaction—as if he hadn't heard it.

I look back at the finger, which has shifted to the whole hand, palm reaching for me, as it were going to grab onto my face like a basketball. I stare at it, a little mesmerized. I can see through it, and yet also see ligatures and tendon connecting the bone.

Apollo turns towards me. "You know, I was thinking with Dymortis turning against his own, he may be running out of options."

This breaks the trance, and I force myself to turn to him. "You may have a point."

Apollo begins walking forward again, straight into the group of Shadow People, his child's body breaking them into a formless fog. One of them avoids the boy, shooting up to the ceiling, then, as Apollo passes beneath, launches itself at him like a football player trying to tackle a quarterback from behind—arms spread, head down, squealing.

And it passes through him with no noticeable effect. Apollo continues walking.

I grab Patrick's upper arm and drag him in the same direction. "Tell me about Leslie," I say, turning to look at him.

He frowns at me. I know he had been as transfixed with what he was seeing as I had, his eyes looking somewhat far-off.

"What—what do you mean tell you about her?"

"Are you interested in each other?"

There are sounds erupting around us, a mixture that can bring chills. It's like a combination of creaking door, squealing bird, nails on a chalkboard, and cats attacking. The forms become streaks of gray light, shooting past us before circling back around to come at us.

I focus ahead, watching Apollo march down the tunnel

"Dang, that's cold," Patrick says.

"Focus. Leslie. Are you interested in a possible relationship?"

"Leslie?" He closes his eyes as I guide him. "Yes."

"She seems very level-headed."

"She's . . . not really my type."

I glance at him and see he's smirking.

"Yeah, I know your type. Basically any female with a nice smile."

"That's not true. I—"

The unearthly screams intensify. More Shadow People have appeared, dozens, hundreds, so many that they have all blended into one swirling mass. It's like walking through some kind of bizarre fog storm. I can literally feel them passing through my body—or at least giving a good impression of it.

"Remember that one girl you dated for like a day and a half?" I say over the shrieks and screeches. "What was her name? Kristin?"

"Krystle. And it was a week and a half."

"Why did she break up with you again? Something about you being too into yourself?"

The mass of gray screeching spinning vapor has intensified to the point that it's all I can see. The beam of the flashlight only seems to make it worse, with the light bouncing off it, like using high-beams in the fog. I turn it off and all goes dark.

"No, she said I was too cute."

I feel the mist brush against my skin.

"Why would a girl breakup with someone over that?"

"I read into it that it implied I wasn't as manly as she thought she wanted."

The shapes produce a strange glow in the dark tunnels, malevolent ghosts trying to scare us into going away. The glowing red eyes bounce around before they come screaming at us.

It's claustrophobic, unsettling and distracting.

"Apollo, I think we made a wrong turn somewhere."

"I agree," he says from somewhere not too far ahead of us. "We should go back."

This is kind of admitting defeat, that the Shadow People have done their job, but I have another idea.

We turn and head back the way we came, the alien creatures not letting up.

* * *

I don't know how long it took us to get back to the staging area, but the ghosts abandoned their attack just a few feet from the entrance. Sylvana and Mr. B are standing near the exit, looking worried.

"Are you okay?" Mr B asks.

"We're fine," I say. "Just a haunted house trick."

"No," Sylvana says, "not a trick. The Shadow People can do real damage."

I turn the flashlight on Patrick, who, I realize, hasn't spoken for several minutes. Eyes wide and glassy, mouth partially open. He looks hypnotized.

Sylvana sees this too, and doesn't hesitate, stepping forward, placing her hand on his forehead. Her ring begins to glow softly.

"In the name of the Father, the Son, and the Holy Spirit, cast the evil from him." She bows her head in prayer.

I mimic her, laying my hand on his shoulder, and praying as well. I feel cold emanating from his skin, even through his shirt and coat. Mr. B follows suit, then Apollo, placing both his hands on Patrick's stomach.

Minutes pass.

Inside Patrick's mind, there is only confusion, the beasts chattering inside his head.

Then, screams, both from Patrick and the intruders. Theirs are cold, squealing, painful. His is blood-curdling.

And then, all at once, it stops. And Patrick collapses to the floor.

Sylvana kneels next to him, gently caressing his forehead.

"He is asleep," she says.

We lay him out so he is comfortable, and I take off my jacket to give him a makeshift pillow for his head.

And then we wait.

* * *

Thirty minutes later, he begins to stir, mumbling. I turn the flashlight on and point it towards him—not directly on him, I don't want to blind him—but enough to see if he's okay. His eyes flutter open, and he looks around, then sits up.

"Where . . . Who are you?"

"It's Collin. Sylvana, Mr. Burkfelt and Apollo are here too."

"Okay." He looks around, rubbing his bald head. "Man, I've got a headache."

"I bet. You just relax." I look over at Sylvana.

He'll be okay, she tells me.

* * *

"So, my idea of going through that underground opening and into The Meadows didn't work out," I say as we stand outside. We're at the corner of the property, at the intersection, but there's no cars, no people, no traffic signal, no power.

"There's only one option," Mr. B says.

"It will be heavily guarded," Apollo says.

I nod. We underestimated Dunraven and Dymortis before. I will try not to again.

I look up at the sky. The clouds are low, and have a decidedly pink hue.

"Red Sky is upon us," Sylvana says.

"I'm still not clear what it means, other than being ominous," I say.

"Yes, it is difficult to know exactly what may happen," Mr. B says. "It is certainly a signal to his people that the end is near. But what he has planned, I do not know."

We stand in silence. Patrick is just about his normal self, only more quiet, still a bit shocked at whatever he went through.

"It may be possible," Apollo says, cryptically.

"What may be possible?" I ask.

"To know what Dymortis has planned." He pauses, and we wait. It's obvious to me he's thinking, trying to sort through whatever idea he has. "You would need somewhere quiet. A place without distraction. No sound. No light. No sensation. A place for complete relaxation, concentration and meditation."

"Perceptual isolation," Mr. B says. "A sensory deprivation chamber."

"Exactly," Apollo says.

I look at each of them.

"I know," I say. "I know where to go, and what to do. I've done it before." I pause. "But I need to go alone."

"Of course," Apollo says. "But we'll walk with you there."

* * *

I step onto the porch of my former home, feeling a peace come upon me. I put my hand on the doorknob and turn to the others. "I don't know how long I'll be."

"That is okay, Collin. You do what you need to do," Sylvana says.

I smile and nod, then open the door and go inside.

Of course, all is dark. It's not hard for me to find my way around, to the stairs, to the second floor, to the spare bedroom.

Despite the deep cold, I begin to get undressed. Coat, shoes, socks, pants, underwear. I stand there for a moment in only my shirt and go to the window, looking out over the graveyard. I see my four compatriots walking through the grass, around the tombstones, heading for what I used to think of as my father's house. They will wait for me there.

At one point, Patrick looks back, and up at me. I hold my hand up in a silent wave, telling him all will be okay. He smile and waves back.

I turn from the window and begin to unbutton my shirt. As I do, I notice my tattoo is glowing blue. Calm settles over me. I let the shirt fall to the floor, then step over to the casket. I open the lid and step in.

I lower myself, holding onto the lid, then lay back, pulling the cover down, settling into the peacefulness. It is not completely dark as the tattoo glows softly, but it begins to dim, and all is black. Warmth begins to fill me, not just on the outside.

I close my eyes and wait.

Chapter 32

"When a man has no strength, if he leans on God, he becomes powerful."—D.L. Moody

With all the events that we'd been through, it takes a while for the peace and calm to come, but I finally feel it settling into me. There comes a point where my mind finally empties, and the line between consciousness and sleep is almost invisible.

I float.

Blackness. Quiet. Darkness. Peace.

I realize I am seeking Jill, whispering for her, hoping she would show herself. After some time, and disappointment, I instead seek Dunraven. This comes almost immediately. The blackness turns dark gray. From the depths, the Earth appears, as if I'm viewing from deep in space. It grows closer, or I'm drawing near. The big blue marble speckled with clouds becomes big, slowly spinning as I get closer. Except the clouds are not fluffy white, nor a stormy gray. They almost all have a red tint.

As I fly in closer—I'm not really flying, but there's no other word for it—there is a vast ocean, not of blue, but more purple, as though the Red Sky has infected it. Then, a large land mass comes into view and I recognize it as India. I glide over it as if I'm a satellite. Up near the far north, there is an immense mountain range—the Himalayas. If I remember my geography correctly, this is Nepal or Southwestern China. As I get even closer, I can see between peaks there is a deep gorge, as deep as the mountains are high. I am being drawn there, sweeping down past stone and rock, sliding closer to the bottom. As I see the ground coming, things slow, until I come to a stop. Of course, it's not really me, not my body, not my physical presence. But I see, hear, smell and feel as if I were.

In front of me is the man I know now as Lord Harod Dunraven XIV. He is sitting on a rock, hunched forward, staring at the ground.

"He pains me," he says. "I thought I could convert him, but he turned on me."

"Stop obsessing, Dunny," another voice says. "We need to focus as it starts to come together."

I see the figure that is speaking. As Patrick called him, an ugly dude in top hat and tails. But he is not dancing or looking very jovial at all.

"How are the ravens doing?" Dymortis asks. "How much as been added to the slurry?"

"You know how many souls have been added to your collection—count them."

Dymortis shoots Dunraven an annoyed grimace. "I have many beasts collecting souls. Humor me."

A long pause from Dunraven. Then: "The last I checked, twenty-two million gallons."

"What is wrong with you Dunny? You can't be distracted by that triviality of a boy."

Dunraven raised his head, and I see just how old and tired he has become. His skin, while never youthful, is deeply lined with wrinkled and spotted with red and dark brown patches. His eyes are droopy, watery and bloodshot, his lips dry and chapped.

"He *pains* me."

"You have some affection for him."

"No," Dunraven croaks. "He worries me as he has escaped all of my traps. All of them."

"He is the Chosen One. What did you expect?"

"You knew and you did not tell me."

"I did not know. I just figured it out before you did."

"You promised me . . ."

"What is it this time?" Dymortis asked. "What have I forgotten now?"

"You have not forgotten. You never forget."

"This is true."

"Then keep your word."

There is a pause of a few moments as Dymortis stares at Dunraven. Then he begins to laugh

"You have always kept it before," Dunraven adds, wearily.

Dymortis turns serious. "Perhaps you should let it go. Let him go. Your fascination is clouding your judgement."

"He can ruin us."

"Only if you let him. We are so far ahead, and you keep doubling back to try to trip him up, slowing us down. If you had let it be, we'd be done now."

"I did what I had to do."

"A bomb on that house? You were in such a hurry, you didn't even check to see if he was there."

A long pause.

"He *pains* me."

A longer pause as they stare at each other.

"Alrighty, I'll keep my word. I'll allow you to have the serum."

"But there are strings."

"Of course. There always are."

A few moments of silence.

"I will turn my attention elsewhere," Dunraven says. "But he will cause a problem."

"I don't doubt it. I just don't think it will be a problem I can't handle. You do. I think you need to trust me."

Dunraven sighs. "I do. You asked me to run things, to put the pieces in place. I need to be wary of those that wish to undermine that."

"I understand. I just don't need you to be distracted. Sometimes a steamroller is better than suspicion. How solid is the ISP?"

"There is some dissension in Russia, which I anticipated. It is under control. China is surprisingly strong, considering I thought they would balk. A few concessions helped. Otherwise, the ISP is in the final stages of locking down every country and continent. The world is in darkness and on the brink of full chaos."

"The Black Souls have been unleashed," Dymortis said.

Dunraven look warily at his master. "Isn't that ahead of schedule?"

"You were behind schedule. It was time. In fact, they made their debut with your son."

Dunraven scowls. "He is not my son."

Dymortis smiles. "That's right. Not your seed, for you have run dry. Oh, that reminds me, that last seed of yours has checked in. I put him in the drooling room. He is not of much use anymore."

"Jacob killed my son?"

"No, not Jacob, but dead just the same. And no one will miss him."

"You should be grateful that he did so much to put the plan in place. Without him, we wouldn't be where we are."

Dymortis smiles at him, eyes twinkling, and nods. I understand that look. It said *You can believe that if you want.*

"My apologies," Dymortis says.

A very long, awkward pause. Dunraven looks around, as if he heard a sound.

"What?" Dymortis asks.

"Do you . . . sense something? Like another here?"

"You are far too conspiratorial. I know that is your talent, to create them, but I think they have come back around to bite you."

Dunraven doesn't react to this, only keeps looking around with his watery eyes.

"You should get back," Dymortis says. "The Shadow People have been keeping track of your friends. They're at Rest Haven. They've pretty much figured out how to avoid the soul inversion."

"Azayakana," Dunraven says.

"Yes . . . the little brat pains *me*. I wish I had killed him when I had the chance. Anyway, you need to get back."

"If they are at Rest Haven, they must be on the hunt."

"Yes, they're sniffing around. Maybe they even think they know."

"It is impossible to find."

"Except nothing is impossible."

"It will bring death to all who touch it."

"Except he cannot die."

Dunraven sighs. It appears he has aged even further in the last few minutes. "Can I receive the serum, please? My bones ache."

"I'm sure they do. It is on the ledge. I must go."

And—blink—he was gone. Not even a puff of smoke. I guess when he doesn't need to impress someone, he doesn't put on a show.

Dunraven slowly got up, as if his arthritic legs were not cooperating. He shuffled over to the rock wall, and felt along the stone. His fingers came up with a small pouch, and he opened it, removed a brown bottle, and popped off the top. He quickly put the bottle to his lips and downed it. He dropped the bottle to the ground, and shuffled back to sit again.

I began to rise, moving back into the heavens. Before I leave the gorge, I see Dunraven raise his head and look around again as if he sensed me there.

* * *

I rise through the atmosphere, above the reddish clouds, the Earth falling below me, seemingly becoming smaller, soon nothing but the size of a basketball, then a marble, then a speck. Once again, I am in complete silence and darkness.

I float.

There is a pain. Not a sharp pain, but dull and throbbing. Small at first, kind of pulsing in my chest. Then growing larger. My heart literally aches. I'm wondering if I'm in cardiac arrest. It is bearable, but uncomfortable.

I focus, trying to push the pain away, and . . . it seems to work. The dull throbbing seems to actually lift away and out of me.

And I am at peace again.

I float.

I lay, wondering if more is to come. Another vision? More pain? Whispering? I wait, and wait.

There is a light knocking.

I open my eyes, though there is nothing to see.

Then, again, light knocking on the lid of the coffin.

I lift my arms and push on the lid. It opens, and I see no one. Compared to the blackness of the coffin, there is plenty of light, although it is still night, and the power is still out.

I sit up, and see a figure in the corner by the window, standing in a shadow.

"Were you tired of waiting?" I ask.

"Yes, Collin," a female voice says. "There is no more to see."

"Sylvana?" I ask. Except it didn't sound like Sylvana.

My heart begins to race as I climb out of the coffin and step towards the shadow.

"Is this another vision? Or are you really here?"

"I am here, Collin."

I walk up to Jill and wrap my arms around her. She is real, flesh and blood, and her skin smells faintly of baby powder. Her arms embrace me, and her lips find mine. The kiss is beyond my dreams, so soft, so warm, so loving. I have missed her so much.

Eventually, it ends, and I pull my head back to look at her lovely face. It is angelic.

"I'm so glad you're here."

"Me too."

"How long can you stay?"

"I'm with you forever, Collin. We never have to be apart." She pulls back, looking at my chest. "It's glowing blue," she says of my tattoo. "It is near."

"What? The Ark?"

Even in the dim light, it seems like her eyes twinkle.

"You should get dressed," she says. "There is a lot ahead of us."

Chapter 33

"A refuge for the coming night. A future of eternal light. No one gets to their heaven without a fight."—Armor and Sword, Music: Geddy Lee and Alex Lifeson / Lyric: Neil Peart

I'm so excited to be with Jill again, I can hardly think of anything else. We walk through the graveyard, and approach Dunraven's old house—the one I grew up in—to see my four friends sitting on the porch. Behind them, I see the door is boarded shut.

"Look who I found," I say, and Sylvana immediately rises and approaches us.

"Jill, it is so good to see you again."

They hug, and the other three come forward also to greet her.

"We should get going," Mr. B says. "The sun will come up soon."

We walk back the way we came, through the cemetery and to the street. We turn left and head to the entrance of the Meadows.

My joy at being with Jill seeps away as we stand 50 feet from the gates, a gigantic Craven perched on top, watching us.

"He knew we would come," I say.

Beyond the one standing guard, I can make out several more on the roof of the main Meadows building.

I hold out my hands, pointing them towards the creature, and as I do, it squawks, flaps its wings and launches itself at us. I feel the power surge erupt from me, and the giant dinosaur bird bursts into flames. The fiery carcass zooms at us, and we duck, the still squealing monster flying over our heads and landing in the street, wings and body flailing in pain.

This sets off the other birds, who take off from their perches, sailing into the air before turning to dive-bomb at us. Four of us—Apollo, Jill, Sylvana and myself—raise our arms to the sky and take aim. Six, eight, ten of the Cravens explode like meteors, falling to the ground, shrieking.

We stand there as the bodies burn, their screams finally going silent while their flesh crackles and pops in the flames. Eerie yellow/orange light surrounds us.

"Look," Jill says, pointing.

The Shadow People have returned, a line of them standing guard, silently floating on the other side of the gates.

I turn to Patrick. "You know what to do."

"Think about basketball," he says, and winks. But his eyes seem wary.

I nod. It's the best I can hope for.

"Ready?" I ask.

The others say yes or nod, and we pause a moment before zipping ourselves over the tall gate. The instant we land, the Shadow People are upon us, hissing and speaking in shrill voices, spinning around us. I do my best to ignore them, like making my way through a swarm of mosquitos.

"*Laus Deo!*" Jill says, and the ghosts shriek in their unearthly voices. But they back off, somewhat, keeping their distance.

We walk to the entrance of the Meadows Polo Club and Apollo pulls on the handle. The door opens easily. Patrick and I pull out our flashlights as we enter the darkened club. Sylvana, Apollo and Mr. B follow suit, and as we step into the lobby, the Shadow People follow us inside, hissing and whispering. We pass through the entry to the restaurant and see something that is as horrific as the bird-monsters and ghost-people we've encountered so far—but it's somehow much more disturbing.

Without the need of the flashlights, we can see ghosts illuminated in the room. They are all naked, engaged in some kind of supernatural orgy. Though there is no sound, the children's faces are writhing in pain, silent screams coming from their mouths.

I close my eyes, trying to will the images away, pushing the horror and disgust away. *This is not real*, I tell myself, except I know it was, at least at some point in time. My wishing it away does no good.

"Let's go," I say, and lead my small troop towards the back. I keep my head down, flashlight pointed at the ground, ignoring the writhing around me.

We reach a door and I throw it open, passing out into a well-maintained area of grass that leads out to the polo yards. I stop and turn to watch the others come through the door, frowns and disturbed expressions on their faces. In the windows, I see the ghosts of children standing at the glass, some silently banging on the glass and crying.

"Don't look back," I advise the others as I turn and lead them out into the grass.

Light from the new day is beginning to glow from the east, but it's muted by ominous red clouds. I look around at the grounds and see a few buildings—one, farther in the distance, is the one that Patrick had been held in, a fortress-like structure.

"What do you think?" I ask, pointing.

"Yeah," Mr. B says. "I would guess that's the most likely."

"Halt!" a male voice calls out. *"Stay where you are."*

We all turn to see four men in black vests, black shirts, black pants and black shoes marching towards us with guns drawn.

"What now?" Patrick asks.

"Regulators," Apollo says.

The men raise their weapons, aiming at us.

We raise our arms, ready to do battle. I just hope I can get—

Then the men begin to transform. Just like in Las Vegas, they morph into the Black Souls, monstrosities that I never could have imagined.

Without waiting for the transformation to become complete, I unleash a burst of energy, and two of the creatures tumble backwards . . . but unlike the Cravens, they do not explode or catch fire.

They just fall back, flailing on the ground. Their kangaroo-like legs attempt to gain purchase on the grass, but have trouble. Sylvana and Apollo also shoot energy at the other two monsters, and as they collapse back on the ground, their guns go off—fortunately, the shots go wild and hit nothing.

"We've gotta figure out their weakness," I say, sounding more panicked than I wanted.

"The back of their heads," Apollo says. "It's the only soft spot on their bodies that isn't armored."

Two of the Black Souls are on their backs, legs flailing in the air, the other two are on their sides, trying to roll over, trying to get up.

Apollo runs up to one of them, kneels down, and sticks his hands out. The zap comes quick, and almost immediately, the monster just stops moving. He then hurries to the other one on its side and does the same thing, silencing it.

The other two are still on their backs, growling and thrashing like giant bugs that can't upright themselves.

"Let's go!" Patrick says, turning to run towards the building in the distance.

The rest of us follow suit, except we zip ourselves there instead of running.

We face the building and its armored door.

I stick out my arms and shoot a blast at it.

Nothing happens.

I look at the others and Apollo, Sylvana and Jill reach out with their arms as well. We all aim and blast at it. The door blows in with a bang and a crash as it hits the ground and slides.

Behind us, we hear the approaching howls of the two Black Souls. We hurry inside, Mr. B, Sylvana and Patrick running into the hallway, Jill and I taking positions just inside the door, out of view.

The beasts burst through the doorway, one after the other, barreling towards Apollo, Sylvana and Mr. B hurrying down the hallway. From behind the monsters, Jill and I immediately take aim, shooting the energy at the back of their freaky heads. The blasts knock both creatures down, sprawling on the concrete, dead.

Jill and I look at each other, and I nod. We do our best to step around the animals, their heads smoking.

I notice as I look down the hall that the lights are on here. The building has power.

We stand, and I look around. There is door after door lining the hallway, each exactly like the other, a drab olive green color. I try the knob of the closest door. It's locked, of course.

With my hand still on the knob, I let out a small surge of energy, and the knob simply falls off. I push the door open. Inside the light is off, but it's easy enough to see the pile of bones that fills half the room. I'm no bone specialist, but they seem human, and small, like those of children. A couple of skulls seem to confirm this.

Apollo tries another door. Inside, more bones. A third door reveals a half-decomposed adult body shackled to a chair. In the corner, more bones.

Door after door reveals varying degrees of death and torture. Bodies suspended from ceilings—both adult and children—piles of bones, decaying corpses. In one room is what appears to be an autopsy table with a female corpse cut open and organs removed.

We continue to move down the hall. Behind us, echoing down the concrete walls, are the sounds of the Shadow People. They approach, floating slowly down the hallway, but keeping their distance. They are dark, smoky shadows in the fluorescent lights.

"Any idea what their weakness might be?" I ask Apollo.

"Evoking the name of our Lord and Savior keeps them at bay, but I don't know what might kill them."

I sigh. These stupid beings are going to be like gnats on us.

We eventually reach the end, and the final door on the left leads to a stairwell. I pause.

"Don't you think that if there are other levels, there would be an elevator?"

The others stare at me, and Mr. B nods slowly. "Yes, I would say so."

"But there isn't one," Patrick says.

I look at the wall he's standing next to. It marks the end of the hall, and looks like it's made of concrete like all the other walls. But there's a crease in it, running horizontal from side to side, something like a very basic design choice, a line to break up the monotony of a slab of concrete. There is nothing else on the wall.

Having half an idea, I look inside the doorway I'm standing in, the top landing of the stairwell. On the wall is a small, plain gunmetal gray door, like that on an electrical box. I pop it open and see two rows of switches, labeled only with numbers. One switch, though, is twice the size of the others. I flip it and immediately the wall on the other side makes a clanking sound and begins to split down the horizontal line through the middle. As it fully opens, it reveals a large cargo elevator.

"*Voilá*," Mr. B says.

"Sure beats tromping up and down the stairs," Patrick says.

We step onto the metal cage, and Mr. B gazes at the buttons mounted on the wall. "Up or down?"

"I think that what we're looking for will be underground," I say. "Probably as far down as possible. Can you choose the lowest floor?"

"There's only up, down, or stop," he says. He presses one, and the doors close, and then we lurch downward.

We pass floor after floor. Six, seven, eight. I tried to think of what floor I rescued Patrick from, but really don't know. Ten, eleven, twelve. I can only guess that each floor is a hallway lined with doors hiding rooms filled with more death and decay. I shiver at the thought at how many thousands of lives had ended here. Fifteen, sixteen, seventeen.

If each floor had thirty, forty, fifty rooms—I didn't bother to count—then the magnitude is both stunning and sickening.

Nineteen, twenty . . . and we lurch to a stop. The entire cage shutters and rattles. The doors clank and begin to open. What's on the other side is beyond what any of us expected.

We stand half-mortified at the sight. If we thought we'd had our fill of the creatures from hell, our fears now overflow. Not only are there a dozen Black Souls, countless Shadow People and even several small Cravens, there are new horrors to take in.

There is something that looks like a cross between a boa constrictor and a crocodile slithering on the floor towards us, jaws snapping wildly—fortunately, it's a good fifty feet away and slow. Another creature has the body of a squid and the head of some kind of lizard. It hisses and shambles along the concrete in a modified wobble. There's a pair of large dogs, the size of Great Dane, but with long jaws filled with big triangular teeth—but that's not the weirdest part. Their coats are a blood-red and seem to glisten like raw, oozing flesh.

A small Craven takes flight and heads for us, squawking. Apollo quickly takes it out, and it lands in a small fiery bundle at our feet. Patrick kicks at it, launching it at one of the squid/dragon things. It bursts into flames, roaring in pain.

"I haven't seen these things in eons," Apollo says. "The Krakens are nasty. Their jaws lock on their victim and don't let go."

"Krakens?"

"Well, these are mini-Kraken. The ones in the ocean are much worse."

"So, what do we do?" I ask as a pair of Black Souls hop on their powerful kangaroo legs in our direction, still staying far enough away to only be threatening. They seem to be sizing us up as we do to them.

"We can't take them all out," Apollo says, stating the obvious as the hallway writhes in creepiness and evil. "I would guess our destination is at the far end, and—"

Another Craven launches at us as one of the snake/croc things slithers closer. Jill throws her arms out and the Craven explodes, spinning to the right and hitting the wall. The snake-odile snaps its jaws, but stops its forward progression.

"—we could just blast our way there," Apollo finishes.

"You mean Orb over and knock down anything in our way?" I ask.

"Yes."

We look out at the group of . . . things.

"Okay. Unless anyone has a better idea . . . let's line up. I'll take the point." I suggest Sylvana and Mr. B flank me, with Patrick on Sylvana's left, and Jill on Mr. B's right.

"Ready? On the count of five."

Chapter 34

"Truth exists; only lies are invented."—Georges Braque

Five.
Four.
Let loose a blast of energy when you go, Apollo told me.
Three.
Two.
One.

Switching to Orb transport and releasing an energy pulse at the same time was a bit tricky, but Sylvana, Apollo, Jill and I manage to pull it off, ending up at the far end of the hallway just ahead of a fireball blast of energy that either evaporated the creatures, or set them aflame.

We stand at the end looking back from where we came, smoldering smoky corpses laying on the floor. Only the Shadow People remain, but they seem to want no more, and quickly evaporate.

We turn, and the wall we face is much like the one we just came from—solid, but with a cut through it as if it were a door. Apollo steps to the side where a keypad is mounted on the wall. It's almost too high for him to reach, but he manages, and taps in a code. It blats back at him as if it were incorrect. He tries again, and another blat. He tries once more, and the keypad beeps.

"Third time's a charm," he says.

The wall makes a metallic clunking sound, and begins to part. We each instinctively take a step back, not sure what will be coming at us this time.

As the two halves of the horizontal door parts, we see . . . another door, this one a deep maroon with another keypad to its right. Apollo approaches and taps in a code. It quickly beeps.

"How do you know the code?" Patrick asks as Apollo opens the door.

"They use a macro-merged computed code sequence with an underlying psypandeo-metric system, and once you know one, it's easy to understand the sequence."

"Of course it is," Patrick says, smirking.

"I cracked it around the time you were captured and brought here, but unfortunately, it was too late for you in that circumstance. Besides, you were in good hands."

On the other side of the door is a staircase, going up.

"I wonder if this is some kind of maze," I say.

"I wouldn't doubt it," Mr. B says. "May have even been created specifically for a day like today."

Up the stairs leads us to a door that opens into yet another hallway. Fortunately, there are no monsters. There are also no doors, just a long corridor, at least a hundred yards long. Once we reach the end, it turns left and from there are a series of corridors that branch off into various directions. It reminds me of the tunnels beneath the cemetery, only better lit and with less dirt.

We split up, each person wandering into a corridor until they come to a dead end, a room with nothing in it, or discovering the way just leads back to the main corridor. Eventually, we make it to the end, which features yet another locked door with a keypad. Apollo applies a code, and the door lock clicks loudly. He pulls it open, and we're surprised to see a man standing on the other side. He looks significantly younger, as if in his forties.

"Welcome," Lord Harod Dunraven says, with a slight smile. He's wearing black slacks, a black shirt, and a long maroon jacket.

The six of us stand warily silent, watching.

"Nice work taking out the obstacles," he says, looking at Apollo. "I knew you'd figure it out."

"I always do."

"Yes, well, I believe you may have erred in coming to this facility as whatever you think you may find here will disappoint you. We cleared out this complex months ago."

He lies, Apollo says to me.

I know.

Dunraven looks at me. "You really should have stayed away. But it's too late now. You're trapped."

"Don't underestimate me *again*," I say. "It's becoming a bad habit."

He actually smiles, then turns his attention to Jill. "Nice seeing you again."

She doesn't reply, but it's easy to feel her fuming.

"It's really interesting, Dunraven," Mr. B says, "how you are able to apply such misery to humanity, and yet understand so little of it."

Dunraven sneers. "Your wife says hello."

Mr. B nods and smiles, but doesn't take the bait.

Sylvana speaks in his place: "I think it's time for you to step aside. Your time has passed."

"Oh, I disagree. It really has just begun."

Sylvana, like Mr. B, smiles. "You don't really think he will take you along, do you?" She pauses, but Dunraven only stares back at her blankly. "His end game is to destroy the Earth, isn't it? What will he do with you? You cannot go where he goes."

There's the tiniest bit of light behind his eyes as this sinks in. "I have always been taken care of—quite well, in fact. He has never let me down."

"And when there is no world to rule?"

"There are many worlds beyond this."

"Of which you will have no access. All the time you spent building your power, and it will be wiped away, and you with it."

"You misspeak the prophecies."

"Do I?" Sylvana asks.

At that moment came a rumbling. I begin to feel the floor shake, then everything seemed to start going sideways. The lights blinked off, then back on. The walls shifted and cracks appeared as everything shook violently for a good twenty, thirty seconds. But everything held as the earthquake finally stopped.

Dunraven stands, smiling. "It has begun."

"So we've truly entered Red Sky?" Mr. B asks.

Dunraven's smile widens. "You have no idea."

But I do, because I'm picking it up directly from Dunraven. "Geomagnetic reversal," I say, "followed by an axial shift."

Dunraven glares at me. "Your parlor tricks are impressive."

"Ah, yes," Apollo says. "Of course. Shift the magnetic poles, causing an earthquake which knocks the Earth off its axis. The planet wobbles, for lack of a better term, and we get knocked off our orbit. The Earth spins out of control, off into space, killing essentially every life form."

"I wish I had killed you, Azayakana, when I had the chance," Dunraven says quietly to the boy.

Apollo cocks his head. "You really do live life looking in the rearview mirror, as Sylvana implied. You're so enthralled with history, you can't look forward. You're so taken with all the things you've accomplished, you don't see where they're leading."

"Does not your precious Bible say not to worry about tomorrow, for tomorrow will bring its own worries?"

"Oh, I'm not worried. I know what will happen." Apollo pauses. "So are we just going to stand here and talk, or are you going to step aside and let us pass?"

Dunraven half-bows and moves to his right. "By all means, be my guest."

One by one, we pass through the door, and I am the last through. I stop and turn to the man I once thought was my father. "Won't you show us the way?"

"I think you will find your way just fine . . . and it won't lead where you think."

I reach out and take hold of his arm. "Then you won't mind accompanying us."

He tries to snap it away, but I hold tight.

Don't make me drag you, I tell him. *I can kill you right here, right now.*

You can't kill me.

But his eyes held doubt. So, I give him a little zap, which makes him flinch and stagger back a step.

I really don't need you, I tell him. *In fact, you're slowing me down.*

His fingers rubs his forehead, trying to massage the headache away.

"Let's go." I jerk him forward.

We're confronted with another corridor, long and doorless. We march down to the far side, only to come to a dead end.

"Where to?" I ask Dunraven.

He shrugs.

I look back down the hall and see Apollo had stopped about halfway. He's staring at the blank wall.

"What is it?" I ask, heading his way and dragging Dunraven with me.

Apollo doesn't answer at first. Instead, he takes a step and places a hand on the wall.

We step up next to him.

"Electricity," Apollo says. "On the other side."

"How do we get in there?"

Dunraven doesn't reply. His face is blank, his eyes empty.

I look around and see a metal panel on the opposite wall. Like an electrical box, it's a gunmetal gray. I raise the hinged door and see another keypad. But instead of twelve keys of the others— ten numbers, an asterisk and a pound sign—this has all the letters and numbers of a keyboard.

The others have joined us. I turn to Patrick and ask him to lift Apollo up so he can look.

The boy stares at the keypad, then taps in something. There's a blatting sound. He tries again. *Blat.* Again. *Blat.* Again. *Blat.* Again.

"This is a more sophisticated code," Apollo says.

I squeeze Dunraven's arm. "What is it?"

He doesn't say anything.

I give him a zap.

His knees buckle.

As he does, another earthquake hits. It's difficult to tell if it's worse than the previous one, but the sensation of the solid ground moving under my feet is more than unnerving. Looking down the hall, I see the walls, floor and ceiling seeming to shift like waves of water, rolling and bulging.

Then it subsides.

"What's the code?" I ask Dunraven.

His eyes are close, his mouth open, I'm holding him up as he seems half-conscious.

I shake him. "Come on, I didn't hit you that hard."

"Nebber," he says.

I look at Mr. B, hoping he has a translation.

"Never," Mr. B says. "You might have given him a stroke."

Drool slides out of Dunraven's mouth, dripping on the floor.

Sylvana steps forward, placing her hand on his forehead. Her rings begins to glow. She doesn't hold it long before Dunraven's head rises, and his eyes become clear again.

"Get your hands off me, you witch," he says.

Sylvana withdraws her hand. "What is the code?"

Dunraven's face becomes angry, he even bares his teeth. "Go ahead and kill me. The results will be the same."

Shaking starts again, but this is noticeably lighter and doesn't last as long.

"Set me down," Apollo says.

Patrick puts the man-child on the floor. The boy holds his hands out, down towards the end of the hallway where we entered.

"What are you—"

Sylvana holds her hand up to silence me.

We stand there for several minutes, waiting and watching. I see something at the far end, a little black blob going through the doorway. Then another, and another. They race towards us, and I realize they are Drats.

"No," Dunraven says.

The robot rats scurry and are soon at Apollo's feet.

"What's the code?" he asks.

Dunraven's eyes are locked on the little creatures. He doesn't know they're not actual rats . . . in some ways, they're much worse.

He shakes his head.

Apollo points a finger at one of the Drats, and the mechanical rodent follows his direction, darting to Dunraven's shiny leather shoes. He kicks at it, sending it flying down the hall.

Apollo sends another, this one jumping on Dunraven's leg and climbing quickly up past his knee, over his thigh, and inside the long red jacket.

Dunraven screams, breaking free of my grasp and jumping up and down, arms flailing. He bats at his clothing, shrill cries and yelps. The rat appear at the nape of his neck, and he swipes at it. The Drat reacts by biting him. Dunraven screams even louder.

The Drat scrambles up on top of his head, and looks down at his ear.

Dunraven collapses onto the concrete, rolling, squealing, screeching, arms slapping at his head madly. The Drat holds firm, and even manages to take a small piece of scalp.

"Okay, get it off, GET IT OFF!"

I look at Apollo and nod. He moves his arm, and the Drat drops off and hurries several feet away, a swatch of skin—with a good chunk of hair connected—still in its mouth.

The old man sits up, back to the wall, looking horrified, and a more than a little crazy. He doesn't take his eyes off the rodent.

"What's the code?" I ask Lord Harod Dunraven.

Chapter 35

"There's no reason, no compromise / Change in seasons, living the high life / I don't know you, so don't freak on me / I can't control you, you're not my destiny"—Godsmack: *"Straight Out of Line"*

Of course, there is no code—or at least not *just* a code.

Still visibly shaken, blood running through his hair, over his right ear and down his jawline, Dunraven reaches into his slacks pocket and pulls out a flash drive, holding it up while not taking his eyes off the Drat.

I take it from him and hand it to Apollo.

"The sequence?" Apollo asks.

"The . . ." He pauses, licking his lips. "It's the one-hundred and twenty-second to six-hundred and forty-first places of Pi, interspersed every six digits with a tri-multiplier sequence beginning with the number twelve."

"At what point do I insert the flash drive?"

"At the tenth tri-multiplier sequence."

Apollo nods. He raises his arms for Patrick to lift him up.

"You know what all that means?" I ask.

"Sure. Starting with the one-hundred twenty-second place of Pi, or three eight four four six zero, insert twelve, and then nine five five zero five eight, insert three six, and so on until the six hundred and forty-first digit of Pi, zero."

"Good. Just checking."

Apollo looks at me and smiles. "This might take a while."

"No hurry," I say, thinking that might change when the next earthquake hits. I turn to Dunraven. "If the code is sabotaged in any way, I'll have to ask my friend Ben over there to pay you a visit."

Dunraven looks up at me warily, the blood from his head dripping onto his burgundy jacket. His tongue tries to moisten his dry lips. "Perhaps it is digits, not places."

"Perhaps?"

He looks away, at the Drat. "Or not perhaps."

"What do you think, Apollo?"

"I think there is a fail-stop where one incorrect entry would set off some kind of self-destruct mode." The boy looked at Dunraven. "He's done it before."

Apollo swings his arm around at the robotic rat and, in a flash, the rodent rushes at the old man, and up the leg of his pants.

Dunraven shrieks and scrambles around backwards on the floor, absolutely terrified.

"Digits! Digits! It's digits!"

"Any other areas you have forgotten to include?" Apollo asks between cries and screeches. "Like letters or symbols?"

"No, no, it's all numbers. Get it off of me!"

He has managed to scoot thirty or forty feet down the hall, panicked at the rat trying to get at his crotch. He lets out a bellow of pain as if the Drat is munching on something very tender . . . and then he passes out.

We all stare at him collapsed on the ground in a crumpled heap.

"That is the worst case of musophobia I have ever seen," Apollo says. "The Drat didn't bite him or even get past his calf."

"Do you think he was telling the truth?" Mr. B asks.

"Yes," I say. "He was too far out of his mind to make anything up."

Apollo returns his attention to the keypad and begins entering numbers.

* * *

"Okay, last few numbers," Apollo says. And as soon as he enters the final digit, the lights go out.

We stand there in complete darkness and silence. Then, a mechanical sound, and a loud clunk as the wall begins to lower. A deep blue light comes from the other side, and as the wall slides down, we begin to see a large black shape perched on a stand. All we can tell is that it's a big box, maybe 5 feet long and 3 feet tall.

"What is it?" Patrick asks as the wall disappears into the floor.

Mr. B begins to answer: "We are looking at—"

Suddenly, there is another loud clunk and the floor of the other room begins to rise as if it were on a lift or elevator.

"What—?" I say as we watch it disappear up into . . . I don't know what. "Where is it going?"

"I don't know," Mr. B says. "But we should go up to the surface."

As the Ark of the Covenant—at least that's what I think it is—rises to the next level, all goes dark again.

"Great," Patrick says.

"We need to find Dunraven and bring him with us," Mr. B says.

"Why? He'll just slow us down," I say.

"We may need him."

Patrick and I feel our way down the hall and find Dunraven's unconscious body. We each take an arm and begin to drag him down the hallway.

* * *

In the darkness, it seems to take forever to get to the stairway and find our way up. But at least the lights are on at the next level. Another couple of levels up, Dunraven begins to wake. Probably having the back of his legs hit each stair helped the bring him around. We get him to his feet, though he still seems somewhat out of it.

"Where did the Ark go?" I ask.

He looks at me warily. "I don't know what you're talking about."

I grab his upper arm and lead him up the stairs.

It's several more flights before we reach the end of the stairway and the main floor, and we have to walk to the far end of the hallway to reach the exit.

Outside, it looks like a nightmare. The sun is blood red, and everything is bathed in a weird, ominous glow.

We go around to the side of the building, but, unsurprisingly, nothing is there.

"Where did it go?" I ask Dunraven.

"Where did what go?"

I stare at him, thinking for a moment. "Okay, if you want to play games, I can too."

I look at Patrick. *Take his arm, we'll Orb him over to the Old House.*

Patrick nods and grabs his right arm as I take the left.

I turn to the others. "We'll be back." And we zip out of the Meadows Polo Grounds.

* * *

We enter through the side entrance.

"Where are you taking me?"

I ignore his question. "I get the sense that Dymortis doesn't trust you enough to give you many powers."

"That is not true," he says as we lead him into the mortuary prep area.

"You can transport yourself around, but that's about it."

"No—" Dunraven says as he understands what might happen.

"Get on the table," I tell him.

He stares at the mortuary table. "No."

Patrick and I drag him over and literally manhandle him onto the table as he kicks and screams. He is surprisingly weak.

"There are straps in that big drawer over there," I say to Patrick.

"No, no, no . . ." Dunraven says as I lay my body over his,

holding him down.

Patrick hurries back with the straps and begins to lock down his legs while I keep Dunraven pinned.

Dunraven either gives up, or he loses all strength, as he nearly goes limp. Patrick applies the straps to his upper body.

I move off him and roll the tank next to the table.

Dunraven's eyes are wide and wild.

"Where is the Ark?" I ask.

He doesn't reply, his crazy gaze darting from me to Patrick.

On the control box on top of the tank, I power it up. I pull the first tube off the tank and move the end featuring a large, sharp needle to the side of his neck.

"Jacob, please . . ."

"I'm not Jacob. Just tell us where the Ark is, and we'll go no further."

"I don't know."

I pause, adding a little more pressure the end of the fat needle pressing against his flesh.

I pick this up: Dymortis, save me.

"He no longer needs you," I tell him. "You've fulfilled your purpose."

Dymortis, please come and save me.

"Last chance," I say.

Dunraven closes his eyes as if in prayer.

"You killed my parents," I say. "You killed my adopted mother. You killed my horse. And you killed Jill." I pause. "I won't even get into the millions of others you devastated throughout the ages, but now it is your turn."

I push the needle into his flesh, and his eyes bulge wide open as he begins to scream.

"You can save yourself," I say as I take the next tube off the embalming machine and move around to the other side of the table. "Just tell me where the Ark is."

He's screaming too much to reply.

I press the needle into the right side of his throat, and the screams intensify.

"Silence," I say, and he actually turns from wails to a sound that is a cross between huffing and puffing, and whining. I go to the tank, and activate the embalming process.

Blood begins to drain through one tube while embalming fluid is injected through the other.

"Where's the Ark?"

"*Ruh . . . ruh . . . ruh . . .*"

"Where?"

"*Ruh . . . uff . . . ruh uff.*"

His eyes close as the last of his life drains out of him.

* * *

After turning off the machine, Patrick and I leave and zip back to the Meadows where the others are. None of them ask about Dunraven.

"It's on the roof," I say. "I'm going up."

"Wait," both Sylvana and Mr. B say in unison.

"What?"

"You can't just go up there and open it," Mr. B says. "We have no idea what will happen."

"You need to calm your mind, Collin," Sylvana says. "You need to have a consultation."

My head is anxious to take action, but my heart is telling me to pause and do it right.

"I'm not in the frame of mind to pray," I say.

"So, maybe that is what you need to pray about." She holds out her hand for me to take. "Come, let us sit before we act."

I'm agitated. I know she's right, but between the adrenaline and anxiousness, I want to defy her.

The others stand in a circle and we all sit, holding the hand of the person next to us. I have Sylvana on one side, and Jill on the other. I close my eyes, and despite my frustration and restlessness, it only takes a minute for my mind to find peace and calm.

Far away from us, but still very clear, the sound of thunder rolls through the sky.

Chapter 36

"O god can I not save one from the pitiless wave? Is all we see or seem but a dream within a dream?"—Edgar Allen Poe, "Dream Within A Dream"

There was no voice. No light through silky clouds. I felt no presence. For a while, I felt nothing.

Then, an image began to appear. Water. As far as my mind's eye could see. Sun glinting off the waves. Then, far ahead, a coastline. No idea what coastline, but soon I'm flying over it and the land it leads to. Miles of green fields, eventually turning to brown, like a desert. Then hills, leading to snow, and mountains. Desolate. Unwelcoming.

The tallest mountain looms ahead, but I slow, and it becomes apparent that peak is not my destination. Instead, a smaller one nearby. I swirl around it, and see near the top, on the top, is a large blue piece of fabric. The same kind and color that covered the Ark of the Covenant.

Around the base of the mountain, fire erupts. Creatures leap from boulder to boulder. Thick black smoke rises. The sky turns red.

And then all goes dark.

* * *

I open my eyes, tears pouring from them as if stung by the smoke. I'm still holding hands with Sylvana and Jill. They are all looking at me.

I let go of their grasps and wipe my face with a sleeve.

"You know where to go," Jill says.

"No," I say. "I have seen it, but I don't know where it is."

She nods. Perhaps she saw it too.

"Describe it to me," Mr. B says.

I frown, blinking, a tear running down my left cheek. "Two mountains, one large, the other smaller, covered in snow."

It is his turn to frown, his brow furrowed as he thinks.

"Masiq," Apollo says, "in the ancient kingdom of Urartu."

Mr. B's eyes clear, and he nods. "The resting place of the Ark—the other Ark."

"What other Ark?" Patrick asks. "I thought there was just one Ark of the Covenant."

"So there is. No, I'm referring to Noah's Ark."

"Mount Ararat," Sylvana says.

"Technically, Lesser Ararat, the smaller of the two. But yes."

"We must take the Ark there," I tell them. "There will be resistance."

I look to each around the circle, and all their expressions are passive, except Patrick, who looks white as a sheet.

"Resistance?" he asks. "Not those creepy fuckers again."

"Patrick," Sylvana says softly.

He nods sheepishly, but still looks pasty.

"When do we depart?" Mr. B asks.

"I was given no insight about that."

A long silence.

"So . . . we leave now?" Apollo says.

* * *

We zip up to the roof. It's a long building, and seems to go on forever. The Ark sits in the middle, slightly off-center, covered in the large cloth. As we get closer, it looks like the cloth is moving, undulating. I stop, and the others do as well.

"What is it?" Jill asks.

We're still a good 30 yards away, but I see something poke up for a second. Then, a head.

"Snakes," I say. Not just a dozen, or two dozen, but hundreds.

"He's not giving up without a fight," Apollo says.

"Neither will we."

Slowly, we approach, keeping our eyes on the teeming mass. When we're within 10 yards, several of the snakes raise their heads towards us and begin hissing. Others begin slithering off the Ark and onto the rooftop, heading for us. They are moving extraordinarily fast.

"Oh, no," Jill says softly.

I put my hands out and send a burst that immediately ignites several of them. Apollo and Sylvana do the same. Behind me, Jill collapses to the ground.

More and more of the snakes move from the Ark to the rooftop, sliding towards us. The flames and smoke block much of our view, and we have to take a few steps back as they come closer. Patrick picks up Jill and hurries her far away from the slithering reptiles.

And that's when we hear the squawks. Above, in the sky, the Cravens have returned.

* * *

Apollo hurries to where Patrick and Jill are, since Patrick doesn't have the ability to use the burst of energy, and Jill has fainted. The boy raises his hands to the sky and begins zapping as many large birds as he can.

I do the same while Sylvana continues to concentrate on taking out the snakes coming at us. Mr. B, also without the power, stands nervously between us. I can't count how many Cravens are circling in the sky, but dozens are swooping in, talons lowered, aiming for our heads.

I am continuously blasting energy into the air, the flaming bodies of the Cravens crashing onto the roof around us. Three or four of the beasts sneak in from my left and come uncomfortably close—close enough to smell their stench. I manage to zap them, but their exploding carcasses crash into me and Mr. B, sending us sprawling. The flaming birds roll past us, one of them still flapping its wings and squawking.

I stand quickly and continue hitting as many as I can, but Mr. B isn't getting up. His head is bleeding, and his eyes are half-open.

There's nothing any of us can do as the creatures keep coming, three or four at a time, then six or seven, then ten. Burning masses of dead and dying birds are falling all around us. And still they keep coming.

I glance back for a moment at the others and see Patrick kneeling by Jill while Apollo zaps and zaps and zaps at the onslaught.

When I look back up, 20 or 25 Cravens are zooming in on us, one big group of terror, talons out, beaks wide. Sylvana, having gotten all of the snakes, turns her attention to the sky, and we do our best to nail all of them at once, a gigantic fireball erupting 20, 30 feet over us, then crashing into the roof several yards away.

Except one made it through, and scoops up Mr. B with it claws, crowing in triumph.

It rises into the sky, the limp body of the Professor dangling beneath it. I scream and let out a burst that decimates the Craven . . . but sends Mr. B falling as well, crashing to the ground.

I scream again, and unleash a torrent of energy, reaching far and wide across the sky, something I didn't even know I could do.

The air becomes fire as hundreds of giant birds begin to fall to Earth, meteors of death plummeting all around us. One lands on Sylvana, knocking her to the ground. I quickly leap at the flaming black creature, grab its legs and heave it as hard as I can away from us. It flies in the air like a beach ball, before going over the edge of the roof and disappearing onto the ground below.

Sylvana is sitting up, patting at her upper body, putting out the small patches of flame on her clothing. Her white hair is darkened and smoldering, so I rush over to extinguish the embers.

"Are you alright?"

She looks up at me, and while her expression is passive, for the first time in my life I see confusion and fear in her eyes.

She doesn't reply, but instead holds out her hand, and I help her up.

Apollo, Patrick and Jill are okay, though Jill is still unconscious. I hurry over to the edge of the roof and look down. Among the dozens of burning and smoldering birds on the grass, I see Mr. B's unmoving body. I climb up on the ledge and zip down, hurrying to his side, my palm touching the side of his face. He is gone.

Thank you, Collin. You are a worthy friend.

I stand on the grass and look to the sky. There is a thin haze from smoke rising into the air, but it is free of Cravens. They are on the ground, where there is only the sound of crackling fire, and the smell of burning flesh.

Through tears, I look up to the top of the building and see Apollo and Patrick looking back down at me. They say nothing, but I know we must continue on.

* * *

I go back up on the roof and hug each of my remaining friends. Jill has come around, looking scared, but healthy. I embrace her for several minutes, not wanting to lose her again, so glad she is okay. As I grab hold of Patrick, I realize these are not my friends—they're my family. Sylvana, my mother; Apollo and Patrick, my brothers; Jill, my wife. Mr. Burkfelt—Malcolm—my father.

I step back, my hands on Patrick's shoulders, and I look him deep in the eyes.

"We've been through a lot together," he says.

"And the worst is yet to come."

He smirks. "I know."

I look around at the others who are either wiping away tears, or not bothering.

"Are you ready to do this?"

Sylvana sniffs, and smiles wanly. Jill rubs the backs of her hands against her eyes and says "Yes."

Apollo, tears pouring down his cheeks, tries to regain his composure, tries to look brave. "Dymortis has killed or tried to kill everyone close to me," he says angrily in his little eight-year-old voice. "It's time to make him stop."

"Then let's do it."

We walk up to the cloth-covered Ark, and I try to consider the best way to handle this.

"So, where is this Mount Ararat?"

"Turkey," Apollo says. He seems to have calmed down. "Eastern Turkey, to be precise, near the border with Iran, Armenia and Azerbaijan."

He might have well as said it was on Jupiter. I only vaguely know Turkey is in some part of Europe. Or Asia. Or the Middle East. I think.

"I guess we all take a corner then?"

"Dude," Patrick says. "Don't you remember that neat trick Sylvana taught you on how to move things?"

I nod sheepishly.

"It's going to take a lot of your concentration due to its weight and the great distance," Sylvana says.

"I would suggest having us go ahead while you transport it," Apollo says.

I frown, thinking this over. Not exactly what I wanted to do, but I can't think of a better alternative.

"He has his beasts there to stop us," I tell them.

"Another reason we should go ahead," Patrick says. "We can help clear the area before you get there."

I smile and nod, not in agreement, but only to not show what I fear.

I step up to Patrick and reach my hand out. I draw a "plus"

sign—a miniature cross—on his forehead. "May God be with you and protect you."

"*Laus Deo,*" he says.

I repeat this with Sylvana and Apollo, and each replies in kind. Then I step in front of Jill.

"To be honest, I don't want you to go," I tell her. "Maybe it's machismo, or arrogance, or silliness, but I feel the need to protect you."

"May God bless you for that," she says, smiling, her eyes still slightly red from crying. "But I can protect myself."

I think of the dreams where she took out the red-headed woman, the old man, and the TV news anchor. "Yes, I know you can." I lean forward and kiss her, a deep, passionate embrace that I've missed so much. And will have to miss for a while longer.

"But, before you go, I have something I want to give you."

I reach deep down inside my front pocket and pull out the ring from Mr. Burkfelt's jewelry store that I got an eternity ago.

"I've been saving this to give you at the right moment."

I reach out for Jill's left hand and slide the ring down onto her third finger. I look up and see tears rolling down not just Jill's cheeks, but everyone's

It is like everything around me had a sudden calmness. The world brightened.

I gaze into Jill's eyes and simply say: "Always."

Wiping away her tears. Jill nods. "Yes—always."

We embrace again, for what seems like a long time, yet not long enough. I open my eyes and see Sylvana her smiling.

I reluctantly pull back, touch her forehead and draw a cross. "May God be with you and protect you."

"*Laus Deo.*"

We separate, and the four line up near the edge of the roof. Columns of smoke rise into the air. Each member of my family takes the hand of the one next to them, and each looks back at me, smiling.

"Go," I say. "Stay true, and pay attention."

They turn back to face the angry red sky. In the distance is a deep maroon cloud, broad and wide. They raise their linked hands, then drop them—instantaneously turning into Orbs and then flashing towards the horizon.

The deep, dark cloud shifts and changes, turning into what looks like a giant enraged face, lightning bolts for eyes. The mouth of Dymortis snarls and snaps at me, still dozens of miles away.

But it is growing closer.

Chapter 37

"Favente Deo Supero" (Latin: "With God's favor, I conquer")

There's a trick to flying. I had figured how to use the Orb transport, maybe even mastered it, but that was beyond supersonic, dropping me at my destination in seconds. Going at a fraction of that while escorting the Ark of the Covenant is much different. I found there's a lot of concentration needed. There's wobbling if I went too fast. There are moments when altitude suddenly lessens as gravity exercises itself. There's the balance between flying low enough that the air isn't too thin, yet high enough that bullets from the ground can't reach me—and there were bullets. Whether it was Dymortis' faction or normal folks wondering what the heck was flying through the sky, it was impossible to know. And I had to keep an eye out on my adversary sending Cravens or other creatures my way.

I eventually find the balance and can maintain both a good speed and altitude. But it still seems to take forever. Fortunately, I managed to get a handle on this before entering the ominous deep red cloud that loomed ahead like the nastiest storm ever. And it turned out, it was.

Hurricane force winds would be accurate. Pelting rain and hail. Massive funnels aimed at me and my cargo. Lightning exploding around me, the thunder that immediately follows is beyond deafening and can be felt as the sound waves blast through my body. It takes every ounce of concentration to stay aloft—forget about staying on course. Occasionally I sense I'm in the wrong direction and correct it, but I'm not sure I'm on the right trajectory.

"Hey Jakey," a voice says during a lull in the storm. "Looks like you're having some trouble." This is followed by a cackle.

I look around and see the ugly old man in top hat and tails leering at me with the crazy smile. He's standing on the top of the Ark.

"Want some help?"

I don't reply.

"Oh, it looks sssssooooo heavy!"

At that moment, the Ark does become heavy, as if a truck was suddenly set on top of it. Holding onto the side of the crate, I drop quite a bit until I can compensate.

"Look, there's no reason to go through this," he says. "I'm sure we can work something out."

Again, I ignore him.

"I can offer protection for your friends. Right now, they're not doing so well. I think the girl has been horrifically injured, and the old lady is weakening fast."

I don't take the bait. Even if he's telling the truth—which I doubt—I'm not going to fall for his bribes.

He tries a different tact. "You've proven your strength and worthiness," he says. "You are formidable, but you've only been playing defense so far. I see something within you that shows you as a great leader, not a follower."

The storm seems to let up. The rain has turned to a mist, and the winds have died down.

"I mean, your God is truly great and mighty, giving you some talents and gifts which you have used remarkably well, but I sense He hasn't really trusted you with all that you are capable of. Think about it: You've shown great restraint and compassion for those who are also followers. You can heal. You've brought a calming peace to those you've been asked to shepherd. You've demonstrated wisdom and foresight. You've been incredibly loyal, and yet, here you are, doing some kind of magical grunt work. You deserve to be placed in a position that suits your greatness."

He pauses, waiting for my reaction. I give him none. The skies are clearing, and while the clouds are still an ominous maroon, they've thinned enough to show a calming blue sky.

"Dunraven was very good at what he did, but even with his devotion, he was never as loyal as you."

Another pause.

My burden has lessened and I'm not struggling nearly as much.

"I can offer you so much more. Literally anything you desire. And your friends too. The girl? The one you love? I can offer her eternal life as well. You can live together in blissful harmony literally forever. Your heart will never be lonely again."

I think of Dunraven. As evil as he was, and as much as I despised him, I can see how he was duped, and in a strange way, I feel for him. Eternal life is only eternal until Dymortis pulls the plug. Dymortis did not come to his aid. He abandoned him. So, as far as anything the guy tells me, it's not believable.

"Imagine, living on a ranch, with your beloved wife and even your horse. Yes, I can bring Ginger back to be with you again. And the professor. The old lady, the little boy, and your best friend can all have a wonderful, peaceful life without a care in the world."

Ginger. The professor. I seriously doubt Dymortis has the ability to bring the dead back to life. But it reminds me of Dymortis' goal, as Mr. B had explained it—that Satan's objective is to not just destroy every soul on Earth, but the very Earth itself. That means any dream of living on a ranch with Jill is just hot air.

"Your stubbornness is admirable," he continues. "It actually shows intelligence. You're an independent thinker who is not easily dissuaded. It takes a lot of balls to keep your word and hold your ground. And that's why I'm so impressed. I've known a lot of people in my time, and I can honestly say there are highly intelligent people who don't have the balls to use their brains, and I've met those with a lot of balls but no brains. You are the first man I've run across in eons that has the perfect balance of both. I'm sincerely impressed. Your children will be stunning."

There's a part of me that wants to engage him, interact with him, if only to let him think there is some part of me ready to listen. And while I am not opposed to deceiving him as he is attempting to deceive me, I just don't have it in me to play that game. His efforts to inflate my ego are pretty transparent, and I don't think I have the ability to be a good enough actor to make him believe I might be interested.

At least he knows not to boldly tempt me with sex and money—although the unsaid implication is there. Instead, he plays to my character, individuality and self-image. Or what he thinks they are. To be honest, he hasn't been too far off the mark. It does sound appealing, but it might be more tempting coming from someone whose existence is based on lies and death.

I look down and still see the ocean—the way it's been for quite a long time now—but up ahead I see a shoreline. Like in my dream, I fly over it, over homes and green fields. I have no idea, however, if I'm on track for Turkey, or just crossing into Australia.

The sky has darkened, not from the storm, but from the sun setting behind me. I look to the horizon, hoping against hope that I might see a mountain—*the* mountain I am searching for. While I don't see a mountain, I do see a faint glow in the darkness ahead of me.

I'll take that as a sign.

"I don't think you want to see my real wrath," Dymortis says, turning from stroking my ego to threatening me. "I could destroy you right now."

"No you can't," I say, interacting with him for the first time.

A pause. "You have no idea what I can or cannot do."

"You can believe that if you wish," I say, and leave it at that.

"You're giving up something truly remarkable for misery and pain."

"Or I'm giving up misery and pain for something remarkable."

"Okay, so you've cast your die. You're playing against the House. The House always wins."

"You're right. The Father's House is a sanctuary and cannot be defeated. So, as Jesus said, 'Get behind me, Satan.'"

Dymortis hisses, then leans in close, his mouth an inch from my ear. "Your God will not save you, but I will destroy you."

"In the name of Jesus Christ, go away."

And, just like that, he was gone.

The glow on the horizon grows stronger. The storm and its clouds have dissipated.

* * *

It turns out the glow may not have been a sign from God, but a natural occurrence—the larger of the two mountains is on fire. It has erupted as a volcano, and is spitting columns of molten lava high into the air. The smaller mountain has its own fires as well, but they appear to be man-made. Hordes of men are all over the sides of the peak, holding torches.

The top is mainly in darkness, but as I draw closer, I can see four figures—the members of my family. I manage to slow and maneuver to where I can land the Ark and myself nearby without crashing.

Jill, Apollo, Patrick and Sylvana make their way over the craggy rocks to where I sit, leaning against the Ark, which is perched crookedly between two large stones.

"I am so glad to see you," Jill says, obviously unscathed. She was not mortally wounded as Dymortis implied.

I manage to get to my feet and embrace her. It seems like weeks since I last touched her, and my weariness and borderline exhaustion has been alleviated.

"Glad to see you, man," Patrick says. "The Cravens were here, but we were able to fight them off."

Apollo looks up at him with a smirk. "We?"

"Okay, okay, you guys did all the work, but I was a pretty good lookout."

"I see there's something like an army trying to climb the sides of the mountain," I say.

"Shadow People," Sylvana says. "They are making good progress."

"Aren't they able to fly?" I ask.

"They can," Apollo says. "I don't know why they're not."

Standing with my arm around Jill, I look out at the erupting large mountain. There is both a menace and a beauty to it. It is quite mesmerizing, and I find it difficult to not look.

"So, what happens—"

Patrick's words get cut off as an earthquake unlike any of the others literally knocks us off our feet. I slip and land on my butt, as does Sylvana. Jill ends up on her side and both Apollo and Patrick fall forward.

It's more than just shaking, it's a motion that feels as if the entire mountain is being demolished. Is it from God? Dymortis? Or just a side-effect of the volcano unleashing its torrent? It doesn't matter. We stay where we are until the shaking ceases. Then we carefully get back on our feet.

The Ark has toppled over. I put my hand on it and raise it back to an upright position. Fortunately, the cloth covering it remains in place. I have no idea what might happen once that is removed.

"Look," Apollo says, pointing.

I turn and see a group of people, eight of them, wearing robes.

"The Soulmadds," Sylvana says, her voice showing her relief.

* * *

The others step over to the group while I decide I need to check out the enemy. I hover and float over to the side of the mountain, looking down. The creatures that had been scaling the side had been, for the most part, shaken loose, sliding down, many of them clear to the bottom.

I float back up to the group of Soulmadds and see they're not only wearing their robes, but holding extras. We put them on, but Patrick hesitates.

"Not sure I should do that," he says.

"Why not?"

"I'm not a Soulmadd."

I look at Sylvana, who smiles slightly and nods.

"You are now. You can pray, right?"

"Yeah. Of course."

"Then you're qualified, at least for now."

He takes the robe, still looking wary. "Isn't thirteen an unlucky number?"

"Only if you're Dymortis," I say with a wink, though I'm not sure he sees it since the glow from the volcano is behind me.

"There is nothing inherently unlucky about the number thirteen, at least Biblically," Apollo says. "Some believe because Judas was the thirteenth apostle and betrayed Jesus, the number is tainted, but the Bible never says this."

"You're not Judas," Jill says as she slips her robe on. "I think you're lucky for us."

He carefully puts the robe on, still not looking sure. "Aren't we supposed to be naked?"

"You can if you like, but I think we will make an exception this time," Sylvana says.

We stand in silence for several moments.

"So, what happens next?" Patrick asks.

I hold out my hands to those next to me. "We pray."

* * *

We each take a turn, with me starting. The lady on my right follows, offering prayer in Latin. It goes around the circle, each short and to the point, mainly asking for God's power and protection in a fight against evil. When the man on my left finishes, I add a closing prayer, requesting guidance in what to do or not do with the Ark.

And, other than the sound of the wind and minor explosions from the volcano, there is silence.

As a group, we turn and face the Ark of the Covenant. It may be my imagination, or light from the lava playing off the cloth, but it seems to be glowing.

I take a few steps when a gigantic fireball erupts from the volcano, blasting into the sky like a nuclear bomb. It lights up the sky like daytime, and even from this far away, I can feel the heat of it on my face.

That is followed by an earthquake that seems even more powerful than the last one. We are all knocked off our feet, and as I sit on my butt, I can watch the rocks, stones and boulders around us literally shake in their place, with several rolling away or tumbling over. As the rumbling continues, I can hear what I imagine is a small avalanche of stone descending down the side of the mountain.

It finally dies down, and we all remain seated until we are sure it is done.

The Soulmadds each make their way around the Ark to find their places, encircling the Holy object.

I walk to the side of the Ark, and take a deep breath.

Chapter 38

"May you have visions of heaven and put them in colors that will never fade."—Rudyard Kipling

I reach out and touch the cloth. It then begins to glow. A warning? Or a welcome?

I lift it and begin pulling it off, cautiously. It's large, and heavy, like a thick tarp, only soft and warm. I manage to remove it completely, and carefully fold it, which takes longer than I anticipated. The radiance dims until it is dark.

The Ark itself is not glowing. It's not easy to see in the dark, but the wood appears both ornate and old.

"Lower your heads," I say to the Soulmadds, and they obey, all bowing their faces towards the ground as if in prayer.

I hold my hand out and make it glow, using it as a kind of flashlight. I see an old, tarnished lock. It is large and thick, but the keyhole looks small in comparison. I ponder this for several seconds, feeling sure that God did not want the lock to be jimmied. Then I remember and reach into the robe, and into my pocket, panicking for a moment when I don't feel it. Then my fingertips find the key—the same that had unlocked Jill's storage locker.

I remove it and it, too, begins to glow. I reach out to place it in the keyhole when a bright light appears in the sky above us, the beam pointing directly on the Ark.

Either God is assisting with the process, or giving a forewarning. I pause, looking up.

A figure, high in the sky, appears, descending quickly. There is a screeching that accompanies it, not a pleasant sound. As the figure draws closer, I understand what—and who—it is.

It lands with a thump, and the screeching stops.

Standing on the top of the Ark is Dymortis, but not the one in top hat and tails, not the small unthreatening one. This one is big, built like the Incredible Hulk, tall and wide. His face is recognizable, but cast in an evil, hateful expression.

"*Give it to me.*" The voice is like that of an animal, growling and menacing.

I slip the key back into my pocket, almost without thinking.

"I will give you nothing."

"*Then I will kill you.*" And he immediately launches himself at me.

It's like being tackled by a football linebacker. I am smothered by his body, and I'm not sure which is worse—his incredible weight, or the stench emanating from him. My head is spinning, dizzy and throbbing. I vaguely understand I hit it on a stone.

His hands wrap around my throat, his tree-trunk legs pinning my arms to the ground.

The pain on my throat is excruciating, and I try to push past it, trying to figure out what to do.

Someone—I'm guessing Patrick—has jumped on Dymortis' back, punching and attacking him as best he can. Dymortis ignores him and keeps squeezing.

I draw up my power as best I can and unleash a burst that seems to explode out of my chest.

As if launched from a catapult, Dymortis is ejected off of me, spinning and flying through the air. Patrick, or whoever was on his back, falls off quickly and lands with a sickening thump on a group of large rocks not far away.

Dymortis' body arcs into the air and begins falling, disappearing out of view between the peak we're on and the volcano.

I manage to quickly get on my feet, knowing Dymortis would come back, angrier.

I'm not wrong as I hear a whooshing sound behind me, and turn as quickly as I can. But too late. Dymortis' arm swipes at my head and sends me flying backwards, smashing into the side of the Ark before collapsing to the ground.

I may have lost consciousness, but if I did, it was only momentary. I work at getting another power burst drawn up, but before I can, Dymortis is on me again, his gigantic hand covering my face and squeezing. His fingers wrap around the side of my head, and he tries to crush my skull.

The power burst this time is more focused and concentrated, but just as powerful. It surges out of me like a combination laser and microwave, surgically entering his chest in a fine beam before exploding outward. His body literally detonates like a bomb in every direction, and my first vision after his palm jumps off my face is his decapitated head flying through the air, spinning, the hateful expression frozen in place.

I lay there watching the head disappear over the side of the mountain.

Several of the Soulmadds approach and help me up. My head is screaming in pain, and I do my best to will it away. It gets better, but doesn't go away.

"He's coming back," a voice says. Sounds like Sylvana.

"I know." I also know I probably can't kill him. I've given it my best shot, twice. How did he get so much power?

I reach through the front of the robe again and fish out the key. It begins glowing again.

As it does, there is squealing from above. I also hear grunting coming from all around us. My brain manages to process this: Cravens are circling, Dymortis's Beasts and the Shadow People— really, Shadow Monsters—are near the summit of the mountain.

Then it happened. Hell opened up high in the sky. As Dymortis appeared, face full of anger, arm extended firmly grasping in his right hand a wooden wand pointed to the skies above. Commanding his enlarged, airborne Black Soul Creatures, with the ones on the mountain about to take flight straight up towards the heavens to join the others. The skies are filled with what looks like millions of flocks, darkening the skies overhead as the swarm of Black Souls amass upward. At a certain height I can see them begin to implode like bomb splatters high up in the atmosphere spreading a dark, plasmatic bloody liquid across the sky.

The ground begins to violently shake as Dymortis swirls his wand, this time creating a massive windstorm that whips upward. It appears to be filled with sand, rising higher into the liquefied mass, plasticizing the liquid into a solid shell, enclosing the Earth into an evil darkness. I stood wide-eyed and breathless watching this supernatural phenomenon beginning to gradually encrust the planet.

Sudden bone-chilling cold and darkness now surrounds us.

I realize there is only one way to defeat them all.

I slip the key into the lock and turn. The latch pops open. My fingers touch the edge of the lid, and begin to open the Ark of the Covenant—something that, as far as I know, has never happened.

The Soulmadds have reformed the circle, their backs to the Ark, facing out where the monsters are coming.

The lid springs open, and immediately, what looks like gold dust swirls and rises out of the vessel creating a looming sparkling cloud. It is hypnotizing. A golden glow surrounds us all.

One of the Soulmadds steps forward and pulls something out of the Ark.

Close it.

I blink several times, a bit surprised at the voice I hear—but I obey, closing my eyes, reaching out, grasping the edge of the lid and pulling it closed. The golden cloud remains, and seems to be growing.

You must assert your authority.

I replace the veil, which does not glow or do anything.

The Soulmadds turn back towards me, and Sylvana hands me a stick.

"The Hazelwood tally stick."

"What do I do with it?"

"It is a source of God's power."

Everyone raises their arms in unison and says: *"Laus Deo!"*

I lift the stick towards the heavens, and feel an immense, almost overwhelming power fill me.

I raise my head to the heavens and yell "I am Sir Coffin Graves. *Casus Belli!*"

Silence, surrounds everyone as the looming cloud begins to swirl. I look skyward and see what appears to be a comet, a bright fiery head followed by a long sparking tail. But I know it is no comet.

The Cravens have circled lower and have begun their attack. The Shadow Monsters have risen over the edge of the mountain and are racing towards us, sprinting at an unbelievable speed.

A lightning bolt strikes out of the tally stick tip across the sky towards Dymortis. Simultaneously, all the Soulmadds—except Patrick, who is still laying on the ground, either unconscious or dead—turn into light orbs and fly into the swirling cloud of gold dust. The intensity of the swirling dust intensifies. Then, it explodes sending streaks of eleven different sparkling comets off into different directions across the fiery-lit skies.

The Cravens and Monsters begin imploding, disappearing into atomic nothingness in a split second. I can feel the displaced air of a Shadow Monster as it passes by me.

The growing Orb comets begin to circle the skies, creating a vacuum. The air seems to be sucked into the center, even the fire and smoke from the volcano being drawn into what I imagine is a Black Hole.

Patrick remains unmoved, and I am able to hold my ground against the gale trying to pull me into the sky.

I can see from all around the atmosphere, from the horizon to the heavens, there are thousands, perhaps millions of pinpoint lights, rising, swirling, drawing closer.

The volcano suddenly explodes with Earth-shattering finality, sending a concussion of sound and energy waves across the land. The chunks of dirt and rock that had made up the larger Mount Ararat spews into the air, fiery masses of earth rising higher than anything I have ever seen. One of the larger portions of the mountain collides with the large comet that I intuitively knew was Dymortis. The explosion of the two objects creates a massive display of fireworks, blooming across the sky and lighting everything up in perfect brilliance.

The pinpoints have come closer, creating a glowing, strobing blanket of light, and I see they are not just points light, but people. Under other circumstances, I would have thought them to be more of Dymortis' minions—but they are chanting, and applauding.

The Soulmadd Orbs descend and land around me. Sylvana pulls her hood down, her face turned up to the sky full of people.

"You have released them, and they are thanking you," she says.

"Who are they?"

"They are good souls that were brutally killed by Dymortis and Dunraven over the ages. They are not just here, but covering the entire Earth. God has given them not just eternal light, but life. The Earth shall no longer be in darkness."

"What about the others who sided with Dymortis? The ISP? The Shadow People?"

"They were sucked into the Vortex with the other evil entities. As Dymortis had purged these good souls into death, the evil ones are taking their place."

The only spot in the sky not covered in light is the hole where the mass of earth exploded upward to take out the Dymortis comet. The absence of light appears as a wound attempting to heal itself.

"Dymortis is working to reconfigure himself," Apollo says. "You must stop him."

I raise the staff again, aiming at the hole which is now turning a deep and pulsing red.

"*Dymortis, in the name of Jesus Christ, and with the blessing of the Lord God Almighty, I hereby banish you from this Earth!*"

The stick erupts with a bolt of lightning, zig-zagging to the center of the abscess, another, final explosion revealing the giant, hateful face of Dymortis, his features locked in a silent scream. The blast sends his image ricocheting into the upper atmosphere, disappearing like the comet it once was into the deep reaches of the galaxy.

Then there is nothing but a chilling silence.

A few minutes later, as we stare like children into the sky, the floating, glowing souls begin to softly fall like snowflakes, descending lightly, drifting off on the winds to the four corners of the Earth.

Before I can ask, Sylvana says in a solemn, almost sad voice: "They are returning to their graves, where they will remain until the Second Coming of Jesus, the Christ."

As if to join them the eight Soulmadds now rise and begin streaking upward.

"Where are they going?"

"They are returning to heaven, as shall I."

"No . . . please, no," I say.

"I must. God is calling."

"Me too," Apollo says.

Her hand reaches out and touches my face, touches it so gently.

"I am very proud of you, Collin. You have honored God, and all of humanity."

The light is dwindling as the Good Souls continue to depart, and in moments, all is dark. Sylvana's hand leaves my cheek, and I realize she is gone. Not a comet, not a pinpoint of light, nothing. She is just gone.

I want to cry, but I know I cannot stand here feeling sorry for myself. She's not gone. She has moved on.

"You need to return the Ark to its rightful home," Apollo says from somewhere in the darkness.

"Okay. Where is that?"

"You will know. Goodbye for now, Collin. It's been a blast." And with that, there's a spark, and then—*zoom*—it streaks into the sky.

I hear someone walking over the stones, coming closer.

"How is Patrick?" I ask.

"I don't know. I laid my hands on him," Jill says, "but he did not respond."

I start to step away, towards my friend, but feel her hand on my arm.

"He's in God's hands now. He will either recover, or not. There's nothing you can do."

"I can't just leave him. I can't—"

Her hand comes up to my face and caresses my cheek. "You don't want to see him this way. Trust me."

I look off into the darkness where Patrick lay. My heart feels heavy, like a boulder. First Mr. B, now Patrick. He died trying to save me.

"He is not dead," Jill says. "I just don't know if God will save him."

I pull her close and wrap my arms around her, not wanting to ever let go. The only one left in my shrinking world.

"*Always,*" I whisper.

"*Always,*" Jill says.

Epilogue

"The antidote for fifty enemies is one friend."—Aristotle

I sit and stare out at the majestic silhouette of the mountains as I've done for most of the days since the catastrophic night in Turkey. Maybe it's a form of PTSD. Or the heavy burden I feel of each soul that perished. I don't know what it is, but I find it difficult to do much.

In the months since then, I've taken no solace in my part of saving humanity, and the Earth as a whole. I know it wasn't me. I was just a conduit. And while so much good may have come out of it, the news that trickled in afterward only laid that much more of a sadness on my heart. However many people were saved, so many more were lost. Reports indicate as many as 3-1/2 to 4 billion people were decimated by Dymortis' ultimate holocaust. Half the Earth, just gone. Whether it was from the diseases, the mass killings, the military's slaughter of civilians, as prey of the Cravens and Shadow People, the massive earthquakes, the bitter cold, the food shortages, no one was left untouched.

The bad news doesn't end there. While there are still plenty of people living, some cities struggle to survive, much less operate. The politicians and policymakers who ran things are gone, leaving a vacuum of leadership and citizens who have grappled with keeping things running. Electricity can go off and on at random. Water, if it runs at all, is not necessarily sanitary. Fuel shortages abound. Police and fire departments—which were either lured to Dymortis' schemes or killed by them—are lightly staffed. In some places, things are working, but just barely. In other places, life has become ultimately harder than it had been in centuries.

Even here, in the shadow of Rocky Mountains, on a 500 acre ranch that is not far from metropolitan Denver, Jill and I have no electricity or running water. Cooking is done on a barbecue or over a campfire. I'm not complaining. It's just the way it is. Based on my occasional walks into the nearest town, things are improving, but slowly. I don't feel bad for us, but for those who don't know how to handle it. They are learning. We are learning.

Jill comes up behind me and her hand caresses the back of my neck. I close my eyes at the soothing, calming effect it has on me.

"I made you lunch, but you have to come in. You can't just sit here all day."

"Yes I can." I pause. "But I won't."

In the distance, I see a figure in a wide-brimmed hat. I watch, and wait. It's black and makes him look somewhat Amish. His limp has gotten better, but still brings him pain. He's never complained, not once. The scar around his neck where he was nearly decapitated may be with him forever, even if the memory of how it got there has been erased. He was more disappointed that he was unconscious during almost all of the battle with Dymortis and his creatures. He still asks us to tell the story, and we do so without embellishment. It's not necessary to add anything more spectacular than what actually happened.

The Great Battle, as we've come to call it, has taken its toll and we can only console ourselves with knowing we did our best, did what needed to be done, and the consequences were regrettable yet unavoidable.

"I made him a sandwich too," Jill says.

I smile. She hand-makes the bread and it is so delightful, I never get tired of it.

"I should go into town to see if I can get feed for Ginger. I only have a day or two left."

Ginger doesn't like being hitched up to the wagon, but does it anyway. It's the way she earns her keep.

"Can I go with you?"

"Sure. But if you're still not feeling well, I can pick up whatever you need."

"No. It's something I need to do. It's Tuesday. Doctor Zuillart will be in town." She pauses as we watch Patrick make his way up the long dirt driveway. He lives in a small house a mile or so away. "Besides, I'm okay now. I only don't feel good in the morning."

"I guess that makes it—"

I stop, frowning. Then I stand and turn towards her. She's smiling.

"You mean . . ."

"I think so. That's why I should see the doctor."

I am literally speechless. I cannot think of anything to say. All I can do is step forward and throw my arms around her. I pick her up and spin her around.

"Wo, wo, wo, cowboy," she says with a squeal. "I don't do dizzy very well!"

I stop the spinning and put her down. "Oh my gosh, I'm . . . I don't know what to say."

"You don't have to say anything. Unless you want to tell Patrick."

I lean in and kiss her, and then give her a long and loving hug.

"*Always*," she whispers in my ear.

"*Always*."

FAVENTE DEO SUPERO

LAUS DEO

STAY
TRUE
PAY
ATTENTION

CPSIA information can be obtained
at www.ICGtesting.com
Printed in the USA
LVHW050030130322
713065LV00004B/25